PRAISE FOR DA[VID KAUFELT'S]
THE FAT BO[Y MURDERS]

"Agatha Christie lovers will find much to savor in David Kaufelt's intricately plotted THE FAT BOY MURDERS, and Sag Harbor residents in particular will enjoy all the familiar locations. . . . (a) finely drawn cast of characters. . . . One of the beauties of the construction is the long list of possibilities on the who-done-it list, right up to the ending. . . . Fear, jealousy, greed, the hots, revenge, real estate development and its frustration, the gradual revelation of a series of sordid pasts, a little jeopardy, and our need to know carry us along happily to the satisfying conclusion."

—The East Hampton Star

"Colorful characters and several surprises keep the reader's attention. . . ." *—Sunday Oklahoman*

"Kaufelt expertly describes the rustic charms and bitter antagonisms of a small seaside town trying to preserve its past while striving to survive economically. . . . There is an abundance of likely suspects, interspersed with ambiguous clues and convoluted local politics. All this leads to a splendid mystery and an extremely unlikely killer." *—St. Louis Post-Dispatch*

". . . a sophisticated little murder mystery. . . . Kaufelt has a pleasing writing style. . . ."

—Topeka Capital-Journal

"A cluttered suburban cozy—first of a new series by Kaufelt. . . . a leisurely, literate finale." *—Kirkus Reviews*

"Secrets from the past collide with the fiscally strained present of the fictional Long Island town of Waggs Neck Harbor to create a swirl of passions in this sprightly first mystery. . . . Kaufelt springs a few fine surprises and fashions a pleasing heroine in plucky, winsome Wyn, whose promised return will be welcomed." *—Publishers Weekly*

Books by David A. Kaufelt

Six Months with an Older Woman
The Bradley Beach Rumba
Spare Parts
Jade (*under the name Lynn Devon*)
Late Bloomer
Midnight Movies
The Wine and the Music
Silver Rose
Souvenir
The Best Table (*under the name Richard Devon*)
American Tropic
The Fat Boy Murders*

*Published by POCKET BOOKS

THE FAT BOY MURDERS

A WYN LEWIS MYSTERY

DAVID A. KAUFELT

POCKET BOOKS
New York   London   Toronto   Sydney   Tokyo   Singapore

For Tom Szuter

This book is a work of fiction. Names, characters, places, and incidents are products of the author's imagination or are used fictitiously. Any resemblance to actual events or locales or persons, living or dead, is entirely coincidental.

POCKET BOOKS, a division of Simon & Schuster Inc.
1230 Avenue of the Americas, New York, NY 10020

ISBN: 0-671-76093-9

First Pocket Books paperback printing July 1994

10 9 8 7 6 5 4 3 2 1

POCKET and colophon are registered trademarks of
Simon & Schuster Inc.

Cover art by Mary Ann Lasher

Printed in the U.S.A.

Author's Note

Sag Harbor, a charming and eccentric eastern Long Island village where I lived for some years, is the inspiration for Waggs Neck Harbor. However, all the characters and events, as well as the establishments and much of the geography, are pure invention.

I'd like to thank: the Carlson family for lending their splendid name; the Sag Harbor Chief of Police, Joe Ialacci, for filling me in on village police procedure; and Molly Allen, Diane Cleaver, Bill Grose, and Frank E. Taylor for their patient support and sure sense of direction.

D.A.K.

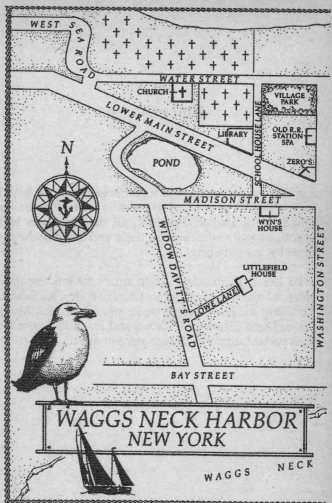

WEST SEA ROAD

WATER STREET

CHURCH

LOWER MAIN STREET

LIBRARY

SCHOOL HOUSE LANE

VILLAGE PARK

OLD R.R. STATION SPA

ZERO'S

N

POND

MADISON STREET

WYN'S HOUSE

WIDOW DAVITT'S ROAD

LITTLEFIELD HOUSE

LOWE LANE

WASHINGTON STREET

BAY STREET

WAGGS NECK HARBOR
NEW YORK

WAGGS NECK

GDS / Jeffrey L. Ward

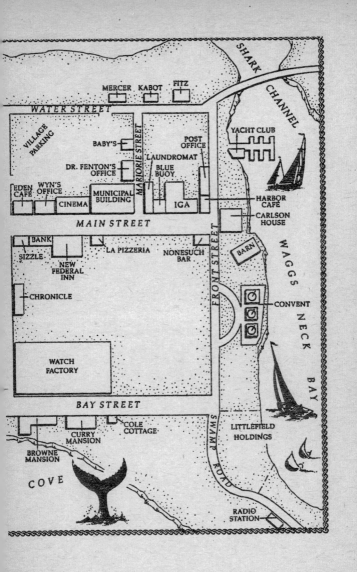

PART ONE

Spring

CHAPTER
One

WYNSOME LEWIS WAS REGRETTING THE CHARCOAL-GRAY jumper she had chosen to wear on that May Monday morning, knowing it made her complexion seem colorless, especially against the yellow-and-blue Disney day. The others, walking ahead with varying degrees of difficulty up the overgraveled pathway toward the old section of the cemetery, also wore blends of grays and blacks, looking like a flock of determined but misdirected winter birds.

Wyn, who was aware that she was often described "as if butter wouldn't melt," today felt it had curdled. She knew what was souring her: she had allowed herself to get involved in this ritualistic burying of the dead not from belief or affection but because it was the thing to do. The "thing to do" was the first of her mother's ten commandments.

Nonetheless I'm here, she thought with grim humor, remembering another of her mother's dictums: might as well enjoy myself. Everything but the weather seemed funereal about the day, from the whispering crowd in the dim church to the white rosebushes lining the route from church to graveyard. The Old Whalers' Cemetery, occupying several acres of prime Waggs Neck Harbor real estate, reminded Wyn of a theme park re-creation—"The Haunted Graveyard"—complete with ancient oaks, falling-down tombstones, and ornate turn-of-the-century mausoleums.

The others had reached the oldest end of the cemetery and were propping themselves up against the stone wall, waiting for the Episcopalian minister, who, as usual, was taking his time. Wyn took hers. She stopped in front of her family's mausoleum, a brownstone Greek temple, and evoked her father, a handsome, even-tempered Realtor whom everyone called Hap, short for Happy. He had been more interested in golf, village history, and amateur photography than in selling real estate, which was just as well as Waggs Neck Harbor property had been stagnant until recently. He had died when Wyn was twelve; she was now thirty-four and still missed him.

Hap had left the house and a little money to his wife, Linda, and his paintings and books—including journals and photo albums—to their daughter, Wyn. The journals contained a daily entry, dating from his twenty-first birthday, plus several monographs on Waggs Neck Harbor village life. Wyn, who worked hard against sentimentality, still kept the journals on top of the desk in her study, where she could see them every day.

Wyn's ex-sister-in-law, Natalie, a psychiatric social worker, enjoyed going on about the havoc Hap's premature death had played on Wyn's psyche. "You married my brother because he's so fatherly."

"I married your brother because at that point he was the most seductive man I had ever met and one of the few Jews. God help me, I thought he was exotic."

"You thought he would take care of you. Like your father. You're still looking for someone to take care of you."

Wyn, who thought she could take very good care of herself, told Natalie to put her psychoanalytic insights where the monkey put the nuts. It was true Wyn had become, like her father, a Realtor, but it was her mother's independent spirit that had pointed the way.

Her mother, Linda, a former Waggs Neck High principal, was now working at City College in Manhattan and living in the West Side condominium Wyn had traded her for the family house. "Don't hide your light under a bushel," Linda often counseled her daughter, implying that was what she herself had done, marrying Hap instead of striking out immediately for the big city. Wyn had tried but it turned out her light had not been nearly bright enough for Manhattan. "That's because you married Nick, a man like your father. You hid your light under his bush."

My mother's Freudian aphorisms, Wyn thought, might give even Natalie pause. Natalie, a firm believer in the psychological language of clothes, would have had a field day at Percy Curry's funeral. Phineas Browne, the mayor of the village, gotten up in an Yves St. Laurent black suit and a shirt so white it hurt to look at it, had grown up with Percy and had elected himself chief mourner. The elderly Cole sisters, Camellia and Ruth, who had been Percy's neighbors since he had been born, had trotted out their ancient funereal black dresses and matching hats. John Fenton, Waggs Neck's general practitioner, a schoolmate of Percy and Phineas, looked handsome in a windblown way in a gray flannel suit and brown suede lace-ups. Colonel (Ret., U.S. Army) Wilfred Mercer, Waggs Neck's own Colonel Blimp, was also in gray, a pipe head sticking out of his hand-stitched handkerchief pocket.

Fitz Robinson, the retired commissioner of New York's finest and Wyn's uncle and friend, wore his all-purpose tweed suit. He was Wyn's mother's brother, as affectionate and caring as his sister was pragmatic and self-serving. They hadn't spent much time together in their youth. Fitz was a decade older and had been sent to boarding school at an early age; Linda, being a girl, had been relegated to the local educational system. Fitz seemed uncomfortable, and Wyn suspected his and her unease stemmed from similar sources: neither had been overly fond of Percy and both had been strong-armed into attending by Phineas.

Maggie Carlson, her half sister Dolly, and Dolly's daughter, Dicie, stood slightly apart from the little group, as befitted the Brahmins of the town. Maggie was in a dark tent of a dress, Dicie in an abbreviated version of the little black dress, and Dolly wore her black Chanel knockoff with Jackie O. sunglasses. Maggie didn't look well, but no one was looking their best.

Even though Percy had grown increasingly eccentric each year, beginning on the day he graduated from high school in 1969, his death was unimaginable. It appeared, the authorities from Hauppauge said, he had been soaking in a bubble bath when he reached up to change the volume on his mother's ancient radio, precariously placed on the commode seat despite any number of Long Island Lighting Company admonitions to keep such devices away from the tub. The unwieldy radio, shaped like a miniature Gothic church, tumbled in and Percy was electrocuted.

"One less Fat Boy," Phineas Browne whispered into Wyn's ear, adding gratuitously and nonsequentially, "It appears he had been drinking."

The minister gave Phineas a long look and finally got the proceedings underway, launching into what he felt had to be said in his usual monotone. Wyn, who had no patience with religion or long-windedness, occupied herself by leaning against the old cemetery stone wall and contemplating the history of that curious Waggs Neck Harbor organization known as the Fat Boys. Her father had served, during his four years in the organization, as the Fat Boys' historian and one of his treatises was devoted to their past. Wyn remembered that the Fat Boys had gotten their start in 1924 when the newly arrived Father Ignatius Quintan declared Greek fraternities taboo in the Mary Immaculate Star of the Sea Catholic Academy, reviling them as hotbeds of cant and sin.

Most of the well-off Waggs Neck Harbor families, whatever their persuasion, sent their children to the academy, where multifaith lay teachers made up the better part of the faculty as a sop to non-Papists. The other option had been to bus the children to nearby West Sea High, in a town light-years behind Waggs Neck, it was believed, in progress and culture.

After Father Quintan banished Greek fraternities, a group of affluent (or "fat," as the slang expression of the day went) Mary Immaculate male students, led by the richest boy in town, fourteen-year-old Bull Carlson, formed a secret but technically not Greek society. Father Quintan chose to ignore the Fat Boys until they became a problem. They never did. Though their rituals changed every few years, the Fat Boys managed to survive for decades, drawing members from the south and monied— or fat—side of town. The stated goal of the Fat Boys was "public service by the elite for the underprivileged." Around Christmas the Fat Boys did collect monies for various charities, but mostly their activities were confined to bullying less well-favored boys and to meetings at which verboten cigarettes were smoked, smutty stories were told, and tentative ventures into the world of pornography were taken.

The Fat Boys' demise came when the Mary Immaculate Star of the Sea Catholic Academy was closed due to rising costs and a perceived lack of need: the red brick Waggs Neck Harbor Public High School had finally been squeezed out of the state legislators. A few boys attempted to initiate a Fat Boys society in the new facility, but the movement died from a general feeling that a secret, elitist club did not belong in a public school and that the word *fat* no longer intimated wealth but had become a term of derision.

Several of the Fat Boys from the final year of Mary Immaculate's existence kept up a Monday lunch tradition at a table set aside in the New Federal Inn's main dining room. The size of the table decreased as members moved away, joined the BPOE, or found more congenial places to be on Monday at noon. In recent times the table was set for just four: John Fenton, Phineas Browne, Wilfred Mercer, Percy Smythe Curry.

Wyn, who was eleven years old when the Fat Boys ceased to exist, never did understand the joys of private clubs and found it hard to imagine wanting to sit across the luncheon table from Percy Curry, with his lightly rouged cheeks and thatch of hair that looked as if he had applied black Carbona shoe polish to it.

"You'd never believe it from what he became, but Percy was a witty boy," Phineas whispered again, breaking into Wyn's reverie as the minister droned on. "He had the drollest delivery and the sharpest tongue. We all left for college after Mary Immaculate but Percy stayed on, his only employment keeping house for that dragon of a mother. The last time I saw him he was strolling up the aisles of Woody's IGA wearing lipstick. Said it was the best thing for chapped lips."

The minister gave Phineas another admonitory glance and finally the crypt was shut, the mausoleum locked. Wyn, moving fast to escape capture by the Cole sisters, who already had Fitz in hand, arrived at her office a few moments before noon, annoyed that the entire morning was gone. She leafed through the sheaf of pink telephone messages her extremely efficient secretary/receptionist, Liz Lum, had waiting for her. The spring real estate season had begun in earnest, and as Wyn was both a licensed Realtor and a real estate attorney, she was in demand.

But as goal-oriented as she was, Wyn couldn't immediately set to work. She sat at Hap's old desk, looking out at Main Street without seeing it, telling herself she had to call Lucy Littlefield and talk to her about the Grasslands contract. But she didn't. She hadn't much liked Percy, but she couldn't help thinking of him and his idiotic death at the age of forty.

Wyn wasn't the only one. She looked across the street and saw Phineas staring down at Main Street from his attic apartment in the New Federal Inn. Phineas was as superficial as thin ice and he got off on making mischief for the sake of making mischief, but Wyn, against her instincts and better judgment, liked him anyway. He genuinely loved the village, he often made her laugh, and best of all, he was so very much who he was, never stepping out of character.

Phineas, catching sight of Wyn, gave her his Queen of England wave, which she returned, wondering how he was feeling about the death of his old friend.

CHAPTER

Two

PHINEAS BROWNE, MAYOR OF WAGGS NECK HARBOR AND
owner–director of that village's only hotel, the New Federal Inn, stood staring down at Wynsome Lewis for a
few moments, distracting himself from Percy's death,
thinking how nice Wyn was to look at. She had the good
sense to wear her nearly white blond hair in a Prince
Valiant do that made her look like both an innocent child
and a woman who knew where to get her hair cut. She
wasn't nearly as sweet as she looked and that was all to
the good.

Phineas, contrary to popular village opinion, believed
her marriage to Nick Meyer and the subsequent divorce
had been the making of her. If the divine Nick (all that
black curly hair and that chronic two-day growth and
those bespoke shoulders and that shoot-from-the-hip delivery) hadn't dumped her, Wyn would have spent her
days in his blue–black shadow, Baby to his Bogart. Now,
she was universally respected if not adored, very much
her own woman, the sort of feminist who did rather than
said.

He gave her the benefit of his reigning monarch wave

and turned his attention to the folded newspaper he carried in his hand, Percy's plaintive young face staring up at him. Picture must have been taken decades ago, Phineas thought, walking across the large, spare space that was once the attic of the New Federal, not wanting to think of Percy, but wondering if he screamed at the end as his mother's old Crosby radio turned him into wet toast. Phineas, not given to introspection, surveyed the enormous space to distract himself. Five years before, at age thirty-six, he had had a mild heart attack and, during the recuperative period, an emotional change of heart. He was over being an interior decorator, bored with his clients' townhouses and penthouses and country houses and villas by the sea. Besides, thanks to certain real estate investments, he was good and rich. As he lay in his Manhattan hospital suite, he decided he would retire to the village where he was born, become an innkeeper, and devote himself to the simple life.

His friends and enemies didn't believe this for a moment, but they underestimated Phineas's heart attack-induced epiphany. Not long after he left the hospital he bought the shabby New Federal Inn, a brick hotel that had stood at the center of Waggs Neck's Main Street for over a hundred years. It took six months to transform it into a splendid neo-Victorian inn, and within a year it was a success, invariably overbooked during the summer, more or less vacant during the other seasons except on holiday weekends.

Returning to one of the half-dozen nicely proportioned mansard windows, Phineas surveyed Main Street and, as always, liked what he saw. Across the street, on the far side of the Municipal Building, stood a row of neat brick shops, one of which housed Wynsome Lewis's office. She had, he noted approvingly, gotten down to work, and was talking earnestly on her telephone, while studying her computer screen. She was, like him, a dedicated workaholic.

Craning his long, thin neck, Phineas could see Carlson

House at the eastern end of Main Street, blocking the view of Waggs Neck Bay. Beyond Carlson House, only partially visible, was Jackson Hall's borrowed yacht sitting serenely astride the bay waters, dwarfing hundreds of other, smaller boats bobbing up and down.

Jackson Hall, arguably the most important living American artist, had recently returned to his hometown and was said to be considering Waggs Neck as a permanent abode. Wyn knew more about it than she was telling, but then she always did. Phineas wanted to talk to Jackson Hall about certain plans he was making for the village, but he wasn't confident of his reception. He and Jackson had not been friends when they were fellow students at the Mary Immaculate Star of the Sea Catholic Academy. In many respects, Phineas's high school years had been the best in his life; and probably the worst in Jackson Hall's. Phineas assumed Jackson wouldn't hold a grudge but he couldn't be sure. His old antagonists invariably possessed extra-long memories.

Thinking about Jackson Hall reminded Phineas of the Fat Boys and Percy and he really wanted to put poor Percy out of his mind. To that end, Phineas resumed his scan of the village. To the west, for about a mile before the pine woods took over, were the increasingly gentrified nineteenth-century workingmen's cottages, one of Phineas's passions. The weathered shingles, the ginger-breaded porches, the narrow gardens coming into bloom all evoked the simple, warm family homes featured in the magazine fiction of Phineas's youth. He had invested those unpretentious houses, now being sought out by upscale weekenders, with the romance of happy families.

It was just as well that he had no view of Bay Street with its cupola-laden mansions where his own unhappy childhood had been spent. Though he had "done over" the family house for his not very sisterly and extremely ungrateful sibling, who used it for weekends, Phineas avoided it. Despite the new decor and Lettitia's gargantuan personality, the oversized rooms were still imbued with the spirit of his father, a mean little man, long dead.

Phineas was usually adept at not allowing ugly thoughts to linger in his mind, but Percy's sad head kept cropping up, like the duck target in the shooting gallery that came each July with the carnival. Percy's house had been one down from Phineas's and as boys they had seen a good deal of one another. When Percy's mother—the appalling Aggie Smythe Curry—ran out of money, she sold their home, known as the Curry Mansion, to summer people with the proviso that she and her late-life issue, Percy, would inhabit the ground-floor rooms "in perpetuity." Perpetuity it must have seemed to the new owners, for Aggie enjoyed a long and noisy old age.

As an adult, Percy, who had inherited his mother's iron constitution, spent his days in a frilly peach-colored apron worn over sturdy brown corduroys, obsessively cleaning during the day, parading around his apartment in mail-order women's clothing at night. When they were boys, Percy had been Phineas's confidant, a cynical witness to Phineas's brilliant machinations, his partner in the deviling of out-of-favor classmates. And Percy had always turned up at the Fat Boy Monday luncheons, interested in Phineas's progress in bringing year-round prosperity to the village. Phineas told himself he didn't actually mean it, but somehow it seemed ungrateful of Percy to have died just when Phineas's plans were about to bear fruit. If he could get his new project, the Pier Mall—a series of shops and restaurants extending into the bay—off the ground, as it were, Phineas felt certain Waggs Neck would experience a well-being it had never had before.

He was aware that the preservationists, led by the formidable Maggie Carlson, viewed him as foolish and even dangerous. A mixed bag of old-time gentry and arts-oriented Manhattan transplants, the preservation lunatics maintained he was ruining Waggs Neck's intrinsic charm while attempting to fill his hotel during the off season.

They missed the point: he loved the village. He wanted to be the mayor who brought good times to Waggs Neck Harbor.

He had become, perforce, the darling of the prodevelopers, working-class-descended Waggs Neckers who would raze Main Street and fill in the bay if they thought it would make them a hundred dollars richer. Phineas refused to be swayed by either group. He had a vision and he meant to see it fulfilled. Privately, he viewed himself as a Fat Boy at Christmastime, an elitist bringing economic relief to the great unwashed.

His attention returned to the folded newspaper. He was reminded of another accident victim, Kate Carlson, who had died over twenty years ago when her family's old stable caught fire.

Phineas thought of Kate, whom he had cared about; and then, again, of Percy. There was now another irreparable hole in the thin, stretched fabric of his universe. He looked up at the exposed beams that supported the New Federal's sturdy roof and closed his eyes. "My friend," he said, finally allowing himself to grieve.

A quarter of an hour later Phineas was at his severe black steel desk, diverting himself by planning the next step in Waggs Neck's march to prosperity: the First Annual Whalers Day Parade. He wondered how he was going to get Jackson Hall to participate. Any event that had Jackson's name attached to it was sure to garner big-time publicity.

It was the Cole sisters who, concerned when Percy didn't take in his morning newspaper, had entered his apartment and found his body in the tub. Now, returning home from the cemetery to their commodious, heavily gingerbreaded Victorian cottage, the younger sister, Camellia, who was once pretty, said she still had not "digested" Percy's death. She glanced out the west windows that faced Percy's door and simultaneously winced and wrinkled her nose, remembering the sharp, acrid odor in Percy's bathroom. "The truth is," she admitted, "Percy's death sticks in my craw like Betty Kunze's twice-congealed salad."

"Don't be ridiculous, Camellia," Ruth Cole, older, wiser, and never pretty, said, busying herself with the tea things.

"You don't suppose he did it on purpose, do you?"

"If so it was an outré way to commit suicide. On the other hand," Ruth went on, playing devil's advocate as she often did, "Percy had nothing to live for."

Camellia was tempted to say, "Who does?" but didn't want to get into an uplifting discussion with her sister. She held their late father's silver German binoculars to her still sharp eyes, training them on the yacht club pier. "Jackson is coming off the yacht."

Glimpses of the artist were infrequent. With characteristic speed Ruth Cole advanced to the window seat, taking the binoculars from her sister's plump, childlike hand. Ruth was deeply offended that in the month since Jackson had arrived, neither she nor her sister had been invited aboard the yacht, much less acknowledged in any way. Jackson Hall had lived with them from the time he was four until he was eighteen, when he left without saying either thank you or good-bye. "We were not the sort of women meant to be parents," Ruth Cole said, bitter after his departure. "We did the best we could with an uncommunicative, difficult boy."

The binoculars were strong and Ruth easily focused in on the familiar face with its slicked-back black hair and the deep cleft in the strong chin. His wide-set eyes were the mud-brown color found in the dried earth of the southwestern United States: rattlesnake eyes. He was wonderful looking but even as a child he had appeared sinister to Ruth Cole.

"Jackson might have come to the funeral today. Not that they were friends but, after all, they were in the same class," Camellia said, retrieving the binoculars. Ruth, staring at the bay, wasn't listening. Camellia, attuned to her sister's moods, asked, "Is something wrong, Ruth?"

"It has only just occurred to me to wonder why Jackson has come back. Considering the way he left."

In between appointments, Dr. John Fenton lay full length on the old, cracked brown leather sofa in his private office, sipping black coffee, reading Percy's brief obituary in the Waggs Neck Harbor Chronicle, getting newsprint ink on his immaculate hands and feeling his own mortality. For no reason he could think of, Percy's death made him wonder if he shouldn't, after all, convince Dolly to marry him.

He had a sudden and repugnant image of Dolly's long-deceased father, Bull Carlson. God help me, John Fenton said, remembering the tyrannical way in which Bull had run the village, thinking Dolly, as his wife, would manage him the same way. Dolly was the middle daughter of the three Bull had by three wives. The wives died young, rumored to have been worn out by Bull Carlson's excessive demands.

The whaling money and the watch factory Bull Carlson had inherited had gone long before he died, and all he had bequeathed to his daughters was the unprofitable newspaper and Carlson House. The eldest, Maggie, had been left in charge and had recently sold the Chronicle to newcomers. The youngest daughter, Kate, had died years before, while Dolly, John Fenton's weekly sexual partner, worked for Phineas as manager of the New Federal Inn.

John Fenton wondered if his life would have been different if Kate had lived. A bell ringing from the outer office announced his next appointment, the hypochondriacal Mrs. Morrell. He stood up and, taking a last look at Percy's photo, balled up the newspaper, slam-dunked it into his trash can, and found himself with another unwanted memory: the night he had helped Kate and Phineas play a silly trick involving poor Percy. It had been the night, John Fenton reflected, that Kate had died.

Colonel (Ret., U.S. Army) Wilfred Mercer stood at the kitchen counter in the refurbished cottage his mother had caused to be moved to Water Street when she sold the big house on Bay Street. That had happened after her husband, Willy's father, left home forever. Father Quintan had arranged for a scholarship so that Willy might finish at Mary Immaculate, a fact publicized with an announcement in the Waggs Neck Harbor *Chronicle*.

If the colonel was allowed one word to describe the following two years he had spent in Waggs Neck, it would have been *mortifying*. Everyone had been aware of his father's desertion. Willy had liked his father, a thin, funny man, always up on sports. Years later, on leave in New York, he was notified that his father had died in a Bowery flophouse. Willie had gone to a New York police station to pick up his father's possessions: five dollars and change; a pair of dime-store bifocal glasses; one of the old tin Carlson pocket watches; and a dog-eared snapshot of a smiling woman and, presumably, her child, taken in front of a suburban house. He kept the watch but discarded the glasses and the snapshot, which made him feel unbearably melancholy.

His consolation in his last two years at Mary Immaculate had been the Fat Boys. He had been happy cruising Main Street in Phineas Browne's convertible with Percy and John Fenton and Kate Carlson, the best-looking, peppiest girl in their class. He hated his new home, that old cottage that had once stood at the rear of their property, and he avoided his mother, believing she blamed him for Wilfred senior's abandonment.

On the contrary, she only blamed herself. Concerned for her son's future, she appealed to Kate's father, Bull Carlson, who had his finger in many pies. Bull pulled out a plum, arranging the appointment to West Point. After graduation, Wilfred was sent not to Vietnam, like ninety-five percent of his classmates, but to London and Whitehall Street on what turned out to be permanent loan to the British Army. The stylized British Army officers' life was tailor-made for him, a Talmudic existence in which the correct response for nearly every situation could be found in the rules book. Over time he became slightly more British than the Prince of Wales.

Retiring after twenty honorable years, he returned to the cottage in Waggs Neck, relieved to find John Fenton in practice, Phineas Browne as mayor, and a Fat Boys' table set aside every Monday for lunch. He even put up with Percy's new affectations—no one's hair was that color—and made it his business to be pleasant whenever the little chap turned up. After all, they had been Fat Boys together at a time when their families were the nabobs of the town and they had to stick together, eh what?

It was funny how Percy had always insisted Jackson Hall was queer when they were kids and Percy had turned out a right little queen, while Jackson, if the press was to be believed, had a string of female conquests miles long.

Percy Smythe Curry's killer, idly strolling down Main Street, glanced into the curtain-shrouded window of the New Federal's main dining room and saw the three surviving Fat Boys sitting down to Monday lunch. Shocked, the murderer returned home. How could they continue that fatuous Monday ritual when one of their own was so newly dead?

Someone had left the newspaper opened to the obituary page. Hands shaking, headache raging, the murderer threw the newspaper onto the floor. It landed perversely, Percy's insipid face staring up like a postage stamp engraving of one of the lesser American presidents. The murderer, who had supposed the obsessive hate would be exorcised with Percy's death, was depressed to find that it was still there, corrosive as ever.

PART TWO

Autumn

CHAPTER

Three

EVERYONE AGREED IT WAS DEFINITELY AUTUMN. THE WIND was up, the sun was pallid, and a fey prettiness had taken over Waggs Neck Harbor, the leaves doing their magical mystery turn. Nearly five months had passed since Percy Curry's death, though his persona was still vivid in several memories.

Maggie Carlson was regretting his death, and not for the first time, when she received the call she had been waiting for from the New York specialist. She took it on the seldom-used extension in her bedroom, not wanting anyone to overhear what she guessed was going to be her own death sentence. The doctor confirmed this in words gratifyingly free of medical babble. The cancer, which had started at her center, had spread everywhere, like the roots of a pesky tree messing up a plumbing system. It was inoperable and there would be considerable discomfort in the coming months. He would contact her physician in Waggs Neck but Maggie said he'd better not. The news would inevitably snake its way out of John Fenton's office and she refused to have her last months—year?—bathed in goopy sympathy and unwanted baked goods.

I'm terminal, she thought, sitting on the edge of her big, messy bed, amused, entertaining a vision of her dead self sitting at a Formica table in the Terminal Café facing Manhattan's Port Authority Bus Station, waiting for a hearselike bus to take her to a final destination. Perth Amboy if I know my luck, she reflected, comforting herself with the thought that everyone was terminal, that she was just more terminal than others.

She returned to the large second-floor living/dining room/office with a freshly made cup of cocoa, spiked with cream and sugar, surprised that she wasn't in the least bit frightened. If the pain gets too much, I'll take myself out, she promised herself as if she were both ball player and coach. Carrying the chocolate to the second-floor "winter" porch overlooking the village, she sat in the old glider and found, on the wicker table where she had left it, the locket her father had given her for her twenty-first birthday.

Though she rarely opened the tricky catch, she did so now, and stared at the photographs in the three hinged frames. Coming face to face with the subjects, one wouldn't suspect a family connection; but seeing their pictures close up, one after another, there could be little doubt. The first was of her father as a boy, handsome and disdainful. I miss him, Maggie thought. After all he did to me, I still miss the son of a bitch.

She was not a woman who normally let herself get sentimental over old photographs, but if there ever was a time for sentimentality, it was now, she told herself. The next frame contained a snapshot of herself as a young woman, taken when she was teaching high school English at Mary Immaculate. Who the hell was she, Maggie asked herself, that barely recognizable, oversized woman with the level gaze and the ironic smile? Her father's daughter, she supposed. Still was, Lord help her. She flipped the picture over with impatience and stared for a long time at the third photo, thinking that it wasn't only sexual love that did peculiar things to people.

Giving in to an impulse, she went inside, found the final Mary Immaculate yearbook with the last photo of Kate, and brought it back to the porch. Taken only days before Kate died in the stable fire, the photo was black and white and one had to imagine Kate's red hair and high coloring. But the photographer had caught her reckless smile and those mean Carlson eyes. Though Kate had been dead for over twenty years, Maggie was never able to think of her without guilt and longing.

Maggie had been the child of Bull Carlson's youth. Dolly, his daughter by his second wife, had been the ignored child of his middle years. Kate had been his final and total delight. Maggie sighed and closed the yearbook. The early October air had a bite to it but she was too indolent to fetch a sweater, sitting on in the creaking glider, looking down at five-o'clock Main Street's mild traffic, feeling remarkably healthy.

Her house—Carlson House—sat at the end of Main Street, its west facade facing the village; its eastern view was of Waggs Neck Bay. "Carlson House blocks the village water vista," Phineas Browne said once too often during a village Tourist Development Committee meeting.

"Why don't you propose a resolution to dynamite it?"

"It was inconsiderate of your father, whom you very much resemble, to build it there."

"You know damn well, Phineas, that it was my grandfather, whom I very much resemble, who built it there."

"I only hope you're leaving the house to the village when you die, Maggie."

There were times when she could have stuck a stick of dynamite up Phineas Browne's scrawny back seat and detonated it without a qualm. And speaking of dynamite, a wonderful silence had descended upon Carlson House in the last few moments, the construction next door having come to a halt. She wondered what the barn was going to look like when the contractors were finally out. Cold, she thought. Spare. Magnificent.

She had needed the money if she, Dolly, and Dicie—

Dolly's daughter—were to continue to live in Carlson House. Selling the barn to Jackson seemed the best way to get it and she had needed someone discreet and smart to handle the negotiations. Wyn Lewis, her old friend Hap's daughter, was the right and obvious choice. Though Maggie was never certain if she quite liked her, there being as much of Linda Lewis's prickly independence in her makeup as there was of Hap's good-natured morality. It was odd that Fitz, Linda's much older brother, was much more like Hap when it came to basic human kindness. He doted—there was no other word for it—on Wyn, but she was a little too much her own person for Maggie's taste; not unlike herself.

And also like Maggie, Wyn had made one mistake early on—a biggie, but Maggie understood it. Nick Meyer had been exotic and erotic and undeniable: the dark and evil cosmopolite seducing the fair country maiden. Unknowingly agreeing with Phineas Browne, Maggie felt that Wyn was all the better for the experience.

Not unexpectedly, Wyn had fulfilled Maggie's belief in her, devising a contract that suited everyone. The first two installments had been paid; the final payment would be made in three years' time. But there was a proviso, thrown in to make the venture seem less like a gift: the third payment would only be made if the barn's view of Waggs Neck Bay remained unobscured.

Maggie had signed the contract in Wyn's office but Jackson had sent a proxy. Maggie had been amused by Liz Lum's mouth-open reaction to Tony Deel, not to mention the raised eyebrows of the dressed-for-success insurance rep. Only Wyn, with her mother's straightforward nonchalance, took his elfin face, black silk jumpsuit, snakeskin boots, and nervous poise in stride.

But as lightweight as Tony Deel appeared, he was still able, the day after the signing, to get the contractors and several teams of workers to start work on the cavernous barn. This was considered supernatural speed in Waggs Neck, where the contractors liked to spend weeks drinking coffee and studying newcomers' blueprints. As an envious Phineas Browne noted, money talks.

There hadn't been a day that summer—even on July the Fourth—when Maggie hadn't been aware of the workmen. The double- and triple-time salaries must have been extraordinary. What they were doing was anyone's guess. Even those Waggs Neckers who fancied themselves amateur architects and went down to the Municipal Building to pore over the filed plans were mystified.

During the first week a tall but inoffensive bleached wood fence had been erected around the barn and the following week full-grown fourteen-foot privet hedges had been brought in from heaven knew where (Windsor Castle, Phineas suggested) and planted in front of the fence. While the renovation was underway, no one, not even Maggie, had been allowed inside that barn where the Carlsons once kept their cows.

Billy Bell, one of the many Bell progeny and a low-level carpenter, came strolling around the front lawn of Carlson House at this moment, his work in the barn ended for the day. Maggie watched as he deposited an apple core under the oak tree that marked the outer edge of her property. He glanced up too late, saw Maggie, and smirked. Billy Bell was too pretty, like an old-fashioned rock star. He had long blond curls, broad shoulders, and thick, cherubic lips usually fixed in the sassy smile he was flashing at her at this moment.

Maggie did not return the smile. She supposed the apple was, like herself, biodegradable, but she still didn't like it. "Billy Bell, pick up that apple core and put it in a proper receptacle." In awe of Maggie but with as much attitude as he could muster, Billy retrieved the core and, tossing it in the air, strolled off, presumably to the Blue Buoy, where he liked to drink beer and play pool.

"Horseball," Maggie said distinctly, watching his retreating broad back and dimpled butt, knowing where the little shot of pity for Billy was coming from, recognizing a kindred, lawless spirit. Sighing, she entered the house, crossed the wide plank floor of the large second-story living room, and stepped out onto the bayfront "summer" porch, looking down on what she could see of the renovated barn. Not much. The near wall had been left pretty much intact, its salt-air-cured pine, once painted blue, now a weathered gray. Beyond the barn and past where the stable had stood, floating casually on the white-capped bay waters, was Jackson's summer command post, an enormous white yacht, on long-term loan from a grateful patron.

Standing in the growing dark, chilled by the cooling wind and this afternoon's news, Maggie shivered. In her mind's eye she could see the cancer in her body taking human form like a fetus in a right-to-life commercial. It grinned, a malignant succubus who had found a new home.

Furious with Death, she went back into the house, stood in the dark second-floor living room, and to her indignation found that her cheeks were wet. Now, when all the years of scheming and deceit and forced waiting were about to pay off, she had only a few months to live. "Damn you, God," she said, walking around her room, furiously switching on lights, taking refuge in anger, wiping away the humiliating tears.

CHAPTER

Four

FITZ ROBINSON FLIPPED OPEN THE GOLD COMMEMORATIVE
watch the mayor of the City of New York had presented
to him when the political winds finally turned and he
was retired as commissioner of police. It was six P.M.,
time to walk over to Maggie's for his early evening drink.
A drink with Maggie was a comforting daily ritual, like
breakfast with Wyn at the Eden Café or lunch with Phineas at the hotel or Sunday tea with the Coles. These
little meals help me pass my days, he thought; smooth-
ing the bumpy road over retirement and bereavement.
They're getting me through what's left of my life.

He looked at the commemorative watch again, saw
that now he was late. Not that Maggie would care; he
could turn up or not; it was that kind of a friendship.
He slipped into his moccasins, put on his ancient "going
to court" jacket, and left the house. He opened the tricky
gate and stopped for a moment, surveying his home with
a mixture of pride and exasperation. It had started out
as a modest clapboard affair built in the late nineteenth
century by a ship's carpenter who would have been surprised to see the working fireplaces Jane had caused to

be installed, not to mention the Jacuzzi, the automatic watering system, the central heating.

Fitz could have sold it to any number of nervous city people searching for the perfect weekend house, made a pile of money, and bought himself one of the spacious watch factory condos—if that proposed project ever got off the drawing board—or one of the new bayfront townhouses where he'd have been more comfortable. But he cherished his house and all its pretty, impractical conveniences (what was he to do with a banana-colored bidet?) because it reminded him of Jane.

Adrift in memories, he closed the gate and stood for another moment atop what passed locally for a hill. Looking down, he saw the new fence and hedges that surrounded the old blue barn like the walls of an ancient town. Jane would have approved of the secrecy and especially of the money involved in taking the barn into a new incarnation.

As he watched, a slim woman with auburn hair emerged, moving with casual self-assurance. Jackson Hall's girlfriend radiated the sort of monied glamour that, despite misgivings, appealed to Fitz. Jane had possessed a similar quality and he guessed that Jessica Stevens came from the same privileged atmosphere his wife had.

Jackson Hall's type, he thought to himself, going back into his house to call Maggie, deciding that he didn't feel like having a drink after all. I don't want to be comforted, Fitz thought. I want to be angry.

Jessica Stevens, unaware of Fitz Robinson's scrutiny, had no trouble finding John Fenton's office, a squat, ugly yellow brick building built in the late 1950s and located in the bank parking lot behind Main Street's shops, next to the tea room called Baby's and across from the Old Railroad Station Spa. It was after six but he said he'd be there, updating his patients' files. He was as good as his word, letting her in himself, writing out the prescription she had asked for.

Though she had taken and passed the New York medical exam, Jessica Stevens's license still hadn't been issued and she needed another doctor to write prescriptions. "All my schooling," she explained as John Fenton handed her the scrip, "was in Europe."

"But you're American, aren't you?" She agreed that she was and then there was an awkward pause until she asked his fee and he said there was none, professional courtesy and all that, and Jessica returned to Jackson's yacht, thinking that John Fenton was a good-looking man without one ounce of sex appeal.

John Fenton, puttering around his office, not all that anxious to go home, had similar thoughts. Jessica Stevens was a beautiful, intelligent woman who did absolutely nothing for him, while Dolly could still, after all these years, turn him on by touching his hand. He was aware that village gossip had him bewitched by Dolly because she reminded him of Kate.

Like a good many boys in the final Mary Immaculate graduating class, John Fenton had been in love with Kate Carlson, but he had taken her death harder than most. Still, he had gone on with his careful plans, avoiding the Army and the war in Asia with a college deferment, graduating from Swarthmore and the University of Pennsylvania Medical School. He was finishing his internship at the university hospital when his father went to his reward and John's dreams of specializing in sports-related medicine were buried with the senior Fenton. Reluctantly, and only after his mother and uncle drove down to Philadelphia to beg and admonish, he returned to Waggs Neck and assumed his father's practice.

It was funny how things became so entwined and nearly incestuous. Dolly, a few years older than John, had left Waggs Neck while he was in college and had gone to live in France with Jackson, yet another Waggs Neck Harbor boy who had been in love with her sister.

When Dolly returned to Waggs Neck with her infant daughter, Dicie, she became the object of grudging admiration. There were no explanations on her part, no tales of adoption or of a foreign marriage gone sour. Dicie was presented to the village as an irrefutable fact: Dolly's illegitimate daughter by Jackson Hall.

John Fenton was then experiencing the frustrations of a young man forced by circumstance—he liked to tell himself—into an old man's routine, his future set out for him like a simplistic map of a rural county with but one main artery. Dolly, disappointed and depressed, came to him for minor medical advice. He had been practicing out of the house then and Dolly had looked so much like Kate in the dappled sunlight in his father's old office that he had bent down and kissed her. Kate had seduced him years before on that same cracked leather sofa.

Dolly was the only patient John Fenton had ever allowed himself to make love to and he felt obliged to offer marriage. It was a relief when she said no. He didn't want to marry and have a family, feeling that he brought enough children into the world as it was. What's more, he was aware that he was a selfish man who relished the solitary peace his quiet existence brought him following the daily dramas played out in his professional life.

Each Saturday night, after they made love, Dolly liked to lie nude and uncovered in the old bed in the doctor's big upstairs bedroom, her pretty hands resting on her oval milk-white tummy while she plotted little retaliations against those she felt had offended her. John Fenton had enough psychology to know that these ceremonial recitations were symptomatic of a larger hurt, that a more important retribution was being considered, if only in fantasy. The vengeful half hours obscurely stimulated John Fenton; and, though he didn't admit this, they frightened him as well.

If John Fenton was the jam in Dolly's life, then Maggie was the glue. There was sixteen years' difference between them and Maggie had been more mother than sister to Dolly and Kate. When Kate died, Dolly had retreated into herself, confused by conflicting feelings of relief and loss. Maggie had gone about the business of mourning with matter-of-fact efficiency.

Their father, on the other hand, had cracked, going to pieces in a cataclysmic way that would have been unbelievable had Dolly not witnessed those sobs escalating into shrieks and screams, spiraling into hysterical fits that required massive doses of tranquilizers to defuse. Shouting for his Kate, Bull Carlson eventually died in the hospital bed they set up in his room, helpless, connected by tubes and wires to hostile machinery.

Not unexpectedly, Maggie took Bull's fall and eventually his death in stride. Dolly pitied anyone who opposed her. Phineas had best take care. He talked seriously of rebuilding and extending the old village pier into the bay, with "glorious restaurants and extravagant shops and a public piazza." It would obstruct Carlson House's view and worse, the blue barn's, causing Maggie to lose that necessary last installment and the wherewithal to keep Carlson House going.

Dolly smiled, not altogether happily, when she thought of Phineas. The best moments of his day were over midmorning coffee when he had her captive and would describe to her his "confidential" goals for transforming Waggs Neck into "the most important tourist destination on Long Island." It wasn't difficult to understand how Phineas had talked the Waggs Neck Tourist Development Committee (TDC) into committing funds for his Whalers Festival, an attempt to draw late October visitors to the village. "The Festival is pivotal," he confided to a disinterested Dolly. If it was successful, TDC would commit funds for the Pier Mall.

There had been more publicity for his Whalers Festival than for any event in village history, thanks to Phineas having convinced his antagonistic sister—by agreeing to make her a substantial loan—to lend her considerable name and presence to the spectacle. Lettitia Browne was a Broadway star, known for her range and durability, and though her dislike of Phineas was legendary, they shared an affection for Waggs Neck Harbor.

Fortuitously, Lettitia had already been scheduled to participate on a national morning television show as a member of a panel assembled to discuss new directions in American theater. The moment the camera was on her, Lettitia, ignoring the opening question, invited her hostess to the upcoming Waggs Neck Harbor Whalers Festival along with—here she turned her remarkable, valentine-shaped face on the viewing audience—"every single one of you watching this morning. We're bringing American theater back to the greater public on Waggs Neck's Main Street and it would be a thrill if all of you joined me on Saturday, October 30th, at ten A.M., on Waggs Neck's Main Street to partake in the fun and spectacle of this marvelous, traditional Yankee parade."

Neither the hostess nor her producers were pleased with this spontaneous commercial but a rival network morning program picked up on the idea and a crew and their redoubtable weatherman/interviewer were scheduled to tape part of the festival for airing on the show. "This will put Waggs Neck on the off-season tourist map," Phineas crowed at the town meeting.

"Right up there with Coney Island," David Kabot said in his sandpapery New York accent that amused as many Waggs Neck Harborites as it repelled. He was a young novelist of the new, concerned persuasion, ecology important to him in the way Vietnam was to an earlier generation of writers. He had become a fixture at the town meetings since he had used his second novel's advance for a down payment on a Water Street cottage not far from Fitz Robinson's.

"Look, Phineas," he said, "I came out here to get away from the noise, the dirt, and the crime . . ."

"If you would be seated, Mr. Kabot . . ."

". . . and what do you think's going to happen to this

cute little village when you start busing in sweaty loads of T-shirt shoppers schlepping boom boxes and babies and used diapers? Think about it, Phineas. Dedicated spenders do not attend parades and outlet shops on pier malls. These year-round tourists you're looking for are not going to plunk down the bucks on your fancy hotel lunches either, Phineas. What they are going to do is pig out on pizza and hot dogs and throw their trash in the gutter and when they can't find a public restroom—because they don't exist—they're going to sneak behind your hotel and the smell's not going to be pretty. This village does not have the cops and the mop-up operation needed to service the kind of crowd you're trying to attract, Phineas. And unless you're going to start charging backbreaking impact taxes, it never will. Phineas, I'm asking you to take a second look at the realities and then do us all a favor, dude, and back off."

"You don't mince words, do you, Mr. Kabot?" an outraged Phineas said in his coolest, high-falutin' voice. "However, I can promise you that all your concerns are addressed in the TDC's master growth plan, mandated by the county fathers."

"Give me a break, Phineas. The master plan's a fiction you and the boys on the village council dreamed up over watercress sandwiches. Come on, man. Cancel this goddamn Whalers Festival and your Pier Mall, whatever the hell that's supposed to be, and address some genuine village problems like the potholes on West Sea Road and sex education for the teenage studs at the high school. If your festival and your pier take off, Browne, it's going to be a disaster for Waggs Neck."

Many Waggs Neck Harborites agreed with David Kabot, despite his ponytail and the tiny emerald stud in his ear. There were several "hear, hears."

But Nat Eden, spokesman for the Main Street Business Society (MSBS), his face red, stood up. "You want us to starve, Kabot, right? Before Phineas came back and did up the New Federal, Main Street was a dying dog. What else we got to sell but tourism?"

Dicie Carlson, who owned a Main Street dress shop called Sizzle, disagreed with everyone, refusing to believe the Whalers Festival would attract hordes. "A few old floats and the American Legion band dweebs?" she said, leaving the Municipal Building with David Kabot. "This is not what you call your dynamite draw." She had the bee-stung lips of a silent screen star, black curly hair that she swept back from her high forehead, her mother's dead green eyes, and the peaches-and-cream complexion associated with legendary English beauties. There were a number of interested observers who thought she was wasting her time with David Kabot.

The same sentiment was also held by Dicie's mother, Dolly, who often asked aloud and to her daughter's annoyance what future there was in a relationship with a young man whose twitchy urban manner unnerved nearly everyone and whose future as a novelist seemed dim. Dolly had been thinking these thoughts again as she stood at her place behind the milk-glass-topped wooden counter Phineas had restored, waiting to seat dinner guests in the long, low-ceilinged, heavily swagged main dining room.

Not that there were many diners at this time of year. Bored with Dicie and David, she was rereading the thick invitation she had received that afternoon as Phineas strolled in.

"Evening, Dolly," he said expansively. "Everything tip-top, my dear? Ah, I see you've received the invitation to the Whalers Festival reception. I thought it only right you should be officially invited. After all, it is being held in your home," he went on, adjusting his gold wire eyeglasses and sucking in cheeks and tummy as he caught sight of himself in the mirror over the fireplace. "Wasn't it kind of Maggie to lend us the keeping room for the reception?"

The keeping room was the width and breadth of the entire house, a brick and stone ground-floor room originally used to store preserves and other comestibles. When Bull Carlson inherited the house, he moved the kitchen to the downstairs pantry and the keeping room became the principal site for entertaining.

Phineas, gleeful about acquiring it for the festival party, was in his ebullient, bitchy mood and Dolly knew that by default she was going to be his target.

And he was wrong. Maggie wasn't being kind. She had offered the keeping room only because Phineas threatened to hold the reception in the library and Maggie wanted the mid-nineteenth-century Carlson House, not the ugly concrete-and-brick 1910 library, to represent Waggs Neck to the nation's morning viewers.

"And what do you think of my greatest coup?" Phineas asked. "Convincing Jackson Hall to be honorary co-chair and special supernumerary guest? You hadn't heard? Really, what luck. He's going to pull in all the rich art groupies."

Gratified to see the color draining from Dolly's face, Phineas, in his delight, did something he rarely did and that was to seat himself in the lobby's oversized chesterfield sofa. "Dumb luck, really. You know how reclusive Jackson's been. But Lettitia was here for the weekend and we were having a regrettable financial discussion in the new Chinese out on the Old Ocean Highway when I looked up and saw him being seated at a table not three feet from us.

"I'm ashamed to say I didn't recognize him. But Lettie grabbed my arm and pointed at him as if she were seeing the Ghost of Christmas Past. 'Jackson,' she croaked, and for a moment I thought she was having a stroke. Not at all like Lettie."

"Phineas, do you think we could not talk about Jackson?" Dolly managed to say.

"I am sorry, my dear, I forget how sensitive you are on the subject," he lied. "Forgive old Phineas but you know I haven't laid eyes on him since we were at Mary Immaculate together. Odd to think that Jackson Hall, John Fenton, Wilfred Mercer, and I are all of an age, though I fancy Jackson and I look younger than the others. Dear me, he's an attractive man. I suppose he was attractive as a boy too, though he looked like no one else on earth: cropped black hair and somber eyes and dun-colored clothes. I'm afraid we used to tease him terribly, but the girls were putty in his hands. Jackson only had eyes for one, your poor sister Kate, may she rest in peace.

"Wildly in love with him, too, but she was full of the devil, poor Kate. Not that I'm telling you anything you don't know. Ah, but I adored Kate and I wonder if that's why you and I get along so well. You look so very like her but you're more sedate. The last time I saw her was just before the fire. It was Mary Immaculate's final dance. Four of us Fat Boys got together with Kate and worked up this marvelous rag. We convinced Jackson . . ." Phineas stopped and looked at Dolly. "Are you well, my dear?" he asked with mock solicitude. "You have the most peculiar expression."

"I'm fine, Phineas. Go on," she said, knowing he would.

"Where was I?" he asked, having lost the thread of his narrative but not the general pattern. This evening's torture, seen as harmless entertainment by Phineas, was called, she knew, Making Dolly Suffer. Phineas had never stopped being a bully. "Oh," he went on, "meeting Jackson in the new Chinese. He couldn't have been more charming. When he told me this summer's rumors were true, that he was planning to live full-time in the barn . . . well, that was when yours truly seized the moment and asked him to be guest of honor at the festival.

"Jackson looked at Lettitia and then at his charming companion, that doctor gal who lives with him, and she nodded encouragement. And then he said, 'Why not? I plan to live in Waggs Neck. I might as well.'

"Needless to say, the media's agog. Think of it. Jackson Hall, at the height of his acclaim, returning to Waggs Neck and being the festival's guest of honor. I'm beside myself. Of course Lettie is the main attraction, we must never forget that, not that she'd let us. What's more, Fitz has got another illustrious native son—the governor—to promise to come, and now, with the TV coverage, he almost certainly will. One hopes the notoriety won't drive Jackson away. And Lettie was so peculiar; nearly rude to him. I wonder what got into her?" He looked at Dolly and saw the tight lips and the clenched hands and thought he might have gone too far. "Dolly," he said, "you're not going to let Jackson discombobulate you, are you? After all these years."

Dolly stared at Phineas without seeing him and said, "It was awful when I heard he'd bought the barn. Betrayed again. This time by Maggie. She would do anything for that damned house. Anything. It wasn't so bad during the summer when he spent most of his time aboard the yacht. But now he's moving into the barn and getting involved in the village. . . ."

"It's water under the bridge, Dolly. Old, old water."

"I can't help what I feel, Phineas."

"What do you feel, Dolly?"

"A terrible hate."

As Dolly was reacting to Jackson Hall's role in the Whalers Festival, her daughter was tiptoeing into the bedroom of David Kabot's shingled, ivy-covered, and heartbreakingly tidy cottage on Water Street. His mother, who had spent her life laboring at a variety of maintenance jobs in Polish Brooklyn, had instilled in him the pride that comes with neatness.

Dicie was slovenly. She got out of the severe black sweater and the elegant black pleated miniskirt and left them where they fell. She kicked off her high-heeled black sneakers, removed a pair of polka-dotted panties and, finally, several pieces of oversized jewelry, all of which came from her shop. After graduating from high school, considering college a four-year waste of time, she had taken the idea of a new, chic Main Street dress store named Sizzle to the local bank loan officers, who had been kind but uninterested in backing an eighteen-year-old girl without education/experience in a business venture. Dolly had freaked when Dicie said she was going to write to Jackson Hall for a loan. "After all, he's my father . . ."

"He never acknowledged you. Not once." Dolly finally agreed to allow Dicie to approach John Fenton and he had been generous. Luckily, Sizzle was operating in the black and the loan was being paid off. Dicie designed most of the clothes and had several local women run them up under her strict supervision.

She maintained her clothing was on fashion's cutting edge, but in reality they were traditional good design, carefully made in contemporary colors and lengths. Both the summer women and certain hip locals had come to look and buy, and there had been gratifying inquiries from major department store buyers about acquiring Dicie's "line." She was late getting to David's cottage because she had been down at the Nonesuch Bar, drinking lite beer with the young-at-heart middle-aged sportswear buyer representing Macy's suburban stores.

Feeling optimistic, taking a quick and naughty look at her nakedness in the bathroom door mirror, Dicie slid into the narrow bed that took up a quarter of the bedroom where David Kabot, a stickler for early bedtime, lay pretending to sleep. "Hold me," Dicie demanded, taking one of his thick forearms and putting it around her.

He obeyed and though he kept his heavily lidded eyes tightly shut, his lips managed to find her neck under the thick black curls.

"Love me?" she asked. He kissed her twice. "How much?" He kissed her neck several times in the manner of a woodpecker attacking a telephone pole and then she placed her lips against his. David Kabot opened his milky blue eyes as Dicie closed her dark green ones and he proceeded, after applying proper and handy precautions, to demonstrate the quality as well as the quantity of his ardor.

Later, while snacking at the counter in his modest, spotless kitchen, she showed him the invitations she had found at the post office—one for each of them, both addressed in Phineas Browne's fine art nouveau hand. David's had been sent in care of Ms. Dicie Carlson, as if he had no identity except that of her boyfriend.

"Asshole," David said, looking critically at his Granola, the blue terry cloth robe Dicie had given him setting off his tan and hairy chest. "Flaming asshole," he said for emphasis, knowing Phineas had hoped to get a reaction by sending the invitation in care of Dicie. "Now he's got your old man on the bandwagon. That's cute."

"I can understand why you hate Phineas, but why does Jackson Hall piss you off so much?" Dicie asked, her mouth full of alfalfa sprouts, peanut butter laced with tofu, and whole wheat muffin. "You don't even know him."

"Neither do you. You're just getting off on your fantasy that he's come to Waggs Neck to find his long-lost little Dice-ums. He's been here how many months and how many times have you seen him?"

"That's beside the point. Jackson Hall is one of the greats of this century." She wiped her mouth with an environmentally sound napkin and said maliciously, "Maybe you could get him to read the new manuscript. Ask him to do the cover. That would sell books."

"I want my book to sell on my talent, such as it is," he said, a little too quietly.

"You haven't met him before, have you? When you were in Paris . . ."

David stood up and, with his usual economic movements, cleared the counter, placing the plates and silverware into the tiny dishwasher, pouring a capful of ecologically approved liquid soap into it, turning it on, not looking at her. "Where'd you get that idea?" he asked over the machine's noise.

"This afternoon I saw you and his girlfriend going into Baby's together, rapping away, looking like best friends. I thought the three of you might have known each other in Europe."

David Kabot turned and rearranged his robe, covering his chest. "Hey, Dice, you mind if I sleep alone tonight? I want to get up early, have my run and get to work. Okay?"

It was an abrupt, calculated rejection, but she wasn't going to let him see she was hurt. "I'm out of here," she said, dressing, leaving without kissing him good-bye, feeling her heart begin to crack and break into little pieces like the stale pink candy they still sold at the Waggs Neck Cinema. She allowed herself only one glance backward and didn't like what she saw. David Kabot was standing by the kitchen window, his troubadour's face tight with fury.

CHAPTER
Five

IT WAS FRIDAY AFTERNOON, THERE WERE EIGHT DAYS TO go until Phineas's Whalers Festival, and the village was levitating with energy. Maggie Carlson, having had her lunch, was reclining on the massive green four-seater sofa, trying to find the impetus to move to her desk and start writing.

Even now, with the *Chronicle* sold and made glossy, she continued to crank out "Letters to Maggie," answering questions of personal tragedy, domestic squabbles, fine points of etiquette.

Succumbing to one last macaroon, she nearly made the move from sofa to desk but Annie Kitchen came noisily into the room and Maggie sighed with relief, sinking back into the sofa. No one could think while Annie cleaned.

Annie, who made a fine art of chronic complaint, indulged herself while she dusted and Maggie listened, soothed by Annie's grumbles about change. "Hear your barn's ready for its owner," she observed as she did something to the new plum-colored stain in the Chinese rug that made it larger and more permanent. "There isn't a house in this village that hasn't been stripped and painted and fireplaced and I don't know what all-ed."

It was true, Maggie thought, after Annie left, that Waggs Neck Harbor exuded a new well-being. Money was being made in the revived carpentry and painting trades; shops once perennially on the verge of bankruptcy were prospering. A real estate broker from East Hampton was making noises about setting up a branch agency and a Japanese restaurant was promised for next season.

There was no doubt that Phineas was having his way, but there had to be an end to this profit fever and Maggie, with little time, was the one to stop it. There would be no string of tacky boutiques sitting on a phony pier extending into the bay. Phineas could tart up his hotel any way he chose and hold a dozen Whalers Festivals a week, but he wasn't going to mess around with Maggie's and Jackson's view of the bay.

Galvanized by the thought of Phineas's pier, she hoisted herself out of the sofa and went to the French windows and looked down at her village. A banner extolling the First Annual Waggs Neck Harbor Whalers Festival stretched across Main Street, and the costly cars of the weekenders were beginning to fill the lot behind Woody's IGA.

When she was young she had desperately wanted to get away from Waggs Neck, but each time she was ready to go, Bull Carlson, unlucky in wives, needed her at home. His first wife, Maggie's wholesome, pretty mother, died when Maggie was young. His second and much-too-frail wife died from a blood disease not long after she gave birth to Dolly. A few years later, Bull Carlson's third spouse—even more refined and delicate than his second—died while bringing the bundle known as Kate into the world.

Maggie had been serious about college, majoring in English, planning a career in journalism. But she had allowed Bull to talk her into returning to Waggs Neck at the end of her sophomore year to care for the house, the newborn Kate, and the three-year-old Dolly. "Only for a year or two," he had said, but as it turned out, she had left in a little over five months and didn't return for four years.

She had had one lover in her life. Someone so unsuitable, so wrong, that now, over four decades later, she wondered why she hadn't protested more. But that relationship turned out to have its own reward, for she discovered that her lover had, in the end, given meaning, substance, and form to her life. One of God's cosmic jokes, she supposed. Like this cancer, eating away at her insides.

Thinking of the cancer made her feel it. She returned to the sofa and lay quietly, "cleansing her mind," as she had been taught in the class Dicie had lured her to at the Old Railroad Station Spa. Breathe deeply, the instructor—a muscular little woman named Patty Batista—commanded. Maggie breathed deeply and the pain receded as the floor lamp behind her was switched on, Dolly coming into the room. "Maggie, what are you doing alone in the dark?" From the tone of her voice, Maggie knew that Dolly was in her managerial mode.

"Allowing myself to be dazzled by the gay lights of Waggs Neck Harbor, pal."

"All right. I know better than to try to get you to talk about what you don't want to talk about. I'm going back to the hotel. Phineas has crossed the thin line into insanity and he's taking me with him. He can't focus on anything, he's so excited about the festival. Dicie is having a makeup dinner with David and for once I'm pleased. A lovelorn Dicie is not what I need now. There's a fresh cheese down in the keeping room pantry and one of those rye breads the German woman does so well . . ."

"Dolly, I won't need dinner tonight. I've been invited out."

"Fitz, Lettie, or Ruth and Camellia?"

"None of the above. I've been asked to the barn. I'm dining with Jackson Hall and his ménage."

The half sisters looked at one another for a long moment, the atmosphere abruptly charged with old, unresolved fury. Maggie had some idea as to how Dolly would react when she announced, last April, after negotiations were complete, that she was selling the old family dairy barn to Jackson Hall. There had been a not-unexpected scene, but its intensity had stunned Maggie. Dolly, usually so tightly zipped, had come undone, reminding Maggie of their father, screaming hysterically, accusing Maggie of terrible disloyalty. Maggie attempted to explain that if she didn't sell the barn for the price Wyn Lewis had gotten Jackson to agree to, they couldn't continue to live in Carlson House.

"Did you think of me once? Of the pain of having him here, living next door to me? Did you think of Dicie? God, you're a cold-hearted bitch, Maggie."

Twenty years had gone by and Dolly was still nursing that same old grievance. Hadn't Jackson given her love and romance? Other women had far less from him. Dolly was still in her twenties when she returned from Paris. She could have had any number of lovers or husbands or lives, but she chose to remain mired in Waggs Neck with her Saturday night trysts with John Fenton, obsessing over a two-decade-old rejection.

"*Bon appétit*," Dolly said and left the room, taking her rage with her. A new cold war could be expected for the next few weeks but they would all survive, Maggie hoped, wryly thinking there was nothing more gut-turning than sibling hate . . . with the exception of stomach cancer. She went to dress, hoping the tomato-red trousers Dicie had made for her were presentable enough for dinner with Jackson and company.

The blue barn had been huge but cozy, redolent with the lazy smell of the cows Bull had kept there. Now it had a modern, alien air of secrecy and distance. Maggie pressed the discreet bell set in the post and in a moment the black-jumpsuited Tony Deel was opening the vault-like door.

Maggie didn't usually cotton to feline men but she had come to admire Tony during the barn negotiations. Wyn Lewis, representing Maggie, had been admirably hard-nosed, belying that never-been-kissed look of hers. But Tony had been a match for her. "Madame," he said, bowing low, like a dancer.

"Mademoiselle," Maggie corrected him, bowing back.

"At our time of life," Tony said, taking her arm as if they were old friends, "we do not make that sort of distinction." She laughed. He was almost forty years her junior.

Maggie accompanied him across slabs of blue slate and through the tall glass entry that replaced the original wooden barn doors. Though Tony looked nothing like him, there was an attitude reminiscent of Jackson and Maggie wondered if it was a conscious imitation.

Her attention was suddenly and thoroughly taken up by the barn. Before its renovation, the barn hadn't been electrified, but now it seemed as if it drew wattage from the entire solar system. A subtle and clever assemblage of lighting played across the interior, making it a stage set for a futuristic theater piece. Heightening this theatricality was a new, huge glass wall, facing the bay, the red lights of Shark Channel Bridge blinking in the near distance like interplanetary radio signals. The panoramic view was startling and yet banal, like the motorized Niagara Falls mural in the Nonesuch Bar.

"Lordy," Maggie said, unprepared for this new-wave extravagance.

"Jackson designed it and I helped a bit. It's glorious during the day when the glass doors slide away and the outdoors seems to come in."

This section of the ground floor was one enormous space divided into areas defined by function. The mostly chromium kitchen lay behind a circular, sculptural counter/

bar. Off to the right, in front of the disappearing glass doors, was the dining room table, a round slab of black marble on a thick glass base. Chrome and leather sofas and a round black and white carpet created a seating area. A steel stairway rose along one wall and led to the upper floor, Jackson's bedroom and studio. Just beyond the kitchen was a corridor that gave access to other rooms. It had been a large barn but it seemed endless now.

"My father, in whatever hell he's frying," Maggie said, "is sizzling."

"Jackson enjoys interior drama." Tony handed Maggie her requested Scotch, keeping a Baccarat brandy glass that he filled with Diet Coke for himself. "I'm addicted to the stuff," he said. "Jackson's addicted to privacy. You wouldn't believe the amount of mail he gets. People who are vague about Rembrandt know Jackson Hall." He said this with naive pride, as if Maggie were unaware of the length and breadth of Jackson's celebrity. He touched a button in the counter, illuminating the wall behind her, turning his Slavic eyes upward. For a moment Maggie thought he had gone into a meditative trance. "His current work," Tony said, still staring upward. "He started it soon after we came to Waggs Neck. Now he's having trouble finishing it; letting go."

Maggie turned and saw the ten-foot-square canvas that had been centered on the wall opposite the staircase. At first Maggie thought the painting depicted a series of horses escaping from a burning stable. But after a moment she realized that the heightened flames of red were three portraits: the two lesser were male and yet to be completed; the pivotal figure, nearly finished, was a woman grown old. Her faded red hair flowed off the canvas, enveloping the men. Her dark eyes, surrounded by a web of fine lines, seemed more challenging than reflective. Her lips suggested fathomless malice.

Even in its unfinished state, the painting was disturbing, thrilling, mesmerizing. Jackson Hall was known for the emotional and sensual power of his paintings, but none of his work affected her as this one did.

Unnerved, she deliberately took her Scotch to a sofa that faced away from the painting while Tony teetered on the arm of its mate, continuing to gaze upward. "Wonderful, isn't it? I think it's his masterpiece."

She was saved from having to invent some answer— of course it was his masterpiece—because Jessica Stevens and Jackson Hall were coming down the steel stairway with a lot of clatter at that moment, her high heels creating a machine-gun rat-a-tat-tat on the metal treads. The room had been lit before their entrance; now it came alive. Though it hadn't been planned—this was their first public meeting—she was in his arms. "God, Maggie, it is good to see you."

The rehearsed words came easy. "If you tell me I haven't changed, Jackson, I'll never believe another word you say."

"Oh," he said, kissing her cheek, releasing her, "we have all changed. Luckily."

Though she had seen him before, of course, now she took her time and really looked at him. He was still too good-looking, his dark hair combed back in a retro gangster style, his flat brown eyes opaque. At forty he managed to look like a boy who knew a great deal more than he should, a boy who was never going to share.

She had met Jessica Stevens—billed as "the miraculous young psychoanalyst"—early in the summer and she seemed nearly as charming, as blessed, as he. They sat across from her making small talk while Tony served drinks; they looked like film stars, impossibly glamorous. It was a pleasure to be with them, though it hurt. It wasn't fair that they should be so good-looking and smart and bright and talented and privileged. As frivolous as was the thought, Maggie couldn't deny it: at that moment she would have signed any pact the devil offered to be either one of them.

Jessica helped Tony serve a casual dinner centered on

"a deceptively innocent curry," accompanied by "a simple little wine." Jackson, who only drank calvados, sipped at the apple brandy throughout. Afterwards, while the others drank peach schnapps, Tony passed around a cigar-sized joint and Maggie, curious, took a few puffs.

Philip Glass's ethereal music was being played on the state-of-the-art stereo system and, through the glass doors, Shark Channel Bridge seemed about to take off for Mars. Maggie herself felt airborne on the magic that filled that enormous cold space. Much too soon it was midnight and Jackson was walking her to the keeping room door.

"It went well, don't you think?"

"Very well."

"Do you like the painting?"

"*Like* is not an appropriate word." She put her hand on his shoulder. "I think you've done it, kiddo."

"If I can only finish the bloody thing."

"You will."

He kissed her cheek and then was gone, Harlequin fading into the night.

Six days later—just two days before the Whalers Festival—on a grim, autumnal Thursday, Fitz was taking tea with Ruth and Camellia. Neither Cole sister hid the fact that Fitz had been invited because he had been given lunch the day before at Jackson Hall's new residence. Wyn had been asked as well but she was, she said, up to her eyeballs in contracts and had to refuse. The luncheon had been one of a series of small meals, one or two guests at a time, to reintroduce Jackson to village society.

"He hasn't bothered to telephone us," Ruth said, "much less give us a meal. We saw him once on Main Street and he looked right through us. What could he have against us? We took him in. We did what we thought best. He was a hard boy to feel affection for but it isn't as if we whipped him every morning and gave him gruel at night."

"Perhaps we should have," Camellia put in.

Fitz had already given them a description of the barn and was on his second cinnamon bun and third cup of Earl Grey, thinking he'd have to take a leak before he left, wondering—this was always a problem—how he'd approach the delicate question of using the bathroom.

"You said there was tension?" Ruth prompted.

"It didn't appear so at the time but in retrospect, yes, there was a definite strain. Though I explained that Wyn had a difficult contract she had to work on, Tony Deel was outraged that she dared refuse an invitation from Jackson Hall. Jackson himself was intrigued.

"But Wyn's not turning up had nothing to do with the unease in the barn that day. It came, I suspect, from Jackson himself. Under all that cinematic charm, he was edgy. He prides himself on his coffee-making ability and at the right moment went off to work a noisy Italian contraption. While he was seeing to that and Tony Deel was cleaning up, I was left alone with Jessica Stevens and I asked if she thought Jackson was happy to be back in Waggs Neck.

" 'Very happy,' she said. 'Like a child who's been sent away and now has been allowed to come home.' Then I asked if she was happy to be here and she said, 'It doesn't much matter where I am as long as I can help him.' She said it nonchalantly, as if she were talking about the weather."

"Or about a patient," Camellia said.

"As a matter of fact, Cammie, I think you're right," Fitz agreed. "It was said very much in that paternal, prescriptive way doctors use when talking about favored patients. But I took the remark at face value. Then I put my big foot in my mouth and said, nonsequentially, that Jackson Hall wasn't renowned for monogamy. She laughed and said, 'He told me he once stayed with a woman for four years. At the end he thought he'd go out of his mind. I've been with him for three and my time is nearly up. I don't regret a moment of it but all the signs are there. He's going to look for a nice homespun beauty to go with the barn. I came with the yacht.'

"There was an awkward moment and to fill it I said that his short attention span with women was probably why he never married. 'Oh, he was married,' Jessica told me. 'Years ago. . .' But she didn't finish because Jackson appeared with the Italian coffee.

" 'What was years ago?' he asked.

" 'Your marriage, Jackson.'

"He gave her a cool look and said, nicely enough, 'That subject is never to be mentioned in my presence. I am against marriage for philosophic reasons.'

"I asked what his philosophy was and he said, 'Art, Fitz, what else?' Then he switched the subject. The luncheon was by way of a peace offering. He and I had a falling-out some time ago. For Maggie's sake—she wants her friends to be friends—and out of plain curiosity, I went, but I don't feel comfortable with him and I don't like him any more now than I did before. After coffee and brandy, he showed me his bedroom–studio and its astonishing view of the harbor. The room was, in keeping with the house, sparsely furnished, but there was a framed photograph propped up against the wall. You'll never guess what it was: an old group shot of the Fat Boys."

"But Jackson wasn't in the Fat Boys."

"He said it was left for him at the Yacht Club. No note but all framed and nicely matted. It smells like Phineas's work. Jackson was going to toss it but he saw that Kate was in the photo, disguised as a real fat boy, a pillow in her jacket, the expression on her face a perfect mixture of bad boy and adorable angel."

"She was so fanciful," Camellia said. "Not really beautiful—not like Dolly—but she made you think she was."

"There was a rough drawing next to the photo, no more than a cartoon really, of a boy standing at the water's edge. In just a few lines Jackson managed to convey an intolerable loneliness. I admired it and he said he was going to give it to Maggie."

"Just like that?" Ruth Cole asked. "Signed? My dear, do you have any idea how valuable it is?"

"Maggie's not going to put it up for auction," Fitz said, a little sharply. "She got it this morning and said it's going to be her contribution to Phineas's exhibit in the keeping room. Phineas asked Wyn if she would lend her painting but decided he didn't want it after Wyn asked what insurance coverage he was providing."

"That particular Jackson Hall always gives me the willies," Camellia said, hugging herself. "Supposedly Jackson gave it to Hap but that's no reason for Wyn to keep it over her mantel. When she first moved back, I offered her Mother's watercolor of Trout Pond but she wasn't interested."

After more talk about "odious Phineas Browne's festival," Camellia agreed to walk with Fitz to the post office. Ruth stayed home, intending to do a little fall gardening before it became "really too brisk." Fitz asked, with a cough, if he could first, uhm, use the facilities.

"Certainly not," Ruth said. He looked up, astonished, to see her teacher's smile. "You know where it is. Go. My Lord, you're an old-fashioned fellow, Fitz. Don't forget to put the seat down when you're finished or we'll have the cleaning lady believing we've taken to entertaining strange males."

"He never fit in as a boy," Camellia said a few moments later as she and Fitz were turning onto Front Street into the bay breeze. "There was something about Jackson that habitually caused uproars to develop around him. He was what my father called a born troublemaker.

"Problem was he was neither fish nor fowl. His parents—one got the feeling they were disreputable—came from the South, Louisiana, I think, and were obscurely related to Mother and Uncle Bull. When they died and

Jackson was sent to him, Bull got us to take the boy in. Bull always resented him. Poor Jackson. He never knew whether he belonged with the factory workers or with the carriage trade and consequently never felt at home with anyone. His being so arty didn't help, either. The Fat Boys gave him terrible trouble over that.

"And then there was Kate. Given her rebelliousness, it was only a matter of time before she got involved with Jackson. Bull was furious. Wouldn't have him in the house. Gossip had it that she was sleeping with Jackson and if that got back to my uncle Bull, you can imagine how enraged he would have been. Of all the men infatuated with Kate, Bull was the most ardent. His dislike of Jackson really was almost pathologic . . ."

She stopped as they reached the dangerous corner where Front and Main streets met. The traffic light had turned red and they both looked up at Carlson House. "I don't know why but I can't help thinking that it would have been better if Jackson Hall hadn't come back to Waggs Neck."

Before parting at the post office, Fitz going to his post office box, Camellia to hers, she said, "I wonder who left that photograph. The Fat Boys despised Jackson. It seems as if—now don't give me that 'Ruth' look, Fitz—it seems as if it was sent as some sort of a warning."

CHAPTER

Six

PHINEAS HAD PRAYED FOR AND RECEIVED A FRAUDULENT summer Saturday for his festival. With the carrot of national television exposure dangling in front of them, the shopkeepers of Main Street had festooned their windows with comedic whales and unconvincing scrimshaw and draped their awnings with the red, white, and blue bunting usually reserved for important republic holidays.

Maggie took her place next to Ruth and Camellia Cole in the rickety reviewing stand set up in front of the Municipal Building. Catching sight of the giant American flag draped across Frank E. Taylor's Antiquarian Book Store, she said, "Would someone please tell me what the hell the nation's colors have to do with Phineas Browne's damn Whalers Festival?"

"You're out of sorts this morning," Ruth remarked. "You're not coming down with anything bad, are you, Maggie?"

Maggie, thinking that she had come down with something very bad indeed, stood up as the American Legion band segued abruptly from "When The Saints Come Marching In" to the national anthem. Professional and amateur hand-held video cameras began to roll. Inspired, the American Legion band members gave it their considerable all.

"Pity that weatherman couldn't be here," the governor was saying to Fitz Robinson down in the first row of the stand. The absent television personality was popular among rural voters and the governor had hoped to catch a bit of his down-home amiability.

"He's judging a fried chicken contest in Panama City, Florida," Fitz informed his old friend. "You would have come off more acidulated than ever next to him anyway." The governor turned, found Wyn behind him on the next tier up, and began a conversation with her about the acreage he owned on the outskirts of the village. Off to the side, the weatherman's replacement, a dedicated blonde, was interviewing Jackson Hall while two remote cameras atop the mobile television van were focused on the crowd mugging for them in front of the Municipal Building.

"He'll get his damn pier after this," David Kabot remarked to Dicie, who was examining his hand, thinking it was a fine, meaty hand. She had caught another glimpse of Jackson Hall—he had been in and out of distant sight all summer—but now the view was blocked and she contented herself with the thought that she would be able to talk to him at the keeping room reception, though she wasn't exactly certain what she was going to say. "Hey, Dad, how come you haven't connected with me in the nineteen years since I was born?" seemed appropriate but ungracious. She wasn't even angry at him. I only want to know him a little bit, she thought, squeezing David's hand as hard as she could for a reaction, getting a squeeze in return that made her say ouch.

They had eschewed the stands and were sitting on the curb in front of the Marjorie Main Launderette, so named because it was located on the corner where Marjorie and Main streets met. The parade began in earnest and they watched the progress of the gargantuan pink fin-tailed 1955 Cadillac convertible into which the Gold Star Mothers had stuffed themselves. This was followed a bit too closely by the inflated whale, which occasionally belched, emitting torpid geysers of brown water, spritzing the Gold Star Mothers in the back seat of the Cadillac.

Dolly was just taking her place in the stand between John Fenton and Willy Mercer, having been involved with various last-minute crises. Lettie Browne arrived a moment later, creating the sort of stir she was mistress of, wearing an out-of-season but spectacular huge half-round lacquered black straw hat and a yellow Galanos dress. Fitz gave Lettie his place next to the governor, squeezing in alongside Wyn as two multibraided members of the Brownie troop, big and soon to-be-myopic eyes opened in awe, presented a bouquet of daisies and baby's breath to Lettie.

Her thanks were drowned out as majorettes from all three Waggs Neck schools—high, junior high, and grade—marched by, twirling in time to their respective school bands. They were followed by the Catholic (Lincoln Town Car), Episcopalian (Rolls-Royce Silver Spirit), Baptist (Taurus station wagon), and Lutheran (Buick Regal) clergy, signaling the end of the parade and the beginning of the speeches.

Phineas gave a much applauded oration, lauding Waggs Neck Harbor's ancient history and painting a verbal picture of Waggs Neck's future prosperity. He concluded by welcoming the governor—"our illustrious native son"—who welcomed another native son, Jackson Hall, who stood up to say it was grand to be home. The crowd applauded, the television and amateur cameras whirred on.

Eventually, the governor shook Jackson Hall's hand, kissed Lettie and several other people on the cheek, grimaced at Fitz and, with apologies, departed midst a flurry of aides for his helicopter and Albany. He insisted on Wyn accompanying him to the airport "to help me decide whether to put that damn land on the market. Taxes on it are killing me." Phineas was annoyed that Wyn was going to miss the reception. "She's so decorous."

He marched the remaining local nabobs off to Carlson House where a nervous Annie Kitchen, in the keeping room pantry, was putting the finishing touches on her fabled poison fudge whale cake.

In the keeping room itself, Tony Deel, pressed into service by Phineas, was coping with the cameraman who was worried about adequate electricity for his lights.

Maggie, Fitz, and the Cole sisters entered the keeping room through its ground-floor door, while Phineas, a stickler for formality, led everyone else through Carlson House's Main Street entry, up the central staircase, through the long service corridor and down the back steps as if he were captaining a medieval pageant.

Dolly Carlson stood at the staircase entry to the keeping room, exhorting guests to watch the television crew's wires crisscrossing the brick floor. David Kabot opined that she looked pretty wired herself. What with the summerlike temperature, the lights, and the people, the keeping room was growing uncomfortably warm, but when Dicie touched her mother's hand, it was as cold as the winter sea.

"Everything seems to be going apace," Fitz said to Tony Deel.

"You think so?" Tony was passing around New York State champagne in shallow plastic cups wrapped in the too-large napkins Phineas had taken it upon himself to design and order. Tony had brought a nearly full bottle of calvados for Jackson and had placed it, for safekeeping, in the broom closet. He had given Jackson a real glass—Jackson hated the texture of plastic—nearly full with the stuff but Jackson hadn't tasted it. He often didn't drink at public events, presumably not wanting to lose control. Just as well, Tony thought. Jackson out of control wasn't pretty. He had set the untasted brandy on a highly polished rosewood console that had been placed several feet in front of the fireplace, creating a sort of corridor filled with guests going to and from the buffet table.

Phineas joined Jackson in front of the console where the ceremony was to take place. "What *are* you drinking?" he asked, as if it were a naughty question. When Jackson told him, Phineas said hopefully, "I don't believe I've ever tasted calvados." None was offered and Phineas contented himself with downing the warm contents of his glass—he had a proper one as well, as befitting his station—setting it next to Jackson's where it would be sure to leave a mark.

"Could someone open a window?" Colonel Mercer asked after Ruth Cole complained. "Decidedly stuffy in here," he added, looking around as if a staff servant might appear to do his bidding. Maggie said she understood the windows would have to stay closed, that the television people would be annoyed if they removed the blackout stuff. She was watching a determined Dolly moving about, getting people to stand against the walls and out of the way of the cameraman.

"There's something wrong with her," Maggie thought. "She looks ill." She started to make her way to Dolly when the producer, in a voice that seemed about to break, asked everyone to take their places.

Billy Bell, wearing a T-shirt advertising New York Seltzer and his inflated pectoral muscles, stood outside the pantry door, making circles with his flashlight on the brick of the fireplace visible over the console.

"I don't suppose you remember our schoolmates," Phineas was saying nervously to Jackson in his jovial civic manner. Two inches taller than Jackson, he was leaning down like a maître d'hôtel greeting a great tipper, his right hand sweeping in a half arc indicating the colonel and Dr. Fenton.

"I remember them." After a brief hesitation, Jackson allowed each to shake his hand.

"We got juice trouble," the crew chief said, as if it were preordained. The producer, running nail-bitten fingers through thinning hair, announced there would be a delay and went with the chief to the mobile van to consider the problem.

Maggie, standing at the foot of the stairs, observed that there was trouble in paradise again. David was wearing his sullen look while Dicie was trying to establish eye contact with Jackson Hall. Fitz had walked around the room via the passage between the console and the fireplace to the buffet and was looking askance at the white cheese wedges. Leave it to Phineas, he thought, to spend a fortune on paper napkins and skimp on the eats.

Annie Kitchen stuck her head out of the pantry and Billy Bell told her, rudely, to stick it back in, that it wasn't time yet. Ruth Cole snagged one of the plastic glasses filled with warm champagne and was staring at Jackson Hall, who appeared oblivious to both her and her sister.

Tony Deel stood near the fireplace, trying to calculate how long it would be until Jackson blew. Phineas was standing too close to Jackson, his head down, his obsequious smile painful to observe. Jackson, Tony knew, wasn't amused.

". . . you, of course, remember Kate," Phineas was saying as if Jackson could have forgotten. Everyone wondered how much longer they'd be cooped up in the ill-ventilated room.

"Time, yet?" Annie Kitchen called through the pantry door, and Billy Bell said in a loud whisper, "No, bitch, it ain't time yet." By now everyone knew Annie was to bring in the whale cake when the lights were dimmed and Billy was to light her way with the flashlight. "A bit of ingenious Phineas choreography," Lettie said to Fitz. "Of all the endless possibilities, why oh why did Fate choose to cast Phineas in the role of my brother?" She removed her hat and, fanning herself with it, stood against the wall watching Phineas chat up Jackson Hall.

Jackson, to her surprise, appeared interested in what Phineas was saying.

"And do you remember how we took you down to the boys' cloak room on the night of the senior dance and Kate got Percy to dress up . . ."

"We're almost ready." The producer had returned and the temporary lights came on, shining through his jug ears, turning them a dark pink.

"She loved her joke, did Kate," Phineas was saying. "It was my idea, I admit, but she thought it was great fun. Still, she only had eyes for you, as the old song would have it."

"Ready?" the cameraman asked.

"What a familiar, angry expression Jackson has," Camellia Cole said to her sister. Ruth was about to say she remembered it well when the inevitable happened and the lights went out. The producer said, with great feeling, "Oh, shit," and asked all present to remain where they were. "All present" began to say something and then thought better of it. Billy Bell's flashlight made circles on the brick fireplace behind the console, creating the only illumination until the lights came on, moments later.

"Doesn't Phineas look idiotic?" Lettitia said. "That smirk."

"Mayor Browne, we are now taping," the producer said though clenched and expensively capped teeth. "If you'll step forward and make the toast, Mr. Bell will give Ms. Kitchen the go-ahead and we can wrap this relatively quickly."

Phineas, still wearing his ingenuous, pleased-with-himself grin, picked up the nearly full glass from the console, swallowed a good deal of it so it wouldn't spill over, choked a little and then moved into the center of the room, holding the somewhat depleted glass high as the lights were dimmed, this time purposely, while all eyes followed the light from Billy Bell's flashlight, illuminating the bottom of the pantry door.

There was a muffled harsh croak, somewhere between a belch and a cry for help, as Annie Kitchen burst out of the pantry, awkwardly balancing the whale cake with its lit birthday candles on a tray in her arms.

This was followed by another unpleasant sound—someone trying desperately to clear his windpipe—but it was difficult to pinpoint where it was coming from, given the cavernlike acoustics of the keeping room. "Must be those cheese wedges," Camellia said aloud, as Annie, holding her cake as if it were a baby, took a few steps forward while the unknown person in distress let out a terrible croak. It seemed to have come from the vicinity of the console but Annie was blocking the view. Without warning, she screamed and threw her short arms up in the air. Ten pounds of fudge, marzipan, and vanilla icing hit the stone floor with a thick, plodding noise, the lights came up, and Annie, to the crowd's dismay, continued to scream. Fitz quickly moved forward and guided her out of the way, revealing the cause of her distress.

A few inches from where the platter fell lay Phineas Browne, his suit covered with vomit and cake, eyes popping and mouth pursed as if in disapproval of such a vulgar finish.

CHAPTER

Seven

THE WEATHER HADN'T HELD. A BRISK NORTH WIND BLEW
in off the bay, shredding yesterday's red, white, and blue
frippery, sweeping it along a deserted Main Street. The
sky was chromium gray, low, threatening, and wintry.
"The way the last Sunday in October is supposed to be,"
Maggie said to herself, sitting at her desk, shuffling accumulated mail, trying to decide which "Letters to Maggie"
deserved answers.

Not that she could. She couldn't do much of anything.
There was no distraction she could think of that would
erase the vision of Phineas, splattered with vomit and
Annie's poison fudge cake, indignant expression on his
face, dead on her keeping room floor. They had been
enemies for a long time and there was no doubt in Maggie's mind that Phineas had been a grade A horseball,
but she had known him forever, he had genuinely loved
their village, and he deserved a kinder finale.

She was not allowed to mourn Phineas undisturbed.
The keeping room was filled with those experienced in
untimely death, its outer door continually opening and
closing with a hollow sound that reverberated through-

out the house. Otherwise there had been a preternatural quiet while investigators, fingerprint men, photographers, and generic scene-of-the-crime experts danced around that ground-floor room, silent and skilled members of a macabre corps de ballet.

Captain Homer Price, Waggs Neck's chief of police, stood at the keeping room entry, a fast-frozen Othello, observing the others concentrating on the detailed, precise gathering of potential evidence: liquids were collected with slender suction tubes; fragments and remnants of human and other materials were picked up with gentle tweezers. All were stored and carefully labeled in sealed, sterile containers, carried out, and meticulously packed in a waiting van. Phineas seemed beside the point, a white chalk outline the only evidence he had been there.

Maggie had gone down to offer coffee. The professionals accepted, but Homer Price—known by the villagers as Captain Midnight—declined with an impatient shake of his head. He had no time for coffee or for Maggie. This was his first murder case and he wanted to get it right.

Homer Price, thirty years old, six feet four inches tall, created in the image of a despotic African god, had been hired away by the Waggs Neck village board from a down-island police force where he had served as second in command. He had been the most qualified candidate they could find: born in Waggs Neck to one of the village's first black businessmen, college-educated, he had through-the-roof scores for the New York State civil service test designated for chiefs of police.

None of the warring village political factions could utter a word against him, publicly. Privately it was said that he lacked experience; that he was overly ambitious; but no one, not in this enlightened day, was about to come out and say that the village elders did not want an Afro-American chief of police.

Maggie went upstairs, thinking that the captain was going to fall on his high-pitched rear end one day, good and hard. She stood at the French doors in her upstairs sitting room, staring out at her village. The shops were closed, the viewing stand removed, the weekenders returned to the city where they belonged.

She sighed—Lord, there seemed to be a lot of sighing lately—aware that she was mourning not only Phineas's death but the village's loss of innocence as well. The last recorded murder in Waggs Neck had occurred in 1898 when a woman named June Frame hit her philandering husband over the head with a game mallet.

The populace were no doubt as titillated then as they were now. Maggie envisioned them in their living rooms, too excited to actually read the newspaper accounts, obsessed by front pages filled with pictures of Phineas, the governor, Fitz, Lettie, Jackson. They would be asking one another throughout the day: Who the hell would want to murder Phineas Browne? Maggie, thinking of all the times she had threatened the dead mayor with bodily harm, felt a blast of chilled air come up the front staircase: someone had opened the never locked and seldom used front door.

Lettie sailed up the stairs and into the room like an important cruise ship docking in a secondary port. She flung her large black hat across the room Frisbee-like and lowered herself into the Boston rocker. She was wearing another Galanos, black, and nearly as costly as the one she had worn for the festival. "You look great," Maggie said, meaning it.

"I took a Valium, had a brandy, and slept the sleep of the pure. I know what you're thinking. You're such an old-fashioned gal, Maggie. I should be weeping buckets, cultivating pouches under my eyes, doing Bette Davis as Mrs. Skeffington after she lost her looks. Not me, my dear. True, he was one's only brother but he had an artificial soul. I despised him."

As Maggie looked at her eminently stylish and, at this moment, not particularly admirable friend, she smelled fear and wondered if it was specific—was Lettie afraid she was going to be knocked off next?—or generic, the kind of awesome dread that murder brings to nearly everyone concerned.

Motherless at an early age, Lettie had long looked to Maggie, as others did, for guidance. With Maggie's support she had left the village early and alone and she invariably returned alone, as if there was something in Waggs Neck she couldn't let go of. Lately, she had spent the season in Manhattan, where she kept a spectacular Fifth Avenue apartment, and the summer in the old Bay Street mansion.

"Vodka," Lettie said, in response to Maggie's offer of tea. "I'll get it myself." She went to the small passage off the sitting room to Bull Carlson's wet bar, where she poured herself two fingers and, as an afterthought, added a cube of ice.

"How are you feeling?" Maggie asked.

"Wretched. John Fenton says they're going to perform an autopsy. Carving up Phineas's body as if it weren't perfectly clear that he was poisoned. And there's going to be an inquest and a lot of disgusting publicity that will probably launch me on an entirely new career. Did you see Barbara Walters?"

"No television."

"One forgets," Lettie said, fitting an oval cigarette into a round jade holder, "just how pure you are, Maggie. You might want to borrow one. We're all over it and my agent called to report that Geraldo, Wimprah, and Phil want to book me. You look marvelous in full color, a gray-headed Buddha in mauve and green. Jackson looks as if he were the one who had been murdered and Phineas . . . how thrilled Phineas would be." She took a long pull at the vodka, put the cigarette out with a stagy, circular gesture, stood up and moved to the French doors.

Though her movements, words, and makeup were, as usual, stylized almost to the point of burlesque, Phineas's violent death had obviously broken through his sister's iron maiden facade. Lettie, looking out at a bleak Main Street, took a white linen handkerchief from a secret pocket and gave her nose a vigorous honk.

"Who are you crying for?" Maggie wanted to know. "Certainly not for Phineas."

Lettie took another gulp of vodka. "I'm an orphan now," she said tearfully, answering Maggie's question, trying out the part. Maggie laughed. "All right. Nonetheless, Phineas would have his long-delayed and only orgasm if he knew that his death had been recorded for the late night news, don't you think?" She turned her elegant shoulders on the dismal Waggs Neck Sunday vista. "Captain Midnight called personally to inform me of the inquest. He sounded delighted."

"I don't suppose they'll leave the investigation up to him," Maggie said. "Although he might do."

"Homer Price couldn't investigate a jaywalking. But they can't take it away from him just yet or the liberals will have a field day." Lettie focused her frosty eyes on her old friend for a long moment and said, in a different voice, "How do you think it happened, Maggie? You don't suppose someone was playing a fool game that backfired? Dropped a couple of spoiled LSD pills in Phineas's breakfast drink, thinking it'd be fun to watch him freak out? Or that the Spanish omelette at the Eden was off?"

"I don't think there's any doubt, pal, that Phineas was deliberately poisoned. Cyanide is difficult to ingest accidentally."

"How do they know it's cyanide?"

"They don't for sure—the medical examiner's report is yet to be written—but John Fenton said Phineas had all the symptoms and as he knelt over him, John said he smelled the well-documented aroma of burnt almonds."

"But who in the world would want to murder Phineas?"

"*Moi*, for one. I threatened it every time he proposed his damned Pier Mall. Jackson, for the same or other, older reasons. David Kabot, Fitz Robinson, and the Cole sisters, at one time or another, threatened Phineas with at least lawsuits. He was a provocative man, Lettie." She stopped for a moment. "And then of course there's you. You're his only living relative. And I don't think Phineas, hidebound egomaniac that he was, ever knew the extent of your animosity. So I guess you inherit what money there is, not to mention the New Federal . . ."

It was Lettie's turn to laugh, not altogether convincingly. "Right. I killed my brother to get my hands on a falling-down Victorian mess on Main Street."

"The New Federal's worth a bundle," Maggie said. And then she had a new thought. "Don't forget that Phineas loved secrets. Made him feel special. There might be all sorts of reasons someone might want to shut him up that we don't know about."

"Like the love affair he was having with the volunteer fire chief's twin brother? Get real, Maggie. Nor do I believe anyone was going to poison him because of a potentially spoiled view. It had to be the touted 'freak accident' of the *National Enquirer.* No one would kill Phineas on purpose."

Fitz Robinson hadn't felt so alert, so alive, in some time, though he couldn't admit that. It would hardly be seemly, this new energy fueled by the murder of an old friend. His right ear hurt from having been held to the telephone for several hours following Phineas's death. He had talked first with various ranks at Suffolk County PD headquarters, then with various ranks of governor's aides.

The powers-that-were and the powers-that-would-be were taking a lively interest in Phineas Browne's death, thanks to television and shared footage. The governor shaking hands and trading fake laughs with the decedent had been the network news's unanimous opening shot. They advised viewers that "the following material" might not be to their liking and then, audience attention riveted, they closed the news with the main event: Phineas Browne dead on Maggie's keeping room floor.

The tail end of that long Sunday morning of telephone conversations was a call from the governor himself. "I'm in a box, Fitz." Fitz tried to commiserate but the governor was too intent on saying what he wanted to say to listen to him. "Hear me out, Fitz. The wise guys up here tell me I can't call Captain Midnight off but I'm not going to let that arrogant son of a bitch fuck this up either. I want you to come on as a special consultant and, in effect, take on the damn investigation. If you can wrap it up in a week, fine. If not, we'll have to do something else. Media's eating me alive. And I'm warning you, there'll be no glory. We're going to have to let your friend, the captain, get the credit. But you should be able to solve this quick. Christ, you know every time someone farts in that town . . ."

"Al . . ."

"I'm not taking no for an answer, Fitz."

"I wasn't going to say no."

CHAPTER
Eight

WYN WOKE UP ON THAT DREAR SUNDAY MORNING AFTER
Phineas's death remembering a whispered conversation
between him and her, held during a Friends of the Library meeting. They were both bored with the issue at
hand—another fund-raising flea market—and Phineas
wanted to know if she had been teased about her name
when she was growing up.

"In high school it was Wyn-or-Lose Lewis," Wyn admitted, retreating slightly. Phineas had notorious breath.
"In college I was known to the fraternity bastards as A
Losing—as opposed to A Winning—Proposition. At NYU
we were too busy doing the law school grind for jokes
but the business law professor got off on calling me Wyn-
some/Lose-some."

"I do think you should use your full name. One really
loathes diminutives and Wynsome is lovely. It's a wonder your mother chose it."

"She wanted to name me Sarmienta after the great Ar-
gentine president–educator, Sarmiento. Luckily my father got to the birth certificate first."

Probity disturbed this reminiscence by emitting her

early morning half-growl, half-sob. Wyn reluctantly got up, flossed and brushed her teeth, put her camel hair coat over her pajamas, and took Probity for a grim walk down School House Lane to the little park where the dog liked to do her duty.

Back in her ill-equipped kitchen, making tea, Wyn looked at the pictures of the people she knew on the front pages of the Sunday papers and found herself reaching for the telephone to call Phineas—to tell him that he was dead.

She wondered if she were in shock. Moving into the dining room, munching toast, facing the autumnal south garden, reading the newspaper accounts for validation, she found it difficult to believe that Phineas, of all people—that foolish, funny, charming, self-centered man—was beyond telephone communication.

When Wyn had made the move from Manhattan back to Waggs Neck, he had become first a client, then an ally, and ultimately a friend. Wyn didn't like all that many people and she found that she was feeling sorry for herself. Nice, she told herself. Phineas is dead and I'm into heavy self-pity.

She couldn't seem to find a comfortable spot to just be in. Balancing her teacup and the papers, she moved again, this time into the long, chilly living room, and stared through the French doors out onto the equally drear west garden, thinking that what she had liked most about Phineas was that confidential way of his, treating her as if they were coconspirators. "My dear, you'll never guess," he liked to say to her, stepping into her office, looking behind him for imaginary eavesdroppers, shutting the door, regaling her with tales of what Old Man Krantz or Billy Bell senior or Roberta Dinacola had said or done to further illustrate the absurdity of village life. "You're as mean-spirited as I am, Wynsome; you like to pretend you're not."

Wyn was, admittedly, somewhat mean-spirited, but that did not signify that she shared all of Phineas's convictions, least of all his grand design for "bringing Waggs Neck, kicking and screaming, into the twentieth century." She was privately against development, liking Waggs Neck as it was: small and quiet and undiscovered.

Nonetheless, she was a licensed attorney and a licensed real estate broker and she enjoyed the heady feeling making money gave her. Thus she often found herself writing contracts for the developers as well as for the preservationists, and sometimes between them. Phineas would grill Wyn about who was selling and/or buying what, but she had always referred him to the public records. "You are the most closemouthed woman I know," he'd complain, looking over her shoulder at the papers on her desk.

He would have loved to have known about the post-contract negotiations Wyn had been trying to effect since last spring between a development company called Grasslands, Inc., and Lucy Littlefield. Lucy lived at the end of Lowe Lane with a variety of unattractive cats and canaries. It was said they all, Lucy included, ate out of the same bowl. She was land rich, having inherited the bayfront second-growth pine forest not far from the convent grounds. Roy Stein, Grasslands' guiding spirit, wanted it so he could erect "a tasteful townhouse development community designed for the empty-nest weekend couple, complete with lavishly landscaped grounds, pool, and tennis court, all in tune with our sensitive ecosystem."

Roy and Lucy had signed a properly witnessed contract for seven hundred and fifty thousand dollars in Wyn's office in the middle of the summer but now Lucy was waffling. Roy promised to sue for performance but his Manhattan attorneys were hesitant after meeting with Lucy, self-described as "one sandwich short of a picnic." If the court agreed with her, the contract would easily be overturned.

Wyn didn't think there was anything seriously wrong with Lucy's mind, only that she enjoyed a fuss. But

Lucy, too, liked money, and Wyn decided she would give it one more try before telling Roy that Grasslands should seek more fertile pastures.

It occurred to her that she should call the village clerk to find out if Lucy was paying her taxes; she had occasionally lapsed in the past. If Lucy was in arrears, that might be another incentive to close the deal.

Sunday morning dragged on. She tried to telephone Fitz, but his line was constantly busy. She switched on CNN, but they were running the same footage of Waggs Neck: Phineas self-consciously welcoming the governor; Phineas cautiously shaking hands with Jackson Hall; and then the final, nauseating scene.

It was simultaneously embarrassing, rude, and fascinating. She tried to be a good person by reading "The Week in Review" in the *Times* but the realization that Phineas had been killed kept getting in the way of the print.

The only call she had was from her ex-husband, Nicky Meyer, wanting to hear about the murder. "Didn't Allie and I stay in his hotel last year when the Benz broke?" Nick and his second wife, the ever peppy Allison Altman Meyer, had been traveling between her parents' house on Shark Island and their own weekend house in Southampton when their car broke down on Main Street and Nick had the nerve to call and ask Wyn to put them up. Wyn, whose spine needed spray starch when she spoke to Nick, had managed to suggest the New Federal. "Were you on the scene?" Nick asked, and when she said no, he wanted to know why not. "Thought all the local biggies were there." Nick liked to suggest that Wyn's family had been the principal founders of Waggs Neck in the late sixteenth century—"old *goyish* family, you know"—when in truth they had only been minor players.

Perhaps it was Phineas's mean, untimely death. Perhaps it was the knowledge that if she didn't finally speak up, she would have to bear her relationship with Nick around her shoulders for the rest of her life like some inoperable deformity. Whatever it was, she was able to say aloud the words she had long been practicing in her mind. "Nick, it's been years since you dumped me. I don't like you one iota better now than I did then. We have nothing in common except a profession and we practice it in very different ways. Please stop with the calls, the birthday flowers—I hate calla lilies—and the humorous greeting cards. I wish you well. I want you to have everything you've ever desired in life including membership in the University Club. But I don't want to know you, Nick. Now or ever." She should have hung up then but didn't. "Wow," Nick said, twice. "Whoever your new analyst is, babe, he knows what he's doing. Seriously, Wyn, Allie and I and the kids are coming out next weekend with some good people we want you to meet and we'd really, really like you to break bread with us. What about dinner, Saturday night? Hey, I have to hang. We got Allie's folks coming for brunch. Never, ever, ever stops. I'll take it as a yes."

"No," she shouted into the phone, too late.

They had met in their senior year at Brown at a fraternity party she hadn't wanted to go to. Where the hell have you been, he wanted to know, circling in like a serious collector on a heretofore undiscovered butterfly. Nick, of course, had been everywhere, a campus luminary, while Wyn had done just what her mother had always begged her not to: hidden her light under a bushel.

This time the bushel had been English lit; who knew what Nick had majored in? Perhaps contemporary ethnicity. Whereas his father, a second-generation Miami attorney, enunciated in the John Barrymore tradition, Nick—who had prepped at Andover—spoke as if he had only just left the *shtetl*. "Such a *shicksa*," he said, taking her to bed on their first date. "Look at that straight blond hair and that adorable nose. Cheek bones up the yin yang. And those long High Episcopalian legs. *Oy vey*, I think I'm in love." He had unruly chocolate brown hair, Shirley Temple dimples, plaintive brown eyes, and a dedicated soccer player's physique. He gloried in his good looks, his Yiddish *schtick*, his quick intelligence. He was the most exotic being Wyn had ever met and yet that paternalistic need of his to take care of her was reminiscent of her father. Wyn, who had a celebrated dry wit in her little literary circle, lost her voice for the last half of her final semester, enslaved.

Trouble with Nick was he never stopped being paternalistic. Even now, when she so clearly wanted him out of her life, he was determined to keep his hand in. "What would you do," Nick wanted to know, "if you had a real emergency? Who would you turn to? Just because we split doesn't mean we're not family."

"Yes it does, Nick."

"You don't mean that." He never forgot a birthday or a holiday, though he did have enough tact not to send a present on their anniversary. "From the first second I saw you, I knew you were an orphan."

"I have a perfectly sound mother."

"You're still an orphan. You got those spit-colored eyes . . ."

"That's very complimentary."

". . . they're just begging for a little affection." Nick also had a mother. "You wouldn't marry her, would you?" that woman had asked at the end of his senior year at Brown, sotto voce behind the menu in the restaurant where he had brought her to meet Wynn, thereby putting the idea in his head. "We're not going to give you one red cent for law school if you marry her," Audrey Meyer went on. "Not one red cent."

They gave him his tuition for Columbia Law and a little extra ("so he shouldn't have to live hand-to-mouth") by way of a healthy monthly check. "That poor kid," Audrey said to her friends at the club. "Living on pizza and

Pepsi. Miss High-and-Mighty from the Middle of Nowhere doesn't cook."

And then there were little expenses. Nick had gotten
someone to put him up for the New York Athletic Club
and he found this great little tailor on Second Avenue
and so on. Wyn gave up her idea of graduate school—
at the time she would have given up almost anything he
wanted her to—and went to work for his cousins who
owned West Side Realty, first as a receptionist and then,
after taking the course and the tests, as a Realtor. "She's
a natural," Cousin Freddy told Nick. "They believe everything she tells them. With a face like that, who
wouldn't?"

By the time Nick passed the New York State law
boards, Wyn was a broker earning seventy thousand a
year selling low-end West Side condominiums, one of
which they had bought.

"Look, I'm leaving you this fantastic apartment and
you got this great career going for you," he said, as he
packed his soft Mark Cross suitcases, having announced
he was divorcing her to marry Allison Altman, whose
father was the principal partner of the law firm that had
hired him at an astronomical salary. "What do you need
me for?" He gave her a check for twenty-five thousand
dollars. "My parents' wedding present to me and Allie,
but, hey, we know you need it more."

She knew that the wedding present was fifty thousand
and very nearly tossed the check back in his appealing
face, but didn't, marking that moment as the one when
she stopped believing in her father's system of fair-play
ethics, when she finally stepped into reality. "Listen,
you're going to be a lot better off without me. Don't cry,
Wyn. Please."

"I'm not crying." She wasn't. She knew Nick was
right.

She thought about using the money to help pay her
way through graduate school, but the idea of spending

her days spreading the joys of nineteenth-century English literature suddenly and forever eluded her.

She decided, she told startled friends, to be an attorney. "Isn't that just a wee bit competitive?" Natalie, her ex-sister-in-law, asked. But she wasn't interested in the drama and theatricality of litigation, Nick's specialty. She had discovered during her few years of selling cooperatives that she enjoyed the dry, careful, legalistic side of the business. She liked researching titles, encumbrances, disputed rights of way. She favored special exceptions and deeds of suspect provenance. The language suggested Trollope, the stories unfolded recalled Dickens. She would specialize in real estate law.

During her two years at NYU Law, she slept with several men, including her former boss, Cousin Freddy; a brilliant fellow student with whom she studied; and once, very much against her spirit if not her will, with Nick. She had been depressed and lonely and there was old Nick, caring and touching and dark and sexy and totally, abysmally seductive.

"Why don't you marry again?" Nick wanted to know, getting into his three-hundred-dollar trousers.

"Why do you care? You don't pay alimony."

"You used to be so sweet, Wyn; I don't know what happened to you. Though I have to admit you're just as neat in bed as you used to be." *Neat*, Wyn knew, was an Allison word. She traded with her mother the little apartment on West Seventy-sixth Street for the family house in Waggs Neck. Linda Lewis immediately secured a job in administration with the City University of New York and was now vice-chancellor for research. Given Linda's drill sergeant's heart and earnest educator's intelligence, Wyn didn't doubt that with luck and in time her mother would be chancellor.

Hap had left Wyn a small, red brick building on Main Street that once housed his own real estate office and was currently occupied by a shoemaker whose rent just about covered the upkeep. She bought the delighted shoemaker out of his lease and set up her law and real estate office, hiring Liz Lum to act as receptionist and secretary. Liz's only drawback was Heidi, a teenage daughter who was, not unexpectedly, driving her crazy.

The practice prospered. Both new and old Waggs Neck trusted Wyn, who had a deserved reputation as a "hard worker" and usually knew when to keep her smart mouth to herself. The money she earned gave her power and responsibility. She didn't often indulge herself but when she did, she did it well: there was a Jaguar in the garage.

She assuaged her social conscience by quietly supporting a long-term group home known as CHARLEE, established under an HRS program. It was supervised by live-in house parents and there was a long list of applicants—teenage girls, most of whom were Afro-Americans, on drugs and/or pregnant. The home, located on a farm on West Sea Road, was chronically short of funds and qualified social workers, but Wyn refused to give it up because of the success it had in turning a number of girls onto a productive life.

Nor did she neglect her sensuality. In the eight years since she had returned to Waggs Neck, she had had four lovers, nice guys, good in bed, but none she wanted to face over the daily breakfast table for the rest of her life. Tommy Handwerk, the most enduring, not to mention endearing, had moved in and it had lasted two months.

She knew she was talked about, but in this modern age only the hard-core gossips cared whom she slept with. In the winter she had a restricted if active social life, much of it centered on such organizations as the Friends of the Library and the Friends of Art in Public Places. When the summer people came, there were cocktail parties and dinners and picnics on the beach and men wondering what the hell she did with herself in Waggs Neck during the winter.

The worst moments came during the high-suicide holiday season (Thanksgiving, Christmas, and New Year's), but she and Fitz managed one way or another, either by going away or with help from Liz, who organized elaborate, artificially festive meals.

If it wasn't what she had planned when, all dewy-eyed, she had married Nick the Rat, it was, on balance, a good life. She liked her books, her dog, her men, her friends, and most especially her work. Sometimes she thought she might like a baby, but she felt no particular urgency and supposed she could always get sweet Tommy to give her one.

Annoyed with herself, grieving over Phineas, Wyn got into sweats and Nikes and wheeled her ten-speed out of the garage. Allowing Probity to run beside her on the deserted Sunday streets, she biked west into the wind out Madison until its little gabled houses with porches gave way to flat-roofed houses with basketball hoops over the garages. She turned around when the pine forest took over, rode back along Madison, took a right at dusty, unpaved Widow Davitt's Road, which led her to Bay Street, where she turned east, passing the old mansions, turning north on Front Street, and entering the convent grounds just as she finally broke a sweat, a signal that she could ease up.

The three Mary Immaculate buildings sat behind a stone wall in the center of twenty bayfront acres facing the choppy bay waters. The buildings, clearly influenced by Eastern Orthodox high-church architecture, featured bulbous cupolas and half-round entryways, suggesting the barren steppes of Mother Russia. They had been designed for a group of Irish missionary nuns by a local architect with a finely developed sense of wrongness: his Waggs Neck Harbor First Presbyterian was a wooden temple of Isis.

Despite the no-trespassing warnings and the closed shutters, the buildings felt occupied. Phineas and her father and virtually everyone in the village over forty had gone to school here and Wyn believed she had missed

out on the good times. She had been born too late, the
public school well established by the time she was ready
for high school, while the convent buildings played host
to a series of doomed retreats, health and beauty spas, fat
farms, substance-abuse sanitariums. The place had been
vacant for the last decade, waiting, David Kabot warned,
for the time-share resort developers to move in.

David may be prescient, Wyn thought, the convent
having been sold by the Archdiocese only this past summer to something called the Bijoux Arts Foundation. Its
sale had been uncharacteristically overlooked by the
Chronicle in its weekly "properties sold" list, which was
odd; the convent changing hands should have been
front-page news. Wyn only learned about the sale while
going through the deeds section at county headquarters,
researching Lucy Littlefield's contiguous forest, and coming upon the new transfer.

She had kept the information to herself but had taken
the trouble to call an old friend, Janet Hayes, at the Foundation Library in Manhattan. Janet faxed her a copy of
the page on which the Bijoux Arts Foundation was listed.
The board had not seen fit to publish either their names
or the size of the endowment. The listing merely gave
an address on East Forty-second Street that sounded as
if it existed to receive mail and offered the fact that it
was a family foundation that did not entertain unsolicited
proposals but gave money to arts projects at the board's
discretion. Janet had written across the bottom in her
generous scrawl that it sounded like another small family
trust and if Wyn wanted her to dig some, she could probably come up with more and would she like to trade
abodes for a weekend soon?

Janet had a clever apartment on Jane Street in the Village but Wyn wasn't tempted—Manhattan and especially
the Village having long ago lost their allure. There was
no real reason for her to bother Janet further, but the
convent sale was odd. She wondered if Roy Stein had
somehow bought it through the foundation and was

planning a much larger project than advertised, but decided not. The Grasslands' chief played hardball but was not especially devious.

Wyn cycled round the three convent buildings, stopping in front of the playhouse while Probity chased a squirrel who easily eluded her. When Wyn was a scholarly tomboy hanging out with the village ragamuffins, the playhouse was often their destination, easily entered but too eerie to invite much destruction. The other kids invariably wanted to get out once they had gotten in, spooked by its enormous dimensions and fading majesty. But Wyn had been intrigued by the domed roof, the intricate balustrades, the carved scrolls of acanthus foliage, the gold leaf moldings and thronelike faded velvet seats. What had the architect been thinking of, she still wondered, plopping a covey of Dublin Town working-class nuns into a St. Petersburg palace? She hoped its new owners wouldn't destroy it.

Whistling for Probity, Win rode out of the convent grounds, to the corner of Front and Main, where the weathered, shingled Carlson House stood. It seemed more deserted than the convent, as if all of Carlson House's inhabitants and ghosts had abandoned it long ago. Observing village law by walking her bike up deserted Main Street, she passed the red brick building Phineas had turned into a fine hotel and wondered if his spirit was haunting his old loft apartment or, more likely, flitting around the mobile TV vans parked illegally in front of the Municipal Building.

The Municipal Building itself was ablaze in fluorescent lighting, half a dozen members of the television press dressed in variations of Desert Storm camouflage, standing around the village board chambers, smoking, drinking coffee, and looking unhappy.

One of the men in camouflage saw her looking in and beckoned to her and Wyn moved on quickly, having a vision of herself being stupid on national TV. She locked her bike in the bike rack in front of her office, warned

Probity to watch herself—she had been fixed but was still
a favorite among Main Street dogs—and let herself in.

Work was usually her best antidote for depression and
she decided she would get Phineas's portfolio and last
testament together; the police would be wanting to know
who stood to inherit what. She switched on the interior
lights, opened the door to her private office, and jumped.
Fitz was sitting in the visitor's chair under the Please
Don't Smoke sign, lighting a White Owl, drinking coffee
from a takeout cup.

"Business call?" Wyn asked, not nicely. Fitz's key was
for emergencies only; she didn't relish him spending his
sunset Sundays occupying her inner sanctum, fouling the
air.

"No," he said, breaking right through her defenses. "I
only wanted to talk to you."

"Here it is in a nutshell," Fitz began and Wyn sat up
in her straight-backed chair. She enjoyed her uncle's
nutshells.

The governor was nervous. Fitz supposed she had
watched television that morning. The network-shared
videotape of Phineas's murder was being broadcast on
all news shows which, lost without a war, were devoting
ten minutes of every hour to it. The governor didn't have
to be told by his press secretary that being shown in his
hometown shaking hands with a murder victim an hour
or so before the crime was "negatory exposure." The
governor wanted the murder solved quickly, efficiently,
and quietly.

The problem, from the governor's point of view, was
Homer Price. He would want as much publicity and
noise as possible, having his own political agenda. Nor
could the investigation be taken out of Homer's hands
without causing exactly the sort of agitation the governor
couldn't afford. What the governor wanted was someone
on his side on the scene and Fitz fit the bill. As an hon-
ored and retired commissioner of New York City's finest,

it would be a courtesy for Price to confer with Fitz, to keep him informed and up to date on developments. "The governor's already talked to him and said we can expect Price's full compliance."

"I bet Homer loved that," Wyn said.

"He hated it but unless he wants to find himself overseeing the incarcerated at the state prison farm for the rest of his career, he'll do what the governor tells him."

"So why are you sitting in the dark in my office blowing smoke rings? Why aren't you over there getting Homer Price's full compliance, solving the murder?"

"I told you: I needed someone to talk to. Usually something like this, I'd go hash it out with Phineas. I miss that arrogant son of a bitch already. I won't say I don't like this chance to get back to work but the truth is I want to find Phineas's killer, Wyn. Why are you looking so pinched and pale all of a sudden?"

"I was just thinking Phineas is going to have fun with this and then I had to remind myself, for the fifth time today, that someone poisoned him and how terrified he must have been. I want his killer punished, too, Fitz."

"Good. You talk to a lot of people. You tell me if you hear anything funny. When you get a chance, I want to know who gets Phineas's money."

"I'll tell you right now. I'm the executor. He left ten thousand dollars to CHARLEE for the express purpose of educating the girls. Maggie, Dolly, Dicie, Annie Kitchen, the Cole sisters, and Willy Mercer each get five thousand dollars. So does Jackson Hall, believe it or not."

"Now that's funny."

"Guilt money I suppose. For treating Jackson so badly when they were kids. The bulk of the estate goes to Lettie."

"A lot of money?"

"Big time."

"Don't notify any of them by letter, will you, Wyn? Tell them first in person. Let me know how Lettie and

Jackson Hall and everyone else takes their good fortune. The sooner the better."

"All right. Where are you going?"

"To see how compliant Captain Homer Price is feeling."

Fitz was surrounded by singularly determined men and women—some of whom he remembered, and not with affection—when he entered the Municipal Building but he kept moving, saying he had no comment, that he wasn't on the case, that he had come to talk to Captain Price on an unrelated matter.

"Yeah, right," was the media's reaction as he was ushered into the captain's office by a thoroughly barbered Raymond Cardinal, the youngest member of the Waggs Neck Harbor PD, who looked as if he might hyperventilate with the effort to contain his excitement.

The captain dismissed Ray and rose from his seat behind the desk, reluctantly offering his hand. Poker-faced, Homer Price still managed to convey his disgust with the governor's scenario. He had his own methodology and it didn't include working hand in glove with a senior citizen, even if he was the governor's buddy and the ex-commissioner of the NYPD. Homer Price would do what he had been ordered to do, no more and a good deal less if he could get away with it.

Fitz remained affable—his standard reaction to hostility—while Homer Price briefed him, staring at the cracked plaster wall behind his head. "There's a roomful of suspects," the captain said in his deadpan voice. "Half of them upwardly mobile storekeepers, half enviro-lunatics. My guess is we're going to find the killer among the lunatics. Phineas wanted to make Waggs Neck a money-making place and the preservationists didn't like that. Anyway, everyone's going to have to be interviewed. Here's the list and any info you want—background checks, et cetera—I'll get you as soon as I can."

"I appreciate that," Fitz said, meaning it. "I'll keep as

low a profile as possible." Looking at the familiar names, he asked, "Do we know if the blackout was engineered?"

"The blackout was real enough. Whoever the poisoner was acted quickly and popped the stuff in Phineas's glass, presumably without anyone seeing him or her do it. Probably could of done it with the lights on, there was so much going on. 'Course they had to be carrying around a certain amount of hydrocyanic acid . . ."

"The postmortem? Already?"

"The prelim. Hauppauge can move fast when they're told to." Price picked up a fax sheet and read from it. " 'The acid was most likely administered in liquid form and was released from its host compound by the large amount of hydrochloric acid found in the deceased's stomach.' "

"In the champagne?"

"Probably, but they haven't gotten that far yet."

"Fingerprints?"

"Whalers Festival napkins were all over the place. The killer's hands may never actually have touched the glass." Homer Price looked down at the fax sheet. "According to the lab, the cyanide acted almost immediately. Hizzoner drank it and sixty-five seconds later he was dead. So, given the time frame, no one outside of that room could have done it. In fact, you could have done it." Homer Price smiled, revealing white, even teeth. "Now me, I could not have done it. I was on my way to East Hampton Airport, riding shotgun while Ray drove and the governor talked real estate in the back with your niece."

"It's nice you have an iron-clad alibi," Fitz said, taking the report, folding it neatly, standing up. "Thanks, Captain, for all your information. Keep me posted."

"Likewise."

CHAPTER
Nine

LETTITIA BROWNE LAY IN THE OVERSIZED WICKER CHAISE longue on that late Sunday afternoon, feeling like a high-strung poodle in an airplane cargo crate whose medication was wearing thin. Thinking hard and fast, she was oblivious to the hard-earned warmth of what had been a solemn, oversized room when she and Phineas were growing up. Her father had left her and not Phineas the house. It hadn't been much of a triumph as Phineas had gotten the money.

Though Lettitia had portrayed Elsie de Wolfe in a PBS telecast, she had never been particularly sensitive to the art and craft of interior decoration. Phineas said her skills lay in self-decoration and she, agreeing, had allowed her detested but skillful brother carte blanche in her increasingly grand habitats. The carte blanche had been expensive and the habitats ruinous. At a cost she didn't want to think of, Phineas had transformed the dowdy old Bay Street family mansion into a comfortable, stylish, and quintessentially Lettitia home. It hadn't made her like him any the more.

Nor did she like the unpleasant telephone conversation

she had just had with a not nice man to whom she owed money; and then there were all the nice men—bankers and such—to whom she owed money. But financial worries, she fervently hoped, were about to be behind her. Hap's and Linda's girl with the irritating name was about to appear and give her, she prayed, the good news.

Not that there wasn't a certain amount of suspense. She wasn't one hundred percent certain she was Phineas's heir, despite his promises. It was pathetic, really, Phineas holding onto their tenuous family ties by dangling great expectations in front of her. Why he wanted that connection was beyond Lettitia, who would have cut and run years before if it hadn't been for the promised money.

She had another unpleasant thought: though Phineas believed he had a lot of money, would *she* think it was a lot of money? That Wyn Lewis had requested a Sunday evening appointment augured well. That Wyn was Phineas's attorney was incomprehensible to Lettitia. She was attractive enough in a cool, Scandinavian way, but she had all of Linda's warmth—which was to say none—and if she had Hap's business sense, Phineas's estate was in trouble indeed. Yet Phineas was no fool where money was concerned and he had sworn by Wynsome Lewis.

It's an ill wind, Lettie thought, her mind returning to her brother's death. The oversized gilt mirror Phineas had insisted upon was not friendly and in the cool blue-gray of the afternoon light Lettie thought she resembled the witch in "Snow White." She was contemplating Swiss surgery—assuming that now she could afford it—when her maid, Mary, came in to say that Miss Lewis had arrived.

Wyn had been asked to wait in the small sitting room off the central hall, where a dozen early American naive portraits covered one wall. Wyn had just decided Lettie's collection, characterized by oversized heads and exophthalmic eyes, was the work of the Diane Arbuses of their day when Mary, the only uniformed servant in Waggs Neck Harbor and proud of it, interrupted these ruminations and led the way to the main sitting room.

Phineas had given the walls dozens of coats of a deep yellow-gold paint applied in every direction so that the finish gave the illusion of an ancient and worn tapestry. The ceiling was sky blue, the wide planked floors were stained nearly black, and the extensive trim was a glossy, lacquered white. Off to the right, at a provocative angle, was a welcome, aggressively wrong note, a white baby grand piano, with silver framed and autographed photographs of Lettie cheek-to-cheek with instantly recognizable celebrities strewn across its closed surface. A dozen ten-foot-high gilt-framed early nineteenth-century Chinese ancestor portraits lined one wall, echoing the American itinerant portraits in the waiting room.

"Phineas did it all," Lettie Browne said. "Decoration was his life." She fitted a cigarette into her jade holder and lit it with her gold Dupont lighter, her hands not quite steady.

Earlier in Wyn's life a woman like Lettitia Browne would have been able to stomp all over her, but Wyn had been expensively liberated. Having survived Nick's mother, not to mention Nick, there were few people who could intimidate her.

But Lettitia Browne surprised her. Wyn had been prepared for snubs, not for the rambling, biographical reminiscence the actress immediately embarked upon, as if Wyn were a magazine interviewer. "We had a disastrous bringing up," Lettie was saying. "Mother dead too early and father a strict disciplinarian. As a result, Phineas spent his life inventing happy homes and I've spent mine playacting. The shrinkers tell me my passion for other people's ancestors"—she pointed a long index finger at the Chinese paintings—"is a need to create a family for myself."

Wyn had seen Lettitia playacting. She had a wide range, one season appearing as Lady Macbeth, the next as Mame. Glamorous without being beautiful, or even pretty, she had a heart-shaped face and a long Browne nose and such an artful amalgam of color in her hair that it was hard to put a name to it. Wyn remembered her as a red-headed Blanche in a televised version of *A Streetcar Named Desire*. Her needy passion had such power it had obliterated the muscular wretch playing Stanley. Under the gloss and volubility, she seemed as needy now.

Mary entered, ending Lettie's autobiographical stream. Beverages were proffered and refused. Mary exited and Lettie, sitting up, switched roles, becoming a society woman meeting with the old family solicitor. Holding one long hand in the other, she asked, "Do you think we might begin with the estate? This may be crass but I want to know who inherits and if it's me, not to put too fine a point on it, how much?"

Wyn informed Lettie that she was the major legatee, that aside from half a dozen small bequests, Lettie got it all. Wyn went on to say that she was the executor and that the estate was large but not complicated and would probably take about a year to settle. Lettie would immediately begin to receive income from the prospering hotel and from the dozens of bank accounts, certificates of deposit, and money market funds on which Phineas had thoughtfully included Lettitia as joint holder. Some of the capital would have to be held until an agreement was reached on state and federal taxes, but a good deal of it could be withdrawn immediately.

"If you like," Wyn offered, "I'll have Phineas's accountant put together a statement for you first thing tomorrow."

"If you'd be so kind. But is there any way you can give me a ballpark figure as to income and net worth?" Wyn dug her notes out of her briefcase/purse—she was going to have to break down and buy a notebook computer—scanned them, and said that Phineas's taxable income was four hundred and ten thousand in the previous year and his estate was probably worth around five million dollars. Out of that, he had left seventy-five thousand to individuals and charities.

"Who the hell would have thought," Lettitia Browne whispered to herself, "that Phineas was worth five million dollars?"

Wyn gave Lettie a few moments to enjoy herself—lottery winners, she supposed, experienced the same kind of euphoric shock—before she made what surely had to be perceived as an ironic statement. "I can't help wondering why anyone wanted to kill Phineas."

Lettie laughed. "Aside from myself you mean? I've speculated, of course. Sex is a good old-fashioned motive, don't you think? I always believed Phineas was nonpracticing but it's possible he was having a secret affair with some hirsute pillar of the community. Though Phineas, Lord love him, would have had trouble keeping a secret like that if his life depended upon it. Perhaps it did." Lettie gave Wyn her second-curtain smile as if to separate herself from such nonsense: this was merely what the playwright wrote.

"Maggie had a solid motive," Wyn said. "If Phineas got his new pier, she stood to lose money and maybe Carlson House."

For a moment Lettie Browne kept still, as intended. It occurred to her that Hap's little girl was more formidable than she appeared. Crushing her cigarette in a porcelain ashtray, she looked up. "Maggie might have killed Phineas but not until she was absolutely certain he was going to get his Pier Mall, and he was still in the testing-the-waters stage, waiting for the reaction to the Whalers Festival."

"I missed the reception," Wyn said. "I'm not sorry."

"I arrived with a gigantic migraine. Phineas had asked me to be the guest of honor and then late in the game he went and asked Jackson Hall to be the guest of honor. You can understand why I was not as gracious as I might have been, especially after I got him all that television attention.

"I tried to find Maggie but she was on the far side of the keeping room, the cameraman and his technician between us. I started to go to her when someone told us to shut up; taping was about to begin.

"So I stayed put—this was Jackson's and Phineas's show—propping myself up against the wall, next to the keeping room pantry door, snagging one of those revolting plastic cups of champagne that looked, smelled, and tasted like one supposes a urine sample does. I could hear Annie in the pantry, complaining in her nasal voice. The lights were blinding. I looked for Maggie again but couldn't find her. Everyone seemed to be clustered on my side of the room where Phineas and Jackson were standing. They seemed uncomfortable with one another. They hadn't been friends when they were young and now Phineas was rewriting extremely minor history, coming on with fictitious fond memories.

"Willy Mercer tried to get me to agree to go with him to a Noel Coward revival—*Hay Fever*—a friend of his is directing at Guild Hall. Fat chance. Out of the corner of my eye I could see Dolly Carlson looking ill, John Fenton solicitous.

"Phineas let out a guffaw that caught my attention and I glanced at Jackson to see if he had said something funny, but Jackson looked as if he were trying not to regurgitate. He was clutching a glass filled with something that looked a lot better than the champagne. When I asked his little amanuensis, Tony something-or-other, to get me whatever Jackson was drinking, I was told the calvados was reserved 'exclusively' for Jackson, who was holding his glass so tightly I thought it might break. Phineas, a sycophantic grimace on his fatuous face, was chatting away, nine to the dozen.

"Then the lights went out and came on again and then they were dimmed and there were those ugly retching sounds. The Bell cretin fooled with his flashlight, Apple

Annie popped out of the pantry, the damned cake seemed to explode, and someone said, 'Jesus, he's dead.'

"I thought it was Jackson. That he had a stroke. But when I looked and saw John Fenton kneeling over Phineas, some unsuspected reservoir of sisterly affection must have broken because I did what I never have done before in my life: I fainted.

"Next thing I knew, I was in Maggie's guest room, John Fenton doing his bedside manner turn.

"I'm not certain I'm yet in touch with the fact that Phineas is dead. He liked having a theatrical sister and though I admit I didn't care for him, neither of us collected spouses or long-term lovers or important human attachments as other people do: we were all we had."

There was the suggestion of artificial tears, dredged up for effect. Wyn tried to bite her tongue—as Fitz would have advised—but she didn't. "Then there's the money, of course."

Lettie gave Wyn the full force of her floodlight eyes. "The money is going to make my life very much easier, I admit. But I didn't kill Phineas. I'm not capable of killing anyone. If I were, there's someone else I might have killed. But not Phineas. I want everyone to believe that."

Wyn wasn't sure that she did. Something about this performance triggered a memory of another, Lettie playing Regina in *The Little Foxes*, sublimely untrustworthy. Surfeited with drama, with the precious room and the hermetic atmosphere, Wyn stood up, saying she would have the accountant send over a statement and that there would be, in time, papers to sign, deeds to be formally transferred.

"You don't like me very much, do you?" Lettie asked. "Well, you're not my favorite, either. You've got your father's angelic face but you're really your mother's daughter and not nearly as nice as you pretend to be."

"Niceness is no more a prerequisite of my profession than it is of yours, Lettie." Wyn looked at her, knowing she shouldn't, but nonetheless saying, "Youth doesn't hurt in either case, however."

"You're not good-looking enough, Wyn, or bright enough or even young enough to get away with a line like that. Get out."

Wyn was already gone.

Too roiled up to go home, Wyn virtually speed-walked across Bay Street to the corner of Washington, where the old ivy-covered, red-brick Carlson watch factory, forever on the verge of condominiumization, stood. She slowed down as she walked across Washington Street, inhaling the moist, damp air, resisting the temptation to beat herself up for provoking Lettie. For it had been a calculated if cheap shot, an attempt to see how far the actress might be pushed before she lost control. Not so very far, as it turned out.

One of Wyn's weaknesses was a tendency toward subtlety and she wondered if this wasn't the case now. Could this be, she asked herself, your simple family murder, a sister killing her brother for money?

As she turned right at Main and glanced in at Dicie's shop with its sophisticated window displays, Wyn thought, nonsequentially, that Lettie was the sort of woman who would always be attractive. Even now, badly frightened—all that loquacity—she had glamour. Wyn speculated as to what Lettie might be frightened of as she approached the hotel, the obvious answer being that she had murdered her brother.

Wyn stood for a few moments on the columned New Federal porch, the meeting place for displaced Manhattan literati during the summer, now desolate under darkening skies.

At the end of Main Street, Carlson House, blocking the view of the bay, commanded attention as it had been meant to do. Two women were in the second-floor sitting room, backlit as if they were on stage. One of the women was pacing nervously, the other standing at the French doors leading out to the winter porch overlooking the village. The woman doing the pacing was almost certainly Lettie Browne; it would be hard to mistake that silhouette. She must have left her house immediately after I did, Wyn thought, and is probably telling Maggie Carlson about her inherited fortune, about Wyn's sassiness, seeking what? Comfort? Reassurance? Collaboration?

Maggie was popularly known as Mother Maggie thanks to her maternal solicitude and motherly bossiness. But she always reminded Wyn of her virginal grade school teachers with their big busts and law-and-order eyes. Maggie stood now—her wide outline unmistakable—at her French doors, staring out at Main Street, the village despot's daughter checking on her subjects for signs of insurrection. For a moment Wyn fantasized that Maggie was looking at her, laying down a challenge.

Telling herself to get real, Wyn entered the New Federal through wooden half doors, the glass insets trimmed with gilt, the lobby filled with a reminiscent bouquet that brought back the castlelike hotels cum golf courses Hap had taken her to when she was a child. Not much of a drinker, Wyn sometimes stopped in the New Federal's lobby–bar for a solitary beer because she found it cozy and sympathetic. The bulbs in the Victorian glass sconces were dimmed to resemble gaslight and there was a fire in the grate. The thick carpets and cushy sofas helped, as Phineas Browne had intended, to create the illusion that one had stepped back in time.

Nick, having spent his one night there with Allison, hated it. "All those dusty *tchotchkes* give me hay fever." He liked his hotels modern, minimal, and really expensive, not being the kind who succumbed to bed-and-breakfast charm, ersatz or otherwise. Wyn was a sucker for ersatz charm.

Effectively destroying the careful atmosphere of the lobby, David Kabot removed a toothpick from his mouth and looked at her with little warmth. "Hey, Wyn," he said.

When David Kabot had arrived in Waggs Neck, fresh on the success of his first novel, he had been interested in Wyn, discounting her half-dozen years' seniority. Wyn found him attractive but young, a rough-hewn Nick, and had let him know she wasn't interested. Though he had soon found Dicie, the rejection still bothered him.

"Taking up the hotel business?" she asked.

"The bartender fell apart when he heard Phineas was iced. Couldn't make a drink if his life depended on it. Least that's what his wife says. Ditto Dolly. Hasn't been out of bed since yesterday. Dicie and I are manning the fort. I used to bartend summers on the Jersey shore. Want a Black Zombie or a Chiquita Banana Double Rum Split?"

She asked for her beer and he asked if she wanted it here in the lobby or in the bar and she said here and he said you got it and went to make it while Wyn closed her eyes, wondering if everyone found simple social intercourse with David Kabot as difficult as she did. Eventually he brought the beer, along with one for himself, and sat down next to her. "You look really, really beat," he said with sincere concern.

"I am." She sipped the beer and looked at him. "Did I ever tell you *Older Woman* disturbed my sleep for weeks?"

"Did I ever tell you that you disturbed my sleep for weeks?"

Ignoring this, she said, "It deserved those reviews."

"Thanks," David Kabot said, sidetracked, torn between embarrassment and ego gratification.

"You're a good writer, David." This was not blarney, Wyn having read and appreciated his two novels. "What are you working on now?"

"*Nada*. I'm blocked," he said conversationally, as if he were confessing to a minor stomach ailment.

"Who do you think killed Phineas?" Wyn asked after

a moment, changing the subject to the one they were both thinking about.

"You know, I can't get it through my head that someone actually iced him. I hated the dude's guts but I didn't *not* like him, you know what I mean? There was something about him that made you admire him at the same time you wanted to knock out his lights.

"Two of the geezers were in earlier, saying it was the preservationists who did it, giving me dirty looks. No one with half a brain wanted the Pier Mall, but only Maggie stood to lose any real money over it. And if she were going to chill Phineas, she'd strangle him, not poison him.

"It's bananas to think," he went on, free-associating, "that anyone would chill him for blocking the view of the bay . . . except maybe for a lot of people who really, really love that view and Maggie, who stood to lose big time if the Pier Mall became an actuality. I don't know. Can you really buy anyone offing Phineas, or anyone, for real estate gain?"

"What *can* you imagine killing for?" Wyn asked.

"Fear. Jealousy. Greed. The hots. Your classic motives."

She sipped at her beer and looked at him. He hadn't touched his beer. He looked unhappy. "You were in the keeping room, weren't you?"

"I didn't see much. Dicie and I were having a fight and fights with Dice-ums take total concentration."

"What was it about?"

"None of your fucking business." Almost immediately he capitulated. "All right. You'll find out anyway. It's already on the harpy hotline. Jackson Hall, who as you know is Dicie's old man, though he won't admit it, has a so-called companion who just happens to be an ex-squeeze of mine. Life gets complicated in Waggs Neck.

"Anyway, Dicie's been crazed since Jackson Hall came floating in last spring. She's been fantasizing about him since she was a kid and I guess she was expecting Daddy to come and put his arms around her and say, 'There,

there, everything's okay, kiddy-bumps, I only ignored you since you were born because I didn't want to mess you up but you know you're my little sweetie-poo now.' Poor kid thought he was coming here for her.

"Sees her on the street and walks the other way. Dicie, who understandably doesn't want to face the reality that her father's an asshole, blames it on Jessica. Then she finds out Jessica is my aforementioned ex-squeeze and World War III is announced.

"Jessica gives Dicie the full treatment at the festival parade. 'Darling!' she says to me, ignoring Dice. '*What* fun: *your* being in Waggs Neck and *my* being in Waggs Neck.' She did it to pull my string but, to mix metaphors, Dicie bit.

"I tried telling her Jessica was an old weekend but that didn't play, 'specially since Dicie knows that I dedicated my first novel 'To J, Who Made This Book Possible.' Dicie, once more snubbed by Daddy, brought it up again in the keeping room and I was just telling her that Jessica hadn't meant much to me, I was too young to know real love, and dialogue along that line when Dicie lost interest—something else had caught her attention—and she stalked off as the lights went out. I stood there feeling like your prize dork. Then I heard someone puking their guts up and all I could think of was Dicie. I started to move toward the door when the lights came on and I found myself next to Jessica, who was comforting Jackson, her arms around him. They got out of the way and I saw Phineas on the floor covered with all that crap, John Fenton leaning over him with that I-smell-almonds look on his puss, and I said something like, 'Holy shit, he's dead.' "

"David?" a child's whiskey voice came in from the corridor leading to the dining room and bar, followed by its owner, Dicie herself. She was wearing a green dress that matched her eyes and would have done for a formal cocktail party except that it was cut off eight inches above the knee. She was heart-stoppingly appealing now, but in ten years, Wyn thought, she'd have real beauty.

"Hey, Wyn. You okay? You look exhausted." She came over and touched Wyn's hand while saying, "David, get off your butt. The Versacis want their check and the Jaycees in the little dining room are getting rowdy. I'll take care of them."

"Dicie," Wyn said, "Phineas left you a bequest."

"How much?"

"Five thousand dollars."

"Wow. That's wonderful. Isn't that wonderful?" Dicie asked David.

"Yeah, wonderful. Try to remember how you got it." He moved moodily off to give the Versacis their check.

"Like you were Phineas's number one fan," Dicie called after him. "Bastard," she said, not letting Wyn take her wallet from her jacket. "On the house." Maggie-like, she put her arm around Wyn and walked her to the door. "You take care of yourself," she said, moving off in the direction of the escalatingly noisy Junior Chamber of Commerce, and Wyn went home.

Probity was waiting for Wyn at the gate and they climbed the front porch steps together, Wyn sorry she forgot to leave lights on. As she opened the unlocked door, she asked herself for the first time since coming back to Waggs Neck that scary, late-night, big-city question: Who the hell is in there waiting for me?

No one, but the fact she asked it brought home the realization that the village was already corrupted by Phineas's murder. Fitz called while she was belatedly switching on lights, to tell her what the captain had said, and Wyn, in turn, described Lettie's reaction to her windfall. "Think Lettie killed her brother for five million bucks?" she asked Fitz.

"Fratricide's one possibility," Fitz said, not exactly answering.

CHAPTER

Ten

LITTLEFIELDS HAD LIVED IN THE MILDEW-GREEN MULTI-gabled Lowe Lane house since it had been built in 1898 and Lucy Littlefield had lived there alone since Wyn could remember. It was seven o'clock, Monday morning, the hour at which Lucy maintained she was at her freshest. Wyn would have hated to see her at, say, noon. They were sitting on the rusting glider on the narrow closed-in porch, its walls lined with the dusty glass bottles Lucy's mother had collected when, Lucy said, the century was young.

Having exhausted the topic of Phineas's murder, they were examining Lucy's latest purchase, a "gender planner" watch bought from a home shopping channel which would, if properly used, assure its owner of conceiving a boy or a girl. "Sixty-nine ninety-five," Lucy said, stirring her spoon around in her coffee mug. "Expensive, but I can, after all, afford it." Lucy lived on Social Security and a family trust that brought her twenty thousand dollars each year, most of which went to pay the taxes on her land.

"If you don't agree to a closing date this week, the

Grasslands people are going to sue for performance, Lucy. You'll end up paying damages and court costs."

"If the little arrow's in the pink, you get a girl. Blue, you get a boy. It's so darned clever."

"Are you scared about something, Lucy?" Lucy seemed frightened, a pinched rabbity look giving her away.

"Why should I be frightened? I've got the world on a string. I can see a rainbow anytime I snap my fingers."

"Why have you changed your mind?"

"I haven't changed my mind. I've still got my old one and it's quite good enough. Ha. Ha." Seeing the expression on Wyn's face, she relented. "I will let you know exactly what I'm going to do tomorrow morning at seven A.M. Will Mr. Roy Stein and those other Grasslands fellows wait until tomorrow morning at seven A.M.?"

"I expect they will, Lucy." Wyn gathered up the coffee mugs and took them into the kitchen, which was, unlike the other rooms, extremely tidy. "By the way," she asked, as she was leaving, "you've been paying your taxes, haven't you?"

"That's for me to know and you to find out, young lady."

Lucy wrapped her lively purple chenille robe around her skeletal body and retreated into the house.

Not guilt-free, Wyn skipped her aerobics class, stopping in at the Municipal Building where, in a very short time, the village clerk informed her that Lucy had not paid her latest village taxes. Putting the top down on the Jag, Wyn drove determinedly to Riverhead, going directly to the county office where the tax rolls were kept on microfiche. "Should have done this a long time ago. When Lucy started having her famous second thoughts." As she suspected, Lucy's county taxes were nearly nine months in arrears. Which was why she was frightened. The tax people, overwhelmed with unpaid tax bills, wouldn't take action for another few months but Lucy, being shrewd and ignorant, a lethal combination, was undoubtedly worried that the sale wouldn't go through if the taxes weren't paid.

Wyn switched off the microfiche projector and almost immediately turned it back on. Something had caught her eye in the entry just above the one for Lucy's property. It was for the convent grounds and it showed the taxes fully paid. What interested Wyn was the fact that Maggie Carlson had paid them. It didn't make sense unless Maggie was a member of the foundation that had bought the grounds and the money was being dispensed through her local account. Out of mere curiosity, Wyn resolved to call Janet Hayes at the Foundation Library again and ask her to do some further digging.

Enjoying her drive back to Waggs Neck along the deserted old highway, Wyn was thinking of all the "gold" bracelets with little bells and "diamond" sterling silver cocktail rings Lucy had been flashing lately—not to mention the gender watch. There should be, Wyn decided, a governor on home shopping channels.

Back in her office she called Lucy and told her the taxes, with a certain penalty, could be paid out of the money she was going to receive, and Lucy immediately capitulated, saying, "Well, that's a relief." Wyn put off having a talk with Lucy about the perils of home shopping. With three quarters of a million dollars to play with, Lucy was going to have to hire a money manager and it was going to be Wyn's job to insist that she did.

She made a note to call Roy Stein to tell him they could, after all, close on Friday. She made another note for Liz to inform anyone interested that Lucy's tax money was coming, and then she set to work writing up a listing agreement she had been putting off. It was for one of the detestable jerry-built condos that had sprung up on West Sea Road and Wyn was looking forward neither to showing it nor to meeting the potential buyers who would be interested. She wondered why she had accepted the listing in the first place and the word GREED in large capital letters came to mind.

So be it. She was leaving to meet Fitz for lunch but stopped when she noticed that Liz was wearing the infamous puckered look that indicated a fight with her teenage daughter, Heidi, who had reached the stage when nothing her mother did was right. "Now I embarrass her," Liz said, scratching her scalp under the brown curls, moving her short, stubby body around in her office chair, setting her appointment book just so. "I put on my brown plaid pants suit this morning and I am told in no uncertain terms that all polyester pants suits are gross. They don't wrinkle, they don't need ironing, they're cheap, they're cheerful, and I can throw them directly in the machine. Why, I would like to know, are polyester pants suits gross?"

Wyn, who silently agreed with Heidi, took the phone call, which was from Fitz, who was waiting for her at the Eden. "Bad girl," Liz said. "You're four minutes late. You want me to type the condo listing first or should I get onto the Etheridges' contract? We can discuss Phineas Browne's murder and the paper work for his heirs when you get back."

"The contract," Wyn said, thanking the gods that Liz's escape from motherhood lay in a dedicated professionalism as she went next door to the Eden to meet Fitz.

He smoked a White Owl, watching with distaste as Wyn knocked back a late breakfast consisting of very soft-boiled eggs, orange sausages, yellowish grits, and sepia corn muffins, covered with butter. "You ever get your cholesterol checked?" he asked.

"One twenty and holding. How's your lungs?"

"Black as a coal miner's. Did you get a chance to watch the tape?"

It was a twenty-minute video made up of the network's tapes and footage shot by the forensic team. Homer Price, almost too conscientious to be true, had delivered it to Fitz the night before, shortly after receiving it and making a copy for himself. Fitz, after viewing the video, had pushed it through the mail slot in Wyn's front door late the previous night.

"I watched it three times and I'm not certain I'm any the wiser. It's difficult to figure out where everyone was standing," Wyn said, laying down her fork. "Tell me if I've got this right: Phineas and Jackson were stage center, in front of the console which had been placed in front of the fireplace. Tony Deel, the doctor, and the colonel were to Phineas's left. David Kabot and Dicie were in front of Jackson and Phineas and between them and the camera-man, who seems to be hovering Vincent Price-like about the ceiling."

"He was standing on a ladder."

"Aha. Anyway, he was in the center. Maggie, you, Jessica Stevens, and the Cole sisters were to the right and Lettie was even farther along, past the pantry. Billy Bell stood more or less in front of the pantry door. Annie Kitchen was on the inside of the pantry. The screen goes black—presumably when the lights blew—and the next image is of Annie coming out of the pantry in half light, that inedible giant Hostess cupcake in her arms. There's a shot of her back as the cake goes in the air and then she fades and is replaced by the fashionable backs of Jackson Hall and Jessica Stevens. They separate after a moment and allow the camera to go in for the close-up of Phineas all America is now so familiar with, John Fenton at his side."

"That's about right."

"Anyone could have slipped behind Phineas and Jackson and popped the cyanide in his drink, which was sitting on the console."

"Theoretically. The lab at Hauppauge is equivocating. There's something they're not certain of but they're not saying just what, yet."

"But they agree it was cyanide? How does one get ahold of cyanide?"

"Anybody with a very basic knowledge of science or

access to a library can figure it out. The Extra-Strength Tylenol victims died of cyanide poisoning. It's very quick and effective. Apricot kernels, one of the health nuts' panaceas when eaten raw, are a prime source if baked. The hippy girl at the Inner Beauty Boutique says she can't keep them in stock. A few years ago a Hare Krishna over in West Sea roasted a bunch of them in a three-hundred-degree oven for ten minutes, thinking if apricot kernels worked raw, they'd be really miraculous cooked. He ate them and was dead in under a minute."

"How did John Fenton pick up on it so quickly?"

"He was the doctor called in on the West Sea case. Besides, Phineas's vomit reeked of bitter almonds."

"Thanks, Fitz, for sharing that with me." Wyn pushed her coffee away. "Who've you talked to so far?"

"David Kabot."

"He's into health food, all right, but do you think he's a dedicated enough conservationist to have killed Phineas?"

Fitz relit the White Owl. No tinfoil ashtray being handy—they were sitting in the Eden's nonsmoking section—he deposited his match on the floor. "Could've. Temperamental enough. In the right place. But why? Yes, he despised Phineas and his Pier Mall, but that's not much of a motive even for a hothead like Kabot. The project was no ways near being a reality and would never be; mostly it was a pipe dream in Phineas's and the Main Street Business Society's heads."

"Phineas was further along than you think, Fitz. Copies of his plans, along with county, state, township, and village permits, are ready for filing. The Pier Mall package was to be presented to the Commission at the next meeting, passage based on the success of the Whalers Festival."

"Boy, that's a well-kept secret. I gather you were his attorney on the deal?"

"I was."

"Don't you think you might have dropped a hint that

Phineas was about to put the last nail in Waggs Neck's coffin?"

"Fitz, it was privileged information."

"All right. But the fact that it was closer to reality than most of us believed would make a stop-the-pier motive more likely."

Wyn signaled Thelma Eden for the check. "Maybe. Anyway, I'm going to talk to Maggie, who is also mentioned, believe it or not, in Phineas's will."

Wyn's progress up Main Street was interrupted by Captain Homer Price, who was coming out of the Municipal Building as she passed it. "Hey, counselor," he said, stopping her, his yellow-flecked eyes squinting with anger. "Want to let me in on the deceased mayor's last will and testament, seeing as how you put everyone else in the picture?"

"I assumed that if I told Fitz, he would pass the information on to you, Homer."

"I like to hear things direct. You want to have a cup of coffee and talk to me or do you need an official invitation, a stenographer, and all that crap?"

The last thing Wyn wanted was another cup of coffee, but knew it was politic to say okay. As they walked, he towering over her in his spit-shined Corfam boots, she absentmindedly asked where he had been during the keeping room ceremony.

"I was in the damn patrol car in front of the damn stretch limo, escorting the governor—and you—to his damn helicopter. We were worried about someone offing the governor, not the damn mayor."

Wyn sat at a rusting metal table at the Harbor Café, formerly the Harbor Gulf Station, keeping her hands in her coat pockets, her collar up, watching Main Street traffic.

The thinning sunlight had become as unsatisfactory as a mini–space heater. Homer set in front of her a cup of dark liquid that looked as if it came from the Gulf station's old grease pit and Wyn described the various bequests in Phineas's will for him.

Homer whistled silently. "That puts his sister right up there at the top of the list," he said. "And he left Maggie money as well. That Phineas was something else again."

"What did you think of him?" Wyn asked, genuinely interested.

"Setting aside all the airy-fairy crap, I found him impressive. He had progressive ideas for the community and he was a man who never gave up. Like a dog with a bone. Look at the Fat Boy lunches. There were only four Fat Boys left but he kept those lunches going year in, year out. You got to hand it to him. Claire, my wife—"

"I know who your wife is, Homer." Claire, a volunteer at CHARLEE, was a chic, even-tempered woman who Wyn felt deserved better than the captain.

"Sometimes I forget who you know and who you don't, Wyn. Anyway, Claire says only a bunch of bachelors could've stared at each other over those rotten New Federal lunches for the past twenty-odd years. Now Percy Curry's offed himself and Phineas got himself murdered, there's only the doctor and Colonel Mercer. They'll probably go on forever having Monday lunch at the New Federal."

The captain deposited their cups in the Harbor Café's red plastic garbage can and said he was going to check on the keeping room. Wyn said she was going to Maggie's and would walk with him. Their progress was carefully observed by the retirees who, weather permitting, sat on the bench in front of the Nonesuch Bar. Wyn knew that by afternoon the town would have her taken into custody for the murder of Phineas Browne.

They rounded Carlson House and stopped for a moment to look at Jackson Hall's yacht out on the bay. "Maybe Jackson Hall will take Phineas's place at the lunch table," Wyn said. "He was in their class at Mary Immaculate, wasn't he?"

"He wasn't a Fat Boy," Homer Price said. "They

wouldn't let him in." He looked at her sideways. "Your dad was a Fat Boy."

"Membership didn't seem to play a key role in his life."

"Obviously, my dad was not a Fat Boy," Homer said with a return to his usual truculence. Mr. Price was an accountant, one of the first professionals to come out of the village's Afro-American community, and had, Wyn knew, both profited and suffered from the experience. She remembered watching him when she was a little girl, sitting behind his desk in his Main Street office, carefully going over his account books, giving the impression of being totally self-reliant. Not unlike his son.

These thoughts were interrupted by Billy Bell, the oversized and cherubic carpenter, far beefier than Homer and nearly as tall. Hired by the captain at five dollars an hour to guard the keeping room, he was sitting just inside the door on a shallow bench, chewing a virulent green gum, studying his large, flat hands, giving off little noxious blasts of stale sweat and drugstore cologne. "How's it hanging, Cap?" he asked, not moving.

Homer ignored this, pushing on into the keeping room, which was cold and dark, the shades drawn, the lights off. Homer switched on the wall lights and withdrew to talk in a low, menacing tone to Billy.

Uninvited but curious, Wyn entered the keeping room, avoiding the chalk outline of Phineas's body, reminded of the videotape. Wyn regretted the video's repugnant intrusiveness. Now that births were visually recorded on a routine basis, Wyn wondered if death, too, were to be made the subject of home videotapes: "Let's watch Grandma die again."

With only the chalk mark suggesting violence, the keeping room was at peace with itself, a vaultlike space, unremarkable except for the Jackson Halls on the far wall. Wyn raised one of the blackout shades, her attention caught and held by the powerful despondency of the artist's early work, reminding her of the Jackson Hall

her father had left her. The boy in the drawing might
have been Jackson himself, a village outcast, contemplating suicide at the edge of the sea. The women in the
paintings were more lively—one seemed to be dancing
madly on the same shore the boy stood on—but there
was a palpable decay about them.

Wyn thanked Homer for the coffee and left, glad to be
away from the place. She walked round to the front entry
of Carlson House, her thoughts taken up by the distinc-
tive, doomed images Jackson Hall managed to create and
the approaching interview with Maggie Carlson.

CHAPTER

Eleven

"I DON'T FOR A MOMENT BELIEVE IT WAS PREMEDITATED, pal," Maggie was saying, having launched into the subject of Phineas's murder before Wyn could inform her of Phineas's bequest. At the same time she was working hard at getting the last miniature marshmallow out of her hot chocolate and into her spoon.

The chocolate was rich and thick and restorative. Maggie herself was a therapeutic sight in an electric orange artist's smock over turquoise trousers and faux jewel-encrusted sandals that revealed the final flourish, pink-painted toenails.

In contrast, her sphinx face was dark and closed while her eyes were as alert and challenging as a preternaturally bright child's. "Nor am I dumb enough not to realize that I top the Most Likely Candidate List. I have a solid motive, I threatened to kill him half a dozen times, and I was standing close to him."

Wyn thought this was disingenuous—Lettie clearly at the top of the list—but she didn't object. Maggie evidently believed, with reason, that anything she said to Wyn would eventually get back to Fitz, that this was a convenient way to plead her case without causing strain between her and her old friend.

Content to be a conduit, Wyn didn't stop Maggie from replenishing her chocolate from an ancient china pot in the shape of an elephant, popping more miniature marshmallows into her mug. They were sitting not so much on the long green sofa as in it, Maggie's feet propped up on a wicker coffee table. "You're like your father, Wyn," Maggie said. "Hap Lewis knew where all the bones were buried, but you'd never have known it from looking at him. You have that same innocent facade. It makes me wonder how much you really know about me. You won't tell, right? All right, let me tell you what you know about me."

"Good," Wyn said, settling in, feeling like a little girl about to be entertained by a familiar story. "Tell me what I know about you."

"You know that I was broke when Jackson Hall offered me a ton of money for my barn with the promise that I'd get more if, within the next few years, nothing obscured his water view. The first installment saved Carlson House for me; the second will enable Dolly and Dicie to keep Carlson House intact, a fiercely megalomaniacal need of mine. Eventually, it's inevitable no matter how many historic registers it's on, some developer is going to raze Carlson House and put up a 7-Eleven but it won't be because of me.

"Understandably, I was vehemently against Phineas Browne and his Pier Mall. I stood to lose money and my heirs their home. Waggs Neck Harbor, as our families have known it for over two centuries, would be history. I trust you will keep this information to yourself but I have been recently told that I am going to die sooner than later and I'll be damned if Carlson House is going to check out with me."

She took a shallow breath and pressed a bell installed in the wall next to her end of the sofa. The gesture brought to mind Lettitia Browne, though her bell was concealed. Was that the difference between the two friends? Lettitia all haute couture subterfuge, Maggie plain and up front? This seemed too easy and Wyn turned her attention to Annie Kitchen, who received Maggie's order for chicken sandwiches with as much attitude as she dared. Wyn was, it seemed, staying for late lunch, her second of the day, and she vowed there would be no skipping aerobics tomorrow or the next day.

"I know you fought a lot, but what did you really think of Phineas?" Wyn asked.

"He was the ultimate prize horseball. I knew him all his life and he was always, from day one, a horseball. You're too young to have known his father. He was a rich man's son, meaner than mud, who made both too much and too little of Phineas. There was a gargantuan fuss when Phineas was born, while Lettie's birth, only ten months later, was barely announced. It was funny how all those kids wound up in the same Mary Immaculate class: Jackson and Phineas because they were the right age; Lettie, because she was so damned smart, she skipped first grade; Kate, who lost a year to illness. You remember my sister Kate, don't you?"

"Distinctly. When I was six years old Kate offered to take me to the Eden for ice cream. My dad gave her money for two double-dip cones, but Kate talked me into a banana split which she ate most of."

Maggie laughed. "That was our Kate. When I was teaching English at the old Mary Immaculate Academy, Phineas used to hint that I gave Kate preferential treatment even though I was harder on her than anyone else. Dear God, that boy made me see red.

"Sucking up to the teachers for a good grade while making fun of them behind their backs. Dubbed me the Graf Zeppelin even though I wasn't nearly as big as I am today." She drank some chocolate. "And proud of it. I've earned every one of these pounds."

"Did the other boys like Phineas?"

"They thought he was cool or hip or whatever word

they used to denote sophistication in those days. He had a car, which was an immediate billet to popularity. And, all right, I'll give him this, he could be generous—he often treated the boys to lunch at the hotel. And even then Phineas had a civic spirit. His senior paper on the history of Waggs Neck architecture deservedly won several prizes.

"One of his least endearing traits was his penchant for elaborate practical jokes. Sometimes they did quite a bit of damage, teens and their warring sensitivities being what they are. Phineas and the Fat Boys made Jackson's life a living hell. They would not leave him alone. Sick slogans carved into the boys' room doors, purportedly offering Jackson's sexual services to all comers. Snakes in his lunch bag. Constant taunts about his masculinity. 'Queer Bait' and 'Queer Meat' and 'Queer this' and 'Queer that.' They equated his painting with his masculinity, but any threepenny psychiatrist could tell you it was their masculinity that was in question. I would have interfered if I thought it would have done any good. I knew it wouldn't. Jackson had to survive his own way."

The sandwiches arrived, along with chips and yet more cocoa. "We going to have a talk, or what?" Annie asked suddenly, hands on nearly nonexistent hips, addressing Wyn, but not looking at her. "I want to know if I got some money coming from Phineas's will. I cleaned for him for years. He promised me something."

Wyn assured her that she was in Phineas's will and that she would get to her as soon as she could. Annie bustled out, mollified. As Wyn and Maggie ate companionably, Wyn felt a misgiving, telling herself she shouldn't be seduced by the cozy comfort of the room and the maternal warmth emanating from the gargantuan woman at the far end of the plump sofa, now playing with an old-fashioned gold locket and chain, the kind often seen in historical romance cover illustrations.

Setting her plate on the wicker table, Wyn got to the

point of her visit. "Phineas left you money as well, you know."

"I don't believe it."

Wyn removed a copy of the codicil pertaining to Maggie from her satchel and read it: "Five thousand dollars to my old adversary, Margaret Carlson, for the preservation of that hideous pile known as Carlson House. To paraphrase Henry James, 'There is something right in old monuments that have been wrong for centuries.' This goes for Carlson House and Maggie as well."

"That horseball." Maggie turned away, using her big, ugly fingers to wipe away the tears. "That sentimental horseball." She continued to shed heavy, pearl-shaped tears. "It's those pills they've got me on. Makes me emotional."

Wyn, uncomfortable, picked up a book that had been on the wicker coffee table. Printed in England, it was a biography of Jackson Hall, interspersed with photographs and prints of his paintings. Wyn thumbed through it, waiting until Maggie regained her composure. "Fascinating, isn't it?" Maggie, composed, asked. "It's going to be published here next year. Borrow it if you'd like."

Wyn said she would and then, impulsively, said, "I was just looking at Jackson's early works in the keeping room and I had a presumptuous thought: that I could have predicted his future from them."

"Anyone with half an eye could have," Maggie said, wiping her nose with a handkerchief she had unearthed from her trouser pocket. "From the beginning his paintings had intestinal fortitude. That's his great secret. He takes his guts and spreads them across his canvases." Wyn, the book in her lap, studied a print of an angular woman and a cubist dog wearing similar expressions. In lesser hands it would have been only amusing, but in Jackson Hall's, the painting provoked fear.

"Mary Immaculate's last headmaster was a pompous ass named Charles Harrison Hart, who also taught senior art. The dirtiest educator I have ever known—one just knew his belly button was crammed full with old lint—and yet he was able to pick up on Jackson's genius.

"He encouraged Jackson, who needed all the encouragement he could get. He was a lonesome child, an orphan living with Ruth and Cammie, neither of whom had a clue as to how to raise a child. Cammie was too soft and Ruth as forgiving as a steel trap.

"His father was killed early on in Korea and his mother—a cousin of ours—had been living in Louisiana when she died. My father was Jackson's guardian and the Coles used to come to him for direction. Bull, as you can imagine, was no Dr. Spock.

"It didn't help that Bull's late-life passion, Kate, fell head over heels in love with Jackson. So did half the girls in town. Not to mention a couple of the boys. He had those flat eyes and long, black hair; tall but not lanky. He moved so nicely. It was a pleasure just to watch him walk. And his voice was wonderfully seductive; not a boy's voice at all but mellow and resonant, filled with wistful kindness. But what was most attractive about Jackson was that he wasn't aware of his extraordinary appeal."

"I saw him at the parade," Wyn said. "He's older, of course, but he doesn't seem to have changed much."

"He's sleeker, but on balance, I agree. He was always an odd mix of unrestrained sophistication and neurotic dependency. There's invariably been some girl he couldn't live without. A girl, as my father liked to say, above his station."

"I forget exactly when he left Waggs Neck," Wyn said, having finished her sandwiches and chocolate, feeling replete.

"When he came into his money. It had been set aside for him by his mother, held in trust by my dear old dad. There's some dispute about how much was in that trust, some believing Bull had used most of it for his own purposes. It wasn't but a couple of thousand dollars. Jackson collected it on the morning of his eighteenth birthday, which came the day after graduation, and then he was gone."

"No one tried to stop him?"

"Kate had only just died in that fire that razed our stables. By the time we surfaced from the trauma, Jackson was long gone and no one had any idea where he was. Later, word drifted back that he was in New York, and still later, when he began to get all that attention, we knew he was living in Paris.

"It was for the best. He'd never been happy in Waggs Neck, thanks to Phineas and Co."

"You don't suppose . . ." Wyn began.

". . . that Jackson, smarting over ill treatment in high school, poisoned Phineas's drink in a fit of nostalgic pique?"

"Several people mentioned that Jackson looked strange just before the lights went out . . ."

Maggie turned and looked at her, her heavy green Carlson eyes widening. "I saw it, too. The keeping room had to have brought back conflicting memories: it was a place where Bull once publicly humiliated him. And then there was Phineas, poor soul, going on about the grand old days that never were."

"What do you think brought Jackson back to Waggs Neck?"

"You know as well as I do it's a village tradition. Our men—and women, look at us—travel but eventually return. Do you know that Jackson's turned my barn into an *Architectural Digest* delight. It really is wonderful. You should see it."

"I expect I will." Putting Jackson's biography into her old briefcase, Wyn stood up and so did Maggie. "As much as I'd like to go on talking, I'd better move on. Is Dolly at home? I have news for her, as well."

"She left for the hotel just before you came. She's been under the weather lately." The two women looked at one another for a moment. "I didn't kill Phineas, you know. You can pass that on to Fitz, if you'd like. The man was a thorn in my not inconsiderable carcass but, and this is an appalling thing to say," Maggie said, echoing Lettitia, "Phineas wasn't important enough to murder."

Headed back down Main Street, diverted by the mild bustle—young mothers, preschoolers in tow, and a few male retirees going about manufactured Monday afternoon chores—Wyn thought one didn't have to be important to be a victim, one only had to be in someone's way.

But more than anything Maggie actually said, Wyn questioned the just-us-girls scene she had produced. Wyn was aware that Maggie regarded her as Hap's bright little girl, Fitz's little divorcée-turned-attorney niece. Maggie was always nice enough, appreciative of Wyn's talents, complimenting her on the contract she had drawn up for the selling of the barn. But more tepid than warm and not nearly intimate enough for the conversation they had just had. Perhaps it was the shock of Phineas's death or the medicine for the unspecified illness, but Maggie had been different.

Had she, after all, poisoned Phineas? She had the motive and God knows she had the backbone, but there was no proof and Wyn's intuition told her Maggie was capable of a great many things but not murder for personal gain.

Passing the bank, Wyn was struck by the fact that Maggie hadn't been interested enough to ask when she was going to receive her bequest. Even with the barn money, Maggie, a renowned pennypincher, should have been more curious about the money Phineas had left her.

Which reminded Wyn that she had forgotten to ask Maggie why she was paying the taxes on the newly transferred convent property. It wasn't important but it was curious that the anonymous Bijoux Foundation was funneling funds through Maggie. Wyn suspected Roy Stein and Grasslands were at the other end of that funnel, that Maggie was picking up a few extra dollars for acting as dispenser, assuming she wouldn't mind a "tasteful" townhouse condominium community a half mile up the road.

These thoughts disappeared as she saw Billy Bell, looking like a Fragonard Cupid who had overdosed on steroids, staring at her from behind the greasy window of the Blue Buoy Bar & Grill. He didn't turn away when she smiled nor did he acknowledge her. The kids called him "Billy Ugh Bell" and Wyn could understand why.

She tapped on her office window and signaled to Liz that she was going across to the New Federal and would be back shortly. Liz nodded her head in acknowledgment, indicating there were no fires to put out, no anxious buyers/sellers calling to take their frustrations out on their Realtor-attorney. The pleasures of the quiet season, Wyn thought, crossing the street and entering the New Federal.

Dolly, standing behind the counter, her back toward Wyn, had evidently allowed Victor (of Waggs Neck Harbor Coiffeurs) to arrange her strawberry blond hair in a severe upsweep. She was wearing a navy dress that suggested a Victorian housekeeper. When she turned, Dolly, despite recent events, appeared to be her usual steely self, her fey good looks offputting.

"Hello, Wyn, what can I do for you?"

When Wyn said it would take a few minutes, Dolly didn't bother to hide her irritation. She didn't like her routine being disturbed. "It has to do with Phineas's will," Wyn persisted, and was finally led down the side corridor to the cramped office Phineas had set aside for his "manageress."

Impatiently rolling a pencil between her fore and index fingers, Dolly listened impassively as Wyn told her about her bequest. "That was thoughtful of Phineas. Is there anything else, Wyn? The murder and being ill and Lettie wanting a full accounting . . . I'm days behind."

But before Wyn could get herself out of the narrow chair, Dolly radically changed her tone, saying, in a rush,

"Who do you think did it, Wyn? What's Fitz saying? To me it's as clear as glass." She continued to put the pencil through its paces while Wyn waited. "I don't know why he hasn't been arrested. He was standing right next to him. He hated Phineas since they were kids. He thinks he's above the law and can do whatever he pleases without facing the consequences."

Dolly's voice had taken on a hysterical note that Wyn hadn't heard before. There was a pause while the pencil broke and Dolly's voice became even shriller. "He kills everything he touches. You know it as well as I do. Jackson murdered Phineas."

"Yo, mama," Dicie called out entertainingly, entering Dolly's sitting room late that Monday evening, wishing she could stop thinking about Phineas's murder, wondering if David was going to be arrested. She believed there was a real chance he might have poisoned Phineas, his disgust with the mayor's "progressive" ideas having bordered on the pathological. As she remembered the events in the keeping room, it had been David who had separated himself from her the moment the lights went out.

She did not share these thoughts with anyone and certainly not with her mother. Dolly was reclining on a petit point upholstered sofa she had brought with them from France almost twenty years before, a cashmere blanket over her shapely legs, the small fire in the grate providing the only illumination.

It looked like a scene from an obsolete fashion magazine but Dolly invariably seemed old-fashioned to her daughter, who sat quietly next to her on the arm of the chaise. Dolly, thankful for the silence, reached for Dicie's hand and held it, staring into the fire. They sat that way for some moments, sequestered in the small, pretty room. It was, characteristically, Dicie who broke the silence. "What's the matter, Mother? You seem so freaked these days. I know you're unhappy that Jackson Hall is here . . ."

"Jackson isn't worth talking about. Phineas's death—"

"Please. You were wired long before he was killed. Phineas's murder was only the icing on the cake."

Dolly laughed and then stopped herself. Death was an odd kind of icing; Phineas a peculiar sort of cake. "I don't know exactly what's been bothering me. Your father turning up and Maggie selling him our old barn. . . . Phineas's murder *was* the icing on the cake, I suppose."

Dicie held her mother's hand tightly. "The ladies who lunch at the New Federal are whispering over their decaffeinated coffees that Maggie killed him. To save Carlson House."

"That's idiotic." Dolly removed her hand. She looked at her daughter and thought no one had ever been so appealing. "What does David think? Are you still arguing?"

"I'm arguing. David's doing his passive–aggressive number." She paused and then went on. "He's seeing Jackson Hall's girlfriend, Jessica Stevens. They have coffee and crumb cake at Baby's. David says, 'Listen, Dice, Jessica and I have been buddies since we were in Paris together and you can take your jealousy and stick it up your nose. You and I have an open relationship. We can see whoever we damn well want . . .' And so on. I know I'm not supposed to be jealous but I can't help it." An exquisite tear followed the lovely curve of Dicie's cheek. Dolly put her arms around her child. It never failed to amaze Dolly what a panacea for pain and anguish this simple act—holding her daughter close—could be. As usual, Dicie, who had begun comforting her mother, ended by being comforted by her.

Wyn, tired, refused a dinner invitation from Fitz and drove over to the new West Sea Japanese restaurant for their Monday night takeout vegetarian sushi special. Giving Probity an early dinner and walk, she uncharacteristically locked all the doors on the first floor. The murdering bastard's getting to me, she thought, wishing she knew who the murdering bastard was. Balancing a glass of white jug wine and a plate of California sushi, she went up to her multi-eaved bedroom and, too lazy to go back downstairs for the splintery chopsticks included with the dinner, ate with her fingers while watching *Murphy Brown* and scanning Sunday's *Times* and the Monday *Wall Street Journal*. Resolutely, she forced herself not to think of leases, contracts, men, or murder. At ten she used her clicker to graze through the channels, found nothing of interest, put out the light, and went to sleep.

An hour later, Probity gave a sharp little bark, the kind she usually gave in her sleep. Only she was wide awake and standing at the far end of the bed. Someone was downstairs. Maybe. Probity was an imaginative watchdog.

Wyn stood at the head of the stairs, Probity next to her, their ears cocked. Nothing except the usual house sounds. Wyn walked halfway down the steep stairs and stood very still again. Cowardly Probity had remained at the top of the stairs, dispensing drool on the runner. Nothing. Wyn went all the way down the stairs, which ended in the living room, switched on lights, and walked around the ground floor, opening closets, checking the basement and the pantry and the half bath. Nothing.

Feeling stupid, she switched off the lights and returned to bed, wondering if Lucy Littlefield was going to be sensible in the morning or if Roy Stein was going to have to sue for performance.

CHAPTER

Twelve

AT SIX A.M. ON TUESDAY MORNING, WYN'S EXTRAVAGANT television, equipped with a timer, turned itself on and a serious anchorman with blow-dried hair began detailing the rapes, riots, and traffic snarls in Manhattan.

She switched him off, gathered up last night's plate and glass, and went down into the living room and felt a draft. It took her a moment to locate its source: one of the panes in the French doors had been carefully removed during the night, the glass set on the brick steps leading into the garden. Outraged, realizing how vulnerable she was in this house, doors locked or not, she set the plate and glass down with a not-quite-steady hand. Mostly it was the thought that someone had removed that pane quietly and professionally, probably moments before she had come down to investigate, that unnerved her. Goose bumps, she thought, surprised, rubbing her arms. The only previous episodes of goose bumps had been caused by her ex-husband putting his thick tongue in her ear.

She thought to look over the mantel: the Jackson Hall was still there, as was everything else in the room. She wondered if she would have felt better if something had been taken. She called Tommy Handwerk, because there was an outside chance he had done it to "throw a little scare into her," to prove his point that a woman like Wyn shouldn't be living alone. But Wyn knew this was wishful thinking along the better-the-known-prankster-than-the-stranger-in-the-night line; that Tommy wasn't capable of committing any genuinely mean act, which may have been the reason she didn't give in and marry him. It wasn't human not to be really down and dirty at some point in one's life.

Tommy's mom, Irene, a cashier at the five-and-dime, enthusiastically woke him, hoping this was a reconciliation call. Wyn had asked Tommy to leave her house in the middle of the summer after an idiotic fight over what movie they were going to watch. He had left—at the time, gladly—but they both continued to regard one another in romantic ways.

"You love him," Natalie, her ex-sister-in-law, diagnosed. "But you don't believe you deserve anyone as fantastic as Tommy. You're waiting for another Nick to come along and walk all over you."

"Natalie," Wyn had said, then and often, "please, I'm begging you, don't social-work me."

Now, a sleepy Tommy said, yeah, he would do her a special favor and replace the pane in the French doors this morning. The house he was adding an attic dormer to belonged to weekenders and could wait.

Before Wyn hung up, she asked if he would also install those Radio Shack motion-detector alarms he liked to talk about. Tommy immediately became enthusiastic, loving Radio Shack products. "Any chance we could grab a hamburger one night?" he asked, and Wyn, vulnerable, thinking of his gentleness and wholesomeness and tattooed biceps, said sure, why not, but it would be a while because she was swamped.

"You're always swamped."

"Leave a bill and I'll pay you right away, Tommy." It

was typical of Tommy not to wonder why the pane was removed. Wyn kept her self-promise to attend the red-eye aerobic dance class at the Old Railroad Station Spa partly as an effort to work off yesterday's calories but also to shift the pane removal into her subconscious. It wouldn't budge. She couldn't come up with a reason, rational or otherwise, as to why anyone would go to the bother without taking something. As Patty Batista urged her on to ten more leg-ups, Wyn finally gave it up, putting it down to a neighborhood kid's practical joke.

Lucy was waiting on her Lowe Lane porch, looking testy, tinted aviator glasses sliding down her prominent Littlefield nose. "It's nearly nine A.M.," she said. She had evidently been on the phone with the tax people and had been reassured. "They can have the darn closing today if they want. I'm ready. Sooner the better. What's holding those darn Grasslands' folks up?" Wyn told her the closing would take place on Friday morning at eleven, that Liz would come by on Thursday morning and explain everything to her, and that maybe she should think about hiring someone to help her handle the money.

"I can handle my own darn money, thank you very much, Wynsome Lewis."

"A qualified money manager can help you make the most of it."

"Tell Liz Lum I'll see her Thursday at seven A.M. As you know, it's when I'm at my freshest." She hesitated. "I don't really trust that Roy Stein. He's short and he limps. Never trust a man that limps." She looked imploringly into Wyn's light gray eyes. "There's no chance this won't come off, is there?"

"It's going to come off, Lucy."

Wyn headed for Main Street and the Presbyterian Ladies' Tuesday morning bake sale held under the undulating marquee of the Waggs Neck Cinema, a minor but classic example of nineteen thirties movie theater architecture. As Wyn stepped under the marquee, conversation among the six stout ladies behind the folding tables stopped abruptly, as if someone had pressed their mutual mute button. Wyn wondered what they had been saying about her, not much caring. They wore frilly but no-nonsense aprons over corduroy-collared stiff tweed fall coats. Their curled iron-gray hair seemed as permanently pressed as that of the bas-relief moderne maiden frolicking above them. The instant chocolate cupcakes, the microwave lemon squares, and the no-cook/no-bake Rice Krispies wedges all looked flatter than they should have. Wyn chose two blond brownies and handed over a dollar bill. "Tommy Handwerk's working on your house again, I understand," Charlotte Cherry said, eyebrows raised, head cocked to one side.

Wyn forced a smile, awed as always by Charlotte's archness, saved from having to reply by the advent of the Cole sisters, who wisely chose Carol Morrell's butter nut loaf at two dollars and fifty cents. "How are you, Wyn?" Ruth asked. Wyn, feeling as if she had stepped into an E. F. Benson novel, said she was fine and asked when she could meet with Ruth and Camellia. Ruth said Thursday would be best as they had errands all afternoon and were to spend most of Wednesday at that very good chiropodist in West Sea.

Wyn, wondering what the chiropodist might have scheduled that would take the better part of Wednesday, and deciding she didn't want to know, said her goodbyes and moved on to the Eden Café, where Fitz was waiting for her in a back banquette. Thelma Eden, her head aglow with neon-pink plastic curlers, was pouring his coffee.

After Wyn's coffee was ordered and the brownies unwrapped, she asked Fitz what progress he was making, having decided to keep the removal of her windowpane to herself. Fitz would have made her notify Homer Price and she didn't want him over at her house, patronizing her.

"I have a number of theories and at least two potential motives," he told her, pushing his plate away, "but I'm not sure I trust any of it."

"Lay your favorite theory on me," Wyn said, "to prove good faith."

"All right. It's been percolating in your brain as well. The Wrong Man Was Killed. The motives for doing away with our late mayor are not substantial. Maggie might have killed him for threatening to block the barn's view, but she would have throttled him with her bare hands, not slipped cyanide into his drink. Lettitia might have killed Phineas for his money, but she wouldn't have done it on a spur-of-the-moment impulse.

"Actually, the final capper to the Jackson As Victim argument came in late last night. The lab has finished its investigations and the ME says the cyanide Phineas drank was dissolved not in champagne but in calvados. If you look carefully at the video, you'll see that Phineas's glass was empty. The glass he raised was nearly full and the liquid in it was dark. What I think happened is that when the producer told him to prepare to give the toast, Phineas picked up Jackson's glass and in his anxiety not to spill it on his nice new suit, drank over half of it. Since he wasn't familiar with the brandy, he wouldn't have noticed an odd taste.

"What's more, Jackson was the only one who drank calvados and he and Phineas were the only drinkers present provided with real glasses. Phineas held on to his until after the lights went out, but Jackson's was sitting on the console for some time. Anyone on their way to the buffet could have easily added the cyanide."

"Isn't cyanide the poison they used to give British secret service agents in case they were captured by the Nazis?"

"Maybe. And speaking of the British secret service . . ."

Willy Mercer had entered the Eden and was looking as if he were waiting for a hostess to seat him at a table by the dance floor. "I still haven't told him about his bequest," Wyn said.

"Here's your opportunity," Fitz said, breaking off half of the remaining brownie, popping it in his mouth, then standing up. "You can give him the good news and, at the same time, try to find out if he knows anything."

"The colonel won't know if he knows anything."

"But you might."

Wilfred Mercer sat bolt upright against the ribbed baby blue vinyl upholstery as if he were the accused in a court-martial. When Thelma plumped down his tea, he looked at the thin restaurant tea bag and the greenish water in the thick china cup with distaste. "Dollars to doughnuts the water's not hot," he said, adding sugar and nondairy creamer, sipping. "Tepid." He wiped the nondairy creamer residue from his graying mustache with his middle and index finger, and it was only then that he was able to look directly at Wyn with his hard-boiled goose-egg eyes.

"Phineas left you a bequest. Five thousand dollars, to be exact."

"Gad, he was a good fellow," the colonel said, not shedding tears but looking as if he'd like to. He had the unreal good looks of an old-time matinee idol. Great nose, Wyn thought, noticing its series of broken veins; he was said to be an afternoon alcoholic. "Doesn't start drinking until noon," Liz reported, "and doesn't quit until he passes out."

Wyn found herself pitying him. He was only forty but he seemed decades older. There was a genuine sadness about the colonel, with his stage Anglo-isms, premature old age, and garrulous, suspicious loneliness. He was the kind of man who often began sentences with the word *sorry*. "Horrible about these murders," he said.

"Murders in the plural?"

"Sorry, one tends to think of these things happening in groups, don't you know? Stories in the newspaper, on the telly. Gets one's wind up." He alternately sipped at the disdained tea and fingered his mustache. "Just been round to visit our local chap-made-good, Jackson Hall. Thought we'd have a cuppa, rake over the coals, what; but that young secretary johnny let me know PDQ that the sahib wasn't to be disturbed this morning.

"Queer setup. Always suspect chaps with male secretaries, not to mention lady doctors. They've even got gals pumping petrol now down at the Getty station."

"Soon they'll have women in the front ranks," Wyn wished she hadn't added. He was doing fine by himself.

"Already have. World's going a million miles a minute and I'm standing still. Not Jackson. Always ahead of his time. You know, I rather thought he wouldn't remember me. We were in the same class in high school but I was keen on sports and Jackson took the artistic line. Then, he never said a word. Now he's turned into a regular talking machine. Had me up to the new place the night after Phineas died. Done a bang-up job, I must say. Couldn't stop talking about the old days. Chatted me up no end. We never did get round to asking Jackson to join the Fat Boys. Don't suppose he would have. Other pursuits. Art, of course. And *l'amour. Toujours l'amour.* His new girl is an eyeful. When I was stationed in England, I'd treat myself to a fortnight in La Belle France once or twice a year. Dear me, we did have gay times, I can tell you. I remember one Boxing Day . . ."

When a break in the colonel's reverie came, Wyn said that it was just as well she had missed being in the keeping room on Saturday. He lit a cork-tipped British cigarette, saying, "Don't suppose you mind?" without waiting for an answer. "I was one of the last to arrive. I had been marching in the parade with the American Veterans of Foreign Wars. Mostly noncoms but good fellows nonetheless. Afterwards, I went up to Carlson House, escorting my two old hens, Ruth and Camellia Cole, both slow as molasses. We went up through the house, using the central hall, and then descended that narrow staircase into the keeping room. Felt as if I had wandered into the proverbial sardine tin. Lost the Cole biddies in the crush, grabbed a plastic glass of champers, and propped myself up against the wall next to Phineas, prepared to watch the festivities.

"John Fenton and I were congratulating Phineas when Jackson Hall returned from a trip to the loo. Old Phineas, terrible snob that he was, always sucking up to the top liners, turned his back on John and myself and immediately began chatting up Jackson about the Old Days.

"You could trot a mouse on Phineas's breath and Jackson kept backing away. Phineas wouldn't stop, however, going on and on, as was his wont, about our school days. I don't think Phineas had any real enemies, but a lot of people didn't like him. He could make the most offensive remarks and never once realize what he had said. Thickest hide this side of a renegade rhino.

"Jackson, who wasn't quite quite in high school, couldn't have enjoyed Phineas's reminiscences. As I recall, he was all right when he took his place next to Phineas, but his face lost all color moments before the electricity cut off. As if he were having a gastric attack. He was staring at his paintings across the room and I assumed something in them ticked off an unpleasant memory.

"Couldn't blame the fellow, what with the close atmosphere and Phineas talking, talking, talking, as if nothing in the world mattered but some ancient prank we had played when we were kids. For a moment the blackout was a mercy because everyone, even Phineas, shut up. Later, when the lights were purposely dimmed, he did as he was told and stepped forward, glass in hand, while everyone's attention was on the pantry door. Then there was that appalling retching sound. I looked around, thinking one of the fair ladies had caught an olive in her throat and was too delicate to spit it out when Annie came out of the pantry and screamed and the lights came up and there was Phineas, poor blighter, on the floor,

John Fenton kneeling over him. Nearly lost my breakfast, I don't mind telling you. Still, RIP, what?"

Stiff from sitting on the Eden's unaccommodating banquette, Wyn checked in with Liz, who said she had faxed off the condo listing and that the papers for Friday's closing were ready but she was waiting on Roy Stein's office to initial a final draft. "You look nervous and cranky," Liz said. "What's up?"

"I'll be back in an hour," Wyn said, not answering. "I'm going to see Jackson Hall to inform him of his bequest."

CHAPTER

Thirteen

TONY DEEL WORE LEOTARDS THAT REVEALED, AS LUCY LIT-
tlefield would say, all of New York. Wyn hoped she
hadn't interrupted ballet practice. Not that he was graceful. His blunt features and discordant movements were
marionettelike, as if he were controlled by some powerful, unseen hand. He was in his early twenties but
looked as if he were still in his teens. That he was very
thin and an inch shorter than Wyn added to the impression that he was contrived, a figure of wires and strings.
But when he smiled, the world-weariness disappeared
and he became a boy wanting to please. He would have
made a convincing Pinocchio.

He led her across the blue stone steps into the huge
white structure that suggested a barn, but barely. "Jackson designed it himself," Tony Deel said, as Wyn took in
the enormous space. "Soaring ceilings make him happy."

"Must've been difficult for him, cooped up on his
yacht all summer." She found herself aping Tony, speaking in reverential terms, talking about "him."

Tony Deel, producing a cup of rich coffee for her and a
Diet Coke for himself, laughed, dispelling the deferential

mood. "The yacht's master suite has sixteen-foot ceilings and is forty feet square. And yes, it was bloody difficult being cooped up on it all summer. For everyone but Jackson. Lest you haven't heard, Jackson Hall subscribes to the czarist school of personal behavior."

Wyn found herself liking the saturnine Tony Deel and his wry delivery. She sat on a tortured modern Italian bar stool that had no right to be as comfortable as it was and, spinning round on its seat, saw the painting.

"He has to work on it down here," Tony said. "It's too big to get up the stairs to his studio."

Wyn felt as if she had been gratuitously punched in the solar plexus. Even unfinished, it had an overwhelming and not especially pleasing force. The gargantuan face that took up the center of the enormous canvas was both familiar and alien, its huge eyes filled with self-loathing and habitual panic. The immense lips were parted as if the woman were about to call out to someone. Or was waiting to be fed. All this seen through a wall of raging fire. Two as yet unrealized figures—a boy and a man, Wyn guessed—were being subsumed by the flames emanating from the central figure, whose malevolent eyes made Wyn feel not so much the observer as the observed.

"He calls it 'Family Portrait,' " Tony Deel was saying, gauging her reaction. "If there is any doubt about his genius, this should put it to rest. And he's only a little over forty."

Wyn remembered Maggie's "guts interpretation" of Jackson's work and found she agreed. Jackson Hall clearly put everything he had on the canvas. "Family Portrait" was, in both the contemporary and old senses of the word, awesome, and Wyn felt humbled. Like nearly everyone else, she held back.

"Unfortunately, all the casebook volatility and neuroses come with the territory. He's a monster, is our Jackson, and I'm his dog Tray. My job is simple: to make certain everything goes his way."

"No fun?"

"Not much, but even when he's at his worst, there are compensations." He looked up at the painting with the fervency of the true believer. "I feel privileged to be allowed to help him. Blessed isn't too strong a word."

The high note Tony's otherwise mellifluous voice hit seemed to stretch hero worship into something less clean. Wyn started to ask if Tony ever painted, but he was still selling Jackson. ". . . at Sotheby's big summer sale, a recent Jackson Hall fetched nearly as much as a Picasso. It was a third-rate Picasso, and a great Jackson Hall, but Jackson Hall is alive."

"Very much so." It was a female voice, buoyant with assurance. Its owner came down the sculptural stairs and stood for a moment in front of the painting, looking as if she had just left a warm and shared bed. Whereas the woman in the painting was a study in tortured reds and yellows, the live woman was a calm composite of auburn and tan.

Wyn had seen her around the village—at the drugstore and once at the Nonesuch Bar—but they hadn't formally met. "You're Wyn Lewis, I'm Jessica Stevens, and now that that's out of the way, wouldn't you like something healthier than coffee?" She descended the rest of the way, took Wyn's hand for a moment in her cool one, and smiled.

She couldn't be more territorial, Wyn thought, if she were a cat peeing in her sandbox. "That's kind of you," Wyn said, "but this is fine. I've come to talk to Jackson Hall."

"Not possible." She was wearing faded jeans, high-heeled half boots made of reptile skin, and a cashmere turtleneck that matched her red-blond hair in texture and color. Her features had a glossy magazine quality, as if airbrushed for perfection. She was, Wyn was obliged to admit, beautiful without makeup, but it wasn't the kind of beauty other women much appreciated.

As she poured herself a glass of colorless juice, Jessica

said, "He's in no condition to be talked to. Your police captain was here and didn't help. The mayor's death was a devastating shock." Like Tony, who had disappeared, she had an accent that was difficult to identify. An American schooled in Europe; or vice versa. "Dr. Fenton also stopped by this morning and shot him full of mega-tranquilizers."

"I thought you were the house physician," Wyn said, thinking that might sound provocative, but Jessica Stevens was probably used to instant hostility from other women.

She answered easily enough. "I don't yet have a license to practice in New York." She finished her juice, looked at Wyn and, changing tack, said, "I'd love to get out of here while he's sleeping. Could we take a walk?"

Jessica led the way past the site where the Carlsons' stable once stood, across the narrow, rocky beach, and onto the grounds of the old convent. Wyn wondered again what the Bijoux Foundation planned to do with the troika of onion-domed buildings, thinking that if Maggie did have a role in the decision, they would be put to good use. Their dried-blood color suited the dreary day. Low, dense clouds, whitecaps on the bay waters, and a chilling southeast wind lent eastern Long Island a Tolstoyian melancholy.

"Jackson's new house, this barn he turned into the furniture wing of the Museum of Modern Art, isn't possible to live in," Jessica was saying.

"You could leave," Wyn said.

"I've tried and I can't. Dictatorial men bring out my maternal instincts. And mothers, of course, are hostage to their children. I'm here till he kicks me out."

"You met in France?"

"I was in my last year of medical school in Belgium. If you've ever been in Brussels, you know why I spent every spare moment in Paris. And there he was, a girl's own fantasy of Mr. Wrong. It didn't take much time.

Jackson likes students and he likes women. Or says he does. He's gone through enough of them. He warned me from the beginning that with him nothing is permanent.

"He has enough temptations. Females get wobbly when Jackson's around. He's literally hot, always in a fever, his normal temperature hovering around the hundred mark. And then he's a certified artistic genius. It's an unbeatable combination."

"You're warning me."

"Deceptive Innocence is his favorite type. I'll give you half an hour before you're unbuttoning his fly. He doesn't hold with zippers."

This conversation was too steamy for Wyn, who not so deftly changed the subject by asking about Jackson's work schedule. They had reached the point where the convent grounds ended and Lucy Littlefield's soon-to-be-sold—Wyn crossed her fingers—swampy pine forest began. Turning back, the two women walked close to the narrow sandy shore. The tide was out and the wind was blessedly at their backs now, pushing them along. "He'll have long periods of great activity," Jessica was saying, "and then abruptly he'll stop and sink into depression, sometimes lasting months."

"What phase is he in now?"

"Hard to say. Since we've come to Waggs Neck he's been the perfect little soldier, heavily into Productive Activity. But he's taking the murder as a personal affront and last night he was suicidal. Which is why I asked Fenton to come this morning. Sometimes we can head off a major depression with Band-Aid chemistry."

"You've been treating him chemically as well as analytically?" Wyn asked, having had several discussions with her ex-sister-in-law on the subject. Natalie was a fervid believer in Prozac.

Jessica hesitated, pulling up the collar of her yellow fur jacket. "My specialty *is* chemical treatment. Jackson's worried that I'll take his genius from him if I regulate his extraordinary highs and lows."

"Is that possible?"

"I don't know. But I do know he's capable of killing himself during his more severe depressive bouts when irrational fear and anger take over." She hesitated for a moment and then decided to go on. "He has never been able to talk about his youth and so, about a year ago, I hesitatingly proposed that he visit Waggs Neck as a kind of Jungian exercise. He not only agreed, but immediately set about moving his entire establishment here. It was evidently the right button to push.

"The summer, aboard the yacht, was fine, Jackson seemingly working out some buried anguish in that yet unfinished painting you saw. It doesn't take a skilled psychoanalyst to figure out that he has a deep-seated hatred of women stemming from what he feels was his mother's abandonment; thus all his conquests, trying to get mommy back and in her place, in bed, under him, so he's in control. I think the painting is a good sign that he's coming to terms with some of that anger. The hideous female is Every Woman and the boy and the man are probably representative of Jackson, watching her destruction with detachment.

"But the murder threw him. He believes that it was he and not Phineas Browne who was meant to be killed. Paranoia is rearing its ugly head and I'm worried."

"There's every chance," Wyn said carefully, "that it's not paranoia."

They had arrived at the barn; the two women looked at one another in speculative silence for a moment before Tony Deel's elfin face appeared at a second-story window. "There you are," he called out. "Jackson Hall will see you now, Miss Lewis."

Jackson Hall's bedroom—studio took up the second floor of the former barn. The wall facing Carlson House was solid but the other three were glass; a series of opaque paper screens were used to regulate light. At the moment the screens were not in place and before Wyn could take in the man, she was confronted by the panorama. Through one glass wall she could see Waggs Neck, looking bygone and toylike, as if it belonged to a child's train set. Framed in the glass wall on the right were the convent grounds and Lucy's spindly forest. The bay was in the center panel, gray-green and whitecapped waters under dark skies. Wyn was reminded of a seventeenth-century triptych: the Town, the Country, the Sea.

"Jessica believes the three vistas add to my alienation."

He was wearing white painter's trousers, a forest green shirt of some soft material, and was, disconcertingly, barefoot. His dark hair was combed straight back. His flat brown snake's eyes were unforgiving. He had a movie star's cleft chin and his voice was deep, dark, foreign, and penetrating. He was holding a cigarette between his teeth like a bad man in a cowboy film. "I am not an addict," he said, puffing on it. "Do not look so disapproving. I only smoke the occasional cigarette."

He stood looking down at Wyn from a white platform of industrial pallets that supported a huge white silk-sheeted mattress. He came off the platform and moved toward her and Wyn understood the "wobbly" reaction Jessica had spoken about.

He was a nice size. He moved beautifully. Without a wasted movement he put the cigarette into a high-tech ashtray and took her hand. His skin was warm, almost hot, as advertised. His muddy eyes did not smile when he did. He had a pouty lower lip. His presence promised warmth and maybe comfort and definitely something agreeably sinister, as if he were about to offer a new and spectacular way to go to hell with one's self.

"I have a sentimental memory of you as a little girl, holding a yellow dog, looking like the Victorian ideal of Child. You could not have been less interested in me. What do I call you now that you are all grown up?" he asked, finally releasing her hand. She felt as if it had been toasted.

"Wyn," she said, moving out of range to a pair of white leather and steel chairs.

"Poor Phineas," he said, sitting next to her after a moment, studying Wyn's face as if he were committing it to memory. "You are here to talk about his death, I imagine." He spoke English as if it were his second language.

"I'm his executor," Wyn said. "He left you a bequest."

"I cannot believe it."

She had brought a Xerox copy of the paragraph naming Jackson as a recipient and she passed it over to him. He read it slowly and intently, giving it all his concentration. Wyn knew it by heart. "Five thousand dollars to Jackson Hall, not that he needs or wants it but as a gesture to atone for any disservice I may have done him in the past." It was the last change Phineas had made, only adding it at the end of the summer, after Jackson Hall had agreed to participate in his festival.

"Had he done you a disservice?" Wyn asked.

"On the contrary. He was one of the Waggs Neckers responsible for my leaving." He looked down at the Xerox. "You know, I had an odd presentiment—a *frisson*—that morning of Phineas's festival. I am not unduly superstitious but I knew something terrible was going to happen. To me.

"I told myself not to be an idiot but the feeling returned again in the keeping room while Phineas was informing me about our shared and supposedly golden youth. It was bloody hot what with the lights and the lack of ventilation and all those people milling round. I was only half listening to Phineas, trying to ignore what I thought of as an irrational feeling, and was looking at two of my early paintings and a drawing—hung too high—on the far wall. I had not seen the paintings since I left Waggs Neck and I was interested in how well the three fit together, how prescient they were, predating the unfinished painting you see downstairs by nearly twenty-five years.

"Phineas was leaning toward me while I was leaning

away. His breath was rancid and we ended up engaged in a conversational gavotte. By the time he was supposed to make the toast, I was ready to give it all up and get myself out of that waiting room to hell.

"During the deliberate and second blackout, I heard the retching noises but I put them down to someone's indigestion. I stood there for those few unlit moments, relieved. The dark and the disappearance of Phineas's dragon's breath were soothing. And then the pantry door flew open, the lights came on, and Phineas was staring up at me accusingly."

He folded his hands, which were, unlike the rest of him, not well made. They were laborer's hands, thick, oversized, the fingers splayed, the nails bruised and blackened. "I am being a poor host. Would you like something to drink? Or eat?"

"No, thank you. I had the Presbyterian Ladies' blond brownies not long ago."

Jackson laughed. It was a nice laugh, completely genuine. "They are not still having their Tuesday morning bake sales, are they? My old aunties, may they end up in some wet, slimy purgatory, used to claim they began the Presbyterian bake sales." He laughed again. "I was not born in Waggs Neck, you know."

Wyn sat back as Jackson, ugly hands folded in unconscious prayer, handsome head turned toward the glass wall that displayed the town, began to talk about his early years. Though she knew most of the story, Wyn was captivated, thinking he had the most beautiful man's voice she had ever heard.

"My parents died early and my guardian, the dread Bull Carlson, parked me with the aunties—you must know them, the Cole sisters? They brought me up according to Bull Carlson's ideas as to how a 'not quite nice' boy should be reared. To be fair, they were merely frustrated spinsters doing orphaned-child duty, never having wanted such a responsibility. They were church strict. Masturbation, not that Camellia could conceive of such an act, would blind you. The human body is not fit to be seen unclad. The sex act is vile and only for procreation.

"Art was Gainsborough reprints and to be vaguely appreciated, not practiced. Fortunately, there was a man at Mary Immaculate—the unbathed headmaster, now gone to his reward—who had the sense to realize that I had a genuine calling. He, himself, was a watercolorist of the fragile lily movement, but Charles Harrison Hart knew.

"So, for that matter, did Maggie. She was teaching English at the time, a subject I never mastered. She did not care. She told me to paint. To paint and paint and paint. There was a colony of Germany refugee artists living in West Sea at the time, A-minus talents. Hart and Maggie got them to look at my work, and after that it was not difficult to get the best of them, Holtz, to give me lessons.

"Of course he and his gang knew better than anyone where I was headed. Holtz himself, eighty and bearded and prideful, begged Bull to let me study with Bonet, then just recently set up in New York. Bull would not hear of it.

"But my mother had left me some money which he was to hold until my eighteenth birthday. The morning after high school graduation, when I turned eighteen, I enlisted your father's aid and he and I confronted Bull and I got my money. It was not nearly what it was supposed to be, but it was enough to get me out. I went away without saying good-bye to anyone, leaving a note for Harrison and two paintings he had liked—the ones on the keeping room wall—and a painting for your father. With a few canvases under my arm, I strolled into Bonet's Eighty-eighth Street studio and, for the next year, that fat French martinet taught me everything he knew, which was considerable. When he realized he could not do anything more for me, he sent me to Paris to study with Schlein, and I never returned."

"What made you come back?" Wyn asked.

"Who can say? I had another birthday I didn't like. Paris is growing ugly and modern and filthy, while the Parisians never get any more sympathetic. Would you believe me if I said I simply needed to shake things up a little? No, I do not suppose you would. You are probably a fine attorney. You are intelligent, which must be half the battle. Not to mention the fact that you are wonderful-looking. I am, I confess, curious. What could have made you choose to do what you do when you had so many options?"

"What really made you return to Waggs Neck?" Wyn asked evasively, not liking his question or even, possibly, her answer.

"And added to your other qualities is the sine qua non of most successes, persistence." His mood changed. He stood up and walked to the wall facing the bay, his back toward her, his posture stiffening. "The truth is I awoke one morning and could not paint, paralysis setting in whenever I approached the canvas. You have met Jessica. Neurotic herself, she is a brilliant therapist. She felt it was important that I return to where 'the Essential Me' began. There is no arguing that who I am and what I am is a result of my early years here.

"Since I have returned to Waggs Neck, I have been able to paint again." He had left the window and returned to stand over her. "You must have seen it," he said, after a moment, moving away. "I am close to being finished."

"Who is she?" Wyn asked. "The woman in the painting."

He held up his ugly hands in a Gaelic gesture, smiled at her, and yawned. "I am beginning to feel the effect of Dr. Fenton's magic pills again."

He looked both preoccupied and fearful, as if he were about to be sick, reminding Wyn of how several people described him just before Phineas died. She said as much.

"The sweating crowd and those lights were getting to

me. I suffer from claustrophobia in addition to my other ailments." He looked at her and smiled again. "The truth is I was afraid. That fey foreboding of the morning returned." He sat down again, next to her, folding his hands. "I felt surrounded by enemies. When I become paranoid, even my best friends appear to have good reasons for getting rid of me. Maggie, for instance, would get the remainder of the money for her barn so she could pour it into the rotting timbers of Carlson House. Dolly Carlson, the self-proclaimed mother of my child, could get revenge. The child herself might have it in for me. Then I have been unable to ignore a number of old faces in the village who have scores to settle.

"And my premonition was not totally incorrect, was it? Only the wrong man was killed. While Phineas and I were doing the Bad-Breath Two-Step in the dark, Phineas took my glass and received the cyanide meant for me. Paranoia aside, I am convinced of that.

"My hope is that the murderer is properly appalled and, having his emotions under control, will go on about his business. I have no great stake in bringing him or her to justice, only a keen instinct for self-preservation. Phineas was a negligible human being, mean as a boy, fatuous as a man." He looked at the Xerox copy of Phineas's bequest and shook his head. "Life is a series of cheap ironies, is it not."

"I think you'd better talk to the police captain."

"I have already talked to the police captain. I do not hold much faith in your Homer Price, but who knows? Meanwhile, I plan to hole up here in my self-made but not uncomfortable prison and attempt to finish what I modestly call my masterpiece and hope that the killer goes away.

"And if he will not, I will depend upon my friends, old and new, to protect me." He held out his right hand, calloused palm up, and, without wanting to, Wyn put hers into it. "I loved your father. When I was very down, he would take me out to the golf course and try to teach me the game. I was hopeless but those days he gave me in the sun on the green fields of the Waggs Neck Harbor Country Club helped me enormously. I think you are equally therapeutic, Wynsome Lewis. People as self-involved as I am are usually audience enough for ourselves. Except when the audience is someone uncommon like you.

"Please, do not let anyone murder me until I finish my painting. *If* I can finish it. It will cap my career and there is self-interest in it for you, as well. Think how much more valuable your painting will be after I am certified a genius."

Wyn wondered how he knew she still had the painting and then had an unpleasant thought: it would be worth more after he was dead.

CHAPTER

Fourteen

LATER ON THAT TUESDAY, ANNIE KITCHEN, ON HER knobby knees, wearing baby-blue Rubbermaid gloves, ammonia making her head spin, was enjoying herself, scrubbing and complaining. "Fine for Miss Mother Maggie Carlson to tell me it's all right to clean up the keeping room," she said, scraping the remains of cake and Jesus knew what from the ancient and pitted brick, applying her favorite brush with fierce determination. "Only she don't have to clean it, does she?"

Eventually, the cake and other remains were gotten up and Annie, cataloguing the sins and follies of her employer, set herself to other sanitizing tasks. She did a "complete" on the pantry kitchen, used Brillo on the oven, defrosted the fridge, and polished the pine cupboard. After several hours' work she was satisfied, sticking her aged Orphan Annie head into the pantry for one last look, reserving a deep sigh for the old porcelain sink that nothing would ever whiten again. Entering the pantry, letting the door slam behind her, she bent down to get at one of the thick paper napkins that had slipped behind the stepladder. "Fancy Pants," Annie said, thinking of Phineas Browne's insistence on "good" paper napkins, as if there were such a thing.

Disposing of the offending article, she retracted her uncharitable thought. "One thing I pride myself on," Annie maintained, "is never saying ill of the dead." It was while she was congratulating herself on this achievement that she heard a noise in the keeping room. A moment of panic ensued. She envisioned the shadowy room on the other side of the thick pantry door and repressed a nearly irrepressible need: to race screaming from the pantry, rush past whatever ghoul (Phineas?) was waiting for her, run outside and shout for help.

Fighting hysteria, she picked up the long, sharp knife that was to have been used to cut the cake, but a vision of herself tripping over the keeping room's uneven bricks, the serrated knife plunging into her own heart, sobered her. There is nothing to be scared of in the keeping room, she told herself, putting down the knife, resolutely opening the door, her heart beating unpleasantly.

At first glance the room was unoccupied and Annie, making the sign of the cross, stepped out of the pantry, closed its door behind her, got a whiff of Old Spice, and screamed. Billy Bell, concentrating hard, was playing his mini flashlight on the brick wall behind the console, just as he had been during the blackout.

White-faced, she asked, "What are you doing here, Billy?" The tremolo in her voice revealed her alarm. He was such a huge, queer lump of a boy. One never knew what he was going to do next.

Billy, not answering, continued to play with his flashlight, transfixed by the circles of light it made on the brick. A smile came to his epicene lips. "None of your fucking business, bitch," he said. And then he was gone.

Wyn spent the better part of Tuesday afternoon on the telephone with an up-island developer looking for an industrial park site; a retired oral surgeon (referred by Nick; she knew she shouldn't have taken the call) who wanted a four-bedroom, four-bath house, in the village, completely remodeled and on a good-sized parcel of land for under one hundred thousand dollars ("that's my max"); Roy Stein, ironing out the last glitches of the Littlefield–Grasslands closing statements.

She felt guilty about still not having formally told Annie Kitchen about her bequest and decided to get that over with, calling Carlson House to make certain Annie was there. When Wyn arrived, Maggie discreetly removed herself from the living room and Annie Kitchen, invited to sit, did so tentatively, on the edge of the Boston rocker facing the green sofa. Her eyes were fixed on her plain little hands, which were held tightly in her lap as if they might break away and do something terrible.

Wyn first read to her and then handed her a copy of Phineas's bequest, which gave Annie five thousand dollars for her loyalty as a "part-time housekeeper." One of the long-running battles between Phineas and Maggie had been over the sharing of Annie Kitchen's services.

"When do I get my money?" Annie wanted to know.

"It may take a month or so, depending upon taxes and such."

"You could hurry it up if you wanted to."

Wyn, having had an emotionally conflicting day, and having little patience with Mrs. Kitchen at the best of times, lost it. "For Christ sake, I'll write you a personal check as a noninterest loan against your bequest, if you want it, Annie."

"That won't be necessary," Annie said, having won the round. "And it isn't necessary to take the Lord's name in vain, either." Annie, seeing the look on Wyn's face, said, "Well, this isn't the way it's done on television."

Wyn, curious, asked how it was done on television.

Annie took a breath and then let out her grievances. "We shouldn't be sitting here in Miss Maggie's living room. We should be in a big wood-paneled office with a huge, mahogany conference table and all sorts of lawyers and heirs sitting around it. You shouldn't look like you just came from choir practice and you shouldn't be a woman at all, matter of fact. You should be a tall man in a pin-striped suit and there should be some woman in a plain dress taking notes. It don't seem right." She crossed her sturdy ankles, bringing attention to dark green socks, ribbed and folded over at the top like a schoolgirl's. Her milk-white face was a study in clench-toothed determination.

Wyn, afraid Annie was going to cry, and at the same time wanting to give her a good smack, tried to pacify her by playing to her recent notoriety. "It must have been frightening standing in the pantry, icing that cake, when the lights went out."

"See, that's just how rumors get started. The cake was already iced. I was waiting for my cue to bring in my poison chocolate fudge whale cake—I swear, as sure as I'm sitting here, that I'll never make it again—and present it to Mayor Browne and Jackson Hall. The TV people set it up that way." She paused for a moment of sham modesty. "They wanted a shot of the cake. And me."

The lights were to have been dimmed, purposely, Annie went on. Billy was to knock on the pantry door, Annie was to light the candle on the cake, knock back, and Billy Bell would open the door. Then she was to sail into the keeping room, cake in her arms, cameras on her as she presented her masterpiece to Jackson Hall and Phineas Browne, who was then to make his toast.

"The cake and I were going to open and close the segment," Annie said, secure in TV terminology. "Billy had been playing with that flashlight all morning, pointing it every which way. Made me so nervous. Finally he gave me my cue, I lit the candle, and when I came out Billy's damn flashlight was shining right in my eyes. So I turned toward where the mayor was supposed to be standing with his glass in his hand, ready to give the toast and, thanks to Billy, I was blind as a bat for a minute, and then I looked down and saw the mayor staring up at me and the cake went up in the air and I screamed and ran back into the pantry."

This reminded Annie of her afternoon scare. Somewhat reluctantly—she had a feeling she should save this episode for a more appreciative audience—Annie told Wyn about Billy's appearance in the keeping room. "I think he finally remembered something he forgot. He got that nasty look on his face and strutted out after calling me . . . well, I don't like to say."

Wyn stopped by Fitz's house and told him how Jackson Hall and Annie Kitchen had responded to their bequests. "So Jackson's aware he was the target," Fitz said, reaching for the telephone. "I'll have to talk to him, but what I'd like to know right now is what Billy Bell remembered."

"Are you calling him?" Wyn said.

"No. I'm not the man to tackle Billy. I'm going to leave that up to the captain."

It was dark by the time Wyn arrived home and she was relieved to find that Tommy had done what he had promised, the pane in place, a plethora of warning decal notices on doors and windows, the turn-key alarm system ready to be activated. She did so, Probity promptly setting off a teeth-chilling noise. Tommy called to see if it was working and Wyn said it was and then he said what about that hamburger and she said she was too tired and he said they didn't have to make love if that's what was bothering her, they could just hold one another and get cuddly. Hearing interested silence on the other end, Tommy said he could pick the burgers up at the Nonesuch Bar along with a couple of brews and Wyn, weakening, not wanting to spend the night alone, the new alarm system not withstanding, liking the idea of getting cuddly, said she had a couple of brews.

CHAPTER
Fifteen

IT WAS LATE WEDNESDAY MORNING BY THE TIME HOMER Price parked his gleaming patrol car in the unpaved, unweeded semicircular Bell driveway. Across the road and above him, the stilt-raised, pressure-treated wood decks of Red Wood Shores were deserted, it being strictly a weekend and summer community. There wasn't much wildlife, either. The sparse and swampy grounds around the Bell house discouraged all but the plainest brown birds.

The Bells' residence leaned to the left. Its unpainted clapboard had resisted what the Realtors called "that charming, weathered look," turning, instead, to a pock-marked oatmeal color that matched the Johns-Manville asbestos roof shingles. The brick chimney had partially fallen down and every one of the old louvered shutters—darlings of the renovation crowd—had something to complain about: slats missing, hinges rusted, frames going, going, gone. In contrast, numerous primary-colored plastic tricycles and choo-choo trains belonging to Bell grandchildren littered the scrubby front lawn.

Homer Price climbed the front steps gingerly and

knocked authoritatively on the front door. As he was about to give up, the door opened and Victor Bell appeared, looking as functionally obsolete as his habitat.

He wore a soiled thermal undershirt, a tight pair of once-blue suit trousers, and a brown knit cap on his long, narrow, bald head. Only his lips, perfect bows, gave credibility to the fact that he was the sire of his more splendid son.

"Billy here?"

"Nope." An unpleasant aroma seeped from Victor Bell's person, its base being bottle-cap wine. There was an attitude to match, Victor Bell believing it "just plain wrong" to have a black man as police captain.

"Expect him home anytime in the near future?"

"Nope."

"He's not living with you anymore?"

"Nope." Victor Bell lifted his cap and scratched his dome. "Billy in deep shit again?"

Homer didn't answer and Mr. Bell chewed over the nonresponse slowly before saying, "Like as not you'll find him over to the Blue Buoy. He took a room down there seeing as how he gets all that money working for Jackson Hall. Out of all my kids, Billy was the last to leave home. Billy is my baby. Guess he's as good as gone now."

The senior Bell as desolate empty-nester didn't play. "You see Billy, you tell him I'm looking for him." The captain would have tapped his forefinger on Bell's chest for emphasis but he didn't want to touch that shirt.

"Sure will. But when Billy don't want to be seen, you can bet your breeches ain't no one going to see him." He waited until the captain was in his car before he said, "Captain Midnight, my mother-loving ass."

Jeremy, thirty-five years old with acne, was the owner–manager of the Blue Buoy Bar & Grill. Jeremy said there oughta be a law. Jeremy said he wanted to see his lawyer. Jeremy said he was going to report the captain to

the authorities. Jeremy, whose shirt collar had gotten
torn, said the least the police could do was pay to mend
it. Jeremy, whose head ached where his ponytail had
been grabbed and his forehead banged against the back
corridor wall, finally stopped horsing around.

He hadn't, he swore, seen Billy in a couple of days.
Yes, Billy had rented one of the rooms above the bar,
but there was a back entrance and he could come and
go at will without being seen. "I would let you go on
up . . . if you had a warrant."

The captain, knowing nothing would be gained by
going through the process of getting a warrant, smiled
at Jeremy. Jeremy, tough little bird, stood his ground. So
the captain took his index and middle fingers and pushed
the offending tavern owner out of the way, giving his
shin a good rap with his pointed boot in the process.
"Thanks, butt hole. I knew you'd cooperate." Jeremy
went back to the bar, complaining sotto voce about jiga-
boo policemen pushing honest white business folk around.

Jeremy's building had once, long ago, belonged to a
dentist, the downstairs devoted to medical offices, the
top floors housing family rooms. Where once the proper
dentist's wife had held teas for village professionals, Jeremy had constructed a rabbit warren of sordid rooms
that he let by the week, the month, the hour.

The captain moved along the cramped, low-ceilinged
firetrap of a corridor, opening doors at will. Two were
occupied, their occupants in no position to object. At the
far end of the hall, facing the village parking lot, was a
door on which was tacked a piece of notepaper with
"B. Bell" neatly written on it in pencil.

The lock on the thin door was easily forced. The captain looked through the cardboard chest of drawers and
found half a dozen T-shirts, an assortment of unappetiz-
ing underwear and socks, a small quantity of marijuana
and Top rolling paper in a Ziploc bag, and a mini
flashlight.

"When Billy comes back, you tell him I'm looking for

him," the captain said to Jeremy, who was standing behind the bar, out of reach. "You also tell him I confiscated his flashlight. You got that?"

Jeremy said yeah, he got it. The morning Blue Buoy regulars snickered as the captain exited and Frank Sinatra sang, on the jukebox, a song about doing it his way. What bothered Homer Price most was that Billy Bell had left his stash behind.

CHAPTER

Sixteen

EARLY THAT WEDNESDAY MORNING, BEFORE HOMER PRICE had gotten round to interviewing Mr. Bell and Jeremy, Tommy Handwerk and Wyn made love. Then he asked her to marry him. "We each got one marriage under our belts," Tommy said, looking so earnest and needy and appealing, toothbrush in hand, towel around no-fat waist, that she almost said yes.

Instead she told him that he was too young and she was too wise and what he needed, she couldn't provide. "Yeah, you can," he said. "Just did." Later, as he mournfully chomped on his Cheerios, he asked if he at least couldn't move back in for a while. "I don't think it's so safe, you living alone, guys coming around taking the panes out of your doors."

She didn't think it was so safe, either, guys (or gals) taking the panes out of her doors. But she wasn't going to have Tommy move back in to protect her. She could protect herself and she told him so.

"The boys think your tits are too small," he said, putting down his spoon, taking her hand, kissing it.

"The girls think you've got a small dick," she said, trying to get her hand back.

"You set them straight." He pulled her into his lap and nuzzled her neck. It wasn't the same as Nick nuzzling her neck with his sandpaper beard; Tommy was fair and only had to shave every other day. Still, it was pretty good. "You're the sweetest-smelling woman, Wyn," Tommy was saying.

"You smell pretty good yourself," she returned, kissing his forehead. He did; even after working on top of a roof on an August day, Tommy's skin smelled like baby powder.

"All right, we're both tens in the smell department but otherwise we're as different as can be, I know that. You're this Yup princess and I'm only a guy who's good with his hands."

He was, Wyn thought, very good with his hands. "Why don't you date other women?" she asked, pretty sure she didn't want him to do that.

"I've tried. Never works out. I love you, Wyn, with all my heart and soul. That's got to count for something."

It counted for a lot, but not enough to make her marry him. She didn't want to marry anyone; not now and not ever. She liked her life the way it was. She kissed Tommy good-bye, raced to the aerobics class, switched off her mind, and allowed little Patty Batista to boss her body around.

Dicie had taken the class as well and afterward they had breakfast together at Baby's, the irresistibly quaint tearoom facing the parking lot behind Main Street. Dicie, chewing on heavily buttered French bread, wanted to know when she was going to receive Phineas's five thousand dollars and then, inevitably, the talk turned to Phineas's murder, which had disappeared from even the most local newscasts.

"What's driving me nuts," Dicie said, "and I don't want this to go any further, is that just before the lights went out, David and I separated. I'd been trying to get my nerve up to approach Jackson all that morning and I decided it was now or never. Jackson got this freaky expression on his face when I moved toward him as if I was a mutant alien coming to collect his brain. Phineas was still talking but Jackson was looking straight at me. I'm a slow study but I finally received the message that he doesn't want to know me. I was going to tell him that he didn't have to when the lights went out.

"Bummer," Dicie said and looked away. "In the old days the outraged family would have strung up a man like Jackson. Now Maggie's selling him our barn and having dinner with him." She sat still for a moment and then looked at Wyn with her silent screen vamp's eyes and said, "You don't think David poisoned Phineas, do you, believing he was chilling Jackson? He buys bags full of those damn peach pits."

Nick's oral surgeon had the skeletal articulation of a grasshopper and was about as verbal. Wyn spent the rest of the morning showing him property that he was never going to buy and the afternoon studying the plat maps for suitable property for an industrial park. In between, she forced Liz to put away her tuna sandwich and treated her to lunch at Baby's, trying to convince her it was time to take the real estate course at the college, to go for her license. "I was terrible at school," Liz said, ordering tuna on French bread.

"Liz, you were valedictorian."

"I hated tests."

"You gloried in them. Listen, I'm going to have to hire another Realtor sooner rather than later and you might as well be it. Then we can hire someone to take your place and you can boss them around. You'd be a sensational Realtor, Liz."

"In my polyester pants suits?"

"You could upgrade to fifty/fifty."

Just as Wyn was leaving the office for the day, a call came through from Janet Hayes at the Foundation Library in Manhattan. "It took a bit of digging, and if you tell anyone I told you I'll swear I never heard of you, but here it is: the Bijoux Foundation board consists of the chairman, Jackson Hall; the secretary, Anthony J. Deel; and the treasurer, Margaret Carlson.''

"So it's not a family foundation after all," Wyn said.

"It said it was in the descriptive material but mistakes do happen, even in the wonderful world of foundations."

There was no reason why Maggie should have announced she was a board member of a foundation almost certainly set up by Jackson Hall for the purpose of acquiring the convent land. But it was a little too coincidental that none of the local newspapers—where Maggie had influence—had reported the sale. The acquisition of the convent land had been the best-kept real estate secret in Waggs Neck Harbor history, and Wyn wondered why.

She decided further speculation wouldn't help so she called Maggie and asked if it was true. "I hope so, pal," Maggie said. "The taxes we've been paying. Jackson decided, after he bought the barn, that he'd better buy up the convent as well, to protect his property, and then he got a brainstorm. It hasn't been made public yet—we're still getting our ideas together—and I'm going to rely on your notorious discretion when I tell you he's planning to turn the playhouse into a museum for modern American painters. The old Mary Immaculate school building will house exhibits and administrative offices, while the annex will be divided into studios where artists can come and work. I haven't been this excited since I discovered Cheez Doodles."

"Phineas would have loved it: Waggs Neck Harbor, Home of the Arts."

"We're trying to keep the ballyhoo to a minimum."

"I won't say a word."

"Who told you in the first place?" Maggie wanted to know.

"If I revealed my sources, Maggie, I wouldn't have them very long." She didn't feel like telling Maggie about the tax rolls and Janet Hayes.

She reached home about five and took an irritatingly

playful Probity down School House Lane just as it began
to rain. Letting herself in through the kitchen door, she
remembered in time to switch off the alarm, and wondered if there was anything to eat. The lone microwava-
ble dinner in her freezer—turkey amandine—was not
appealing. Wyn was always ravenous when she felt anxious and she felt anxious now, realizing the replaced broken windowpane was not to be easily forgotten.

She wondered how she was going to get through the
evening, thinking it would be a mistake to call Tommy
Handwerk. "Next thing I know, we'll be shuffling off to
Buffalo." Antsy, she read the alarm controls instruction
booklet, examined the restored French door, and studied
her Jackson Hall, which had unaccountably begun to give
her the creeps. After twenty minutes of this, she gave in
and called Fitz. He said he'd be delighted to give her
dinner.

Just as Wyn was reaching Fitz's house, Jackson Hall
was stepping onto the New Federal's porch. He removed
his taxicab yellow rubber raincoat and matching hat, gifts
from Tony Deel, and draped them over one of the old
green rocking chairs, discreetly chained to the side rail-
ings. He stepped into the lobby and looked around, im-
pressed by what Phineas had wrought.

When they were growing up, the New Federal had
been only respectable, catering to traveling salesmen
and, in the summer, overflow from the swank eastern
Long Island resorts. Then, it had faded prewar flowered
wallpaper, moth-eaten American Oriental rugs, upholstered sofas needing new springs. The Victorian mag-
nificence that was now the New Federal's lobby was
attractive and inviting. A success. Just as when he had
played those practical jokes as a boy, Phineas had been
painstaking, anxious to make everything seem real.

Jackson could hear the members of the Fiori family
celebrating Joe Fiori's half-century birthday in the small
dining room as he walked over to the untended counter

and read through one of the menus, tickled by the high-flown restaurant French. He remembered the old New Federal's thinly sliced pot roast, oversized canned peas, chewy mashed potatoes. His aunts would bring him for sullen Sunday afternoon meals, his treat of the week.

It had been Camellia, supposedly the weaker sister, who had been the least caring, afraid, he supposed, of competition for Ruth's attention. They had both let him know by countless gestures that he was a charity case, in their house and under their care only because their cousin Bull Carlson had decreed it.

Bull himself would be at the head of the big oval table in the New Federal dining room's bay window on those long-ago sepia-colored Sundays, his red-haired daughters and occasional guests trying to look attentive to his pronouncements as they snuck forkfuls of potato and beef into their mouths. When a sated Bull left the dining room, he would bow to the aunties, ignoring Jackson. A cowed Dolly had followed his example. But Kate and Maggie used to give him big smiles, hoping to take the sting out of their father's rejection.

He heard a sound behind him and turned. Dolly Carlson stood in the doorway that led from the dining room to the lobby, petrified, a mannequin in a *tableau vivant*. She had successfully avoided him since he had returned.

"Jackson," she said.

"*C'est moi*, Dolly. Your dress suits you. Phineas must have chosen it. You never had an eye for that sort of business."

"What do you want?"

"I thought we might talk."

"We might have talked twenty years ago but not now."

"I want you to tell her the truth, Dolly. It is time."

"I have," Dolly said at the moment that the Cole sisters emerged from the dining room, where they had partaken of the veal Prince Orlaf. They looked exactly as they had then, Jackson thought, right down to their good jet evening earrings.

"Jackson," Ruth said, not missing a beat in her march across the lobby. "Dolly." Camellia didn't say anything, her eyes down, as she swam along in her sister's wake. Jackson still couldn't decide which sister was the pilot fish and which the shark.

He turned to Dolly but then the Fioris began to troop out of the small dining room. Some of them knew Jackson from what they called the old days and stopped to shake his hand. By the time he was finished with them, Dolly had her coat on. It was a thin raincoat, too stylish, made of some gold material, out of step with the dark, proper dress. "Since you're determined to have this conversation," Dolly said, the coat seemingly giving her new strength, "we can have it while you walk me home. There's no reason to air the past in the New Federal's lobby."

She gave a set of keys and concise instructions to the night man, and, dismissing him, turned toward Jackson, every gesture filled with anger.

"You still have Bull's temper, don't you, Dolly?" Jackson asked. "Kate had it, as well."

"I'm nothing at all like Kate," Dolly said, stepping out onto the porch. The rain had subsided into a desultory drizzle. A vintage Army Jeep painted red pulled up and Dicie's head emerged. "Sorry we're late, Ma . . ." She stopped and looked up at Jackson Hall but he wasn't seeing her. He was staring at David, and not with joy, through the Jeep's streaked windscreen.

There was a moment of silence and then David said to Dolly, "We thought with the rain that you'd want a ride."

"It's nearly stopped," Dolly said. "You two go on. Your father," she said to Dicie, "is going to see me home."

Dicie watched her mother and Jackson Hall walk up rainy Main Street toward Carlson House. Then she looked at David, assuming that the reason he and Jackson Hall hated one another was Jessica Stevens. "Life is totally tubular," she said, putting her head on his flannel-clad shoulder, closing her remarkably young eyes. "Don't you think?"

"Totally," David Kabot said, kissing her forehead, his thoughts elsewhere.

"It's been a long Wednesday," Wyn had said earlier, when she sat down at her uncle's kitchen table with a little groan of relief.

"It's almost over," Fitz said, serving perfectly poached sole. One cycle in the top rack of the dishwasher, he maintained. Fitz had become an avid reader of newspaper food sections and box top recipes. "You haven't lived until you've tasted my turkey chili."

They tried not to discuss the murder over dinner, but resolve disappeared with the salad. Wyn raised questions about Tony Deel's background, Jackson Hall's New York love life, and Lettie Browne's early career. Fitz thought they were good questions, said he would have Albany supply him with answers, and then forbade further talk about the case, decreeing that noncontroversial topics were the key to healthy digestion.

"What did you do to those little potatoes?" Wyn, who was decidedly not a cook, asked, somewhat interested. Fitz, leading the way into the snug, underlit living room, explained. He played Billie Holiday on his excellent stereo system and they settled down to brandy. "Miss Brown to You" came in and took over the room, a sassy antidote to the prissiness of Jane's decor.

"It would have been our tenth anniversary," Fitz said matter-of-factly. "What is the tenth, anyway? Silver?"

"I never remember stuff like that," Wyn said. Above the mantel was Jane's portrait. A well-known society painter had captured Jane's nervous good looks but hadn't been able to make her sympathetic. No one could, Wyn thought. She had been a much handled and somewhat fatigued debutante when she met Fitz. Aging on the vine, desperate to marry, she had lowered her sights. Coming from a background of Newport mansions, Manhattan townhouses, and Swiss finishing schools, she was an unlikely wife for the commissioner of New York City's police.

Fitz had been admittedly "ripe for the picking," meeting Jane just when his long relationship with a married woman had come to an end. Jane, so pretty and so brittle, seemed like another but superior mistress. "During the early years of our marriage we lived in Jane's mother's old Fifth Avenue apartment," Fitz said, sipping at Hennessy. "We were so busy with our own lives, we seemed to meet only in bed. She had her decorators and her dress designers and I had my police and my politicians."

"You seemed to like 'tomatoes,' " Wyn said. "While Jane went for 'tomahtoes.' " She was sitting in one of the whippet and cabbage rose chintz-skirted ladies' chairs that flanked the fireplace—another of Jane's legacies—feeling bitchy. Wyn had adored her uncle all her life and had liked his unmarried state. When he married, Wyn had felt abandoned. Jane was not about to play auntie to her husband's niece.

Looking at her portrait, Fitz said, "She was attracted to me in the beginning because of my 'down to earthness.' She saw herself as Katharine Hepburn; I was to be Spencer Tracy. Her idea was that the commissioner spot would launch me as a national politician. She had fantasies of entertaining solemnly in the White House, leaving her mark through the glamour of her table settings.

"Even though I told her from the beginning that I wasn't interested in politics, Jane only heard what she wanted to. She was disappointed but she never stopped thinking of me as her protector, especially when she was in her fragile-flower mood."

"An expensive bloom," Wyn said, unable to stop herself.

"I know. She could be needlessly mean and she enjoyed bringing out the worst in people—you, for instance—but I loved her, Wyn." He bowed his big, bovine head and, without warning, began to cry. After a moment he honked into a huge handkerchief and sighed. "For a long time I thought we had a great marriage."

He looked up with pale, accusatory eyes and said, "You knew otherwise; I guess everyone did." Wyn poured more brandy, Fitz lit a White Owl, and in a moment the room was filled with its cheery old-time aroma, soothing them both. "From the beginning Jane had affairs. Hell, forget 'affairs.' 'Affair' implies some longevity. These were one-night stands. It was a compulsion. She had to have every man. Soon as she had him, she was finished with him. It was the 'how good could he be if he wants me?' syndrome.

"She married me because I had the bad luck to be a conservative in the sex department. I didn't go in for hopping into bed, one-two-three. She thought I was rejecting her so she had to have me. To have me, she had to marry me. What a dumb dope." He laughed, knocking ashes into a heavy glass ashtray. "When I found out Jane was everyman's pincushion, all the air went out of me. I felt like a deflated football, good for nothing. I made noises about a divorce and she became more discreet and I learned to live with it. I didn't think I had any options.

"Eventually, she stopped coming out to Waggs Neck. She had liked it, once, but now she thought it was 'precious.' She preferred Paris with her sisters. She had her own money and so did the sisters and off they'd go, at the drop of a hat: to buy clothes, to play in the art world, to get laid.

"But after years of shutting my eyes to her little hobby, of finding some satisfaction in the fact that she always came back to me, Jane announced she was having a real, long-term, big-time romance. She was in love, she said, starry-eyed. Really in love, she said. For the first time in her life. I suppose I was expected to jump for joy but she didn't give a damn how I reacted. She was besotted."

He puffed on his cigar for a moment, letting his eyes

move back to the painting. "Whether you liked her or not, you have to admit she was a beauty." Wyn followed his gaze, taking another look at the glossy, distant woman. "When she swallowed those pills, I know she didn't give one damn thought to me. She was punishing him, the negligent boyfriend."

He stopped looking at the painting, poured more brandy, and stared up through the blue smoke at nothing Wyn could see. "Had that bastard left her a pinch of pride, Jane would still be alive. After she got his good-bye note, she flew to Paris to see him. She wasn't always stupid about herself. She needed, she said, for him to let her off lightly. She knew what she wanted: excuses, a fake illness, a simulated repentance. Anything but that silent, total rejection.

"Jackson Hall killed Jane as sure as if he put a pistol to her head and pulled the trigger. She was only another conquest to him, a little older than he was used to, but willing to do whatever he asked. He wouldn't even let her into his house, much less see her. When he told her to get lost, Jane went back to her fancy Paris hotel suite and took it literally."

He upended his brandy glass. "I'm blitzed," he said, smiling hazily at Wyn. "There was a time when I might have killed him but I wouldn't have missed, Wyn, believe me."

Wyn, head reeling from the brandy and the wine, left Fitz in the light of the dying fire, his dead White Owl held in his hand like a teacher's pointer. Billie Holiday was singing "I Wished on the Moon."

With the motion detector alarm switched on and Probity snoring on her miniature settee, Wyn lay awake in her big bed, nauseated and hairy-tongued and much too sober, finally admitting to herself that Fitz was capable of killing Jackson Hall. What she didn't know was whether he was capable of lying to her about it or of carrying on a pretend investigation.

CHAPTER

Seventeen

CONSIDERING THE BRANDY SHE HAD POURED DOWN HER throat the night before, her morning headache was no surprise. "I feel nine hundred years old," she told her tail-wagging dog as she forced herself to put on panty hose, a skirt, a silk blouse, and low heels for her Thursday morning appointment with Ruth and Camellia Cole.

Somehow she got herself downstairs and let the relentlessly cheerful Probity out the kitchen door to do what she had to do in the yard. This was no morning for gaily tripping down School House Lane. She was searching in her bare cupboard for caffeine of any kind when she realized she hadn't switched off the motion detectors and that no screeching alarm had ensued when she came downstairs.

"Goddamn Radio Shack," she said, adrenaline rising. Sure enough, the little red lights on the detectors were off. But so was the little red light on the range when she tried to boil water. "Goddamn LILCO," she said, feeling shaky, cursing her heels and hangover as she made her way down the precarious basement steps to check the recently installed circuit breakers. The breakers responsible for her first-floor electricity were in the off position. Wyn snapped them back and wondered if the alarm system had caused an overload.

She was drinking Japanese green tea—the only hot beverage she could find—sitting on a particularly uncomfortable sofa her mother had purchased in 1956, not a good year for upholstery, when it struck her. The new alarm system hadn't caused an overload. Someone had gotten into the basement—easy enough, there being no lock on the outer basement doors—and switched off the breakers. This helped clear her head.

Her first thought was Tommy. His hopeful mother woke him and a sleepy Tommy, finally goaded into curiosity, wanted to know what the hell was going on. Wyn said she was spooked by all those television home alarm commercials and wanted to make her house secure. "Lock on the basement doors isn't going to make much difference," Tommy said, agreeing to install it anyway, first thing.

Wyn knew he was right: there was no way she could make her house impregnable. It wasn't that kind of a house. Whoever was doing this could always find a way in. For what purpose, she wondered, was he or she tormenting her? For the hell of it, she supposed, thinking of all the mindless crimes, serious and otherwise, that had affected her neighbors in New York.

She determined that nothing was missing or damaged, but just when she was leaving to see the Coles, she saw that the Jackson Hall painting had been removed from its nail and was leaning against the mantel. Was someone in the process of stealing it when she and Miss Probity blundered down, scaring them off?

This, more than anything else, gave her the willies and she found herself dialing Tommy's number again, ready to surrender, to ask him to stay with her for a few days. She had the receiver in hand and then put it back on the cradle. "I'm damned if I'm going to use Tommy Handwerk as my bodyguard," she told herself. "I'm already using him as a lover." She slammed out the door, slammed back in, causing a snoozing Probity to yelp, and called Liz to make certain she went to Lucy's house to go over the closing statement.

The meeting with the Cole sisters took place over morning tea. Wyn was provided with a cup of oolong (just what I need, she thought, after Japanese green) and a slice of the Presbyterians' butter nut loaf, and she found her stomach settling down in the Coles's violet sachet-scented sitting room. She enjoyed visiting the Coles, who, when provided with an audience, played dextrous verbal Ping-Pong with one another. All Wyn had to do was sit back and enjoy the match.

Ruth received the news of Phineas's bequest matter-of-factly, saying it had been thoughtful of Phineas but they didn't, praise the Lord, need it and Wyn could tell that bright little CHARLEE director they would turn it over to her when the time came. "You do such fine work there, Wyn," Ruth was saying, about to embark on a laudatory summation of the CHARLEE program.

But Phineas's bequest had already launched Camellia into a reminiscent cataloguing of his achievements. "Every time one thumbed through a copy of *House & Garden* at the dentist's, there was Phineas with some face-lifted blonde sitting on the arm of an eighteenth-century hunt chair. During those days he rarely came home."

"Not much in the way of society for young homosexuals in Waggs Neck," Ruth said, impressing Wyn with her worldliness.

"Phineas always had money," Camellia went on. "Never needed to work. But even after he retired, he couldn't sit still. Look at the success he made of the New Federal."

Ruth, staring out the bay windows at the weeping willow tree, said, "Poor Phineas. Always passionate about the wrong things."

"Well, what about his sex life?" Camellia asked, missing the point. "Isn't sex one of the great motives for murder?"

"Phineas," Ruth said, "led an entirely celibate life."

"Hard to believe," Wyn put in, thinking of her own libido, then blushing, for perhaps the third time in her life. She supposed that the Cole sisters had led an entirely celibate life and if they hadn't, she didn't want to know about it. Ruth noticed Wyn's self-consciousness and laughed. "For your generation," Ruth said, "sex is like broccoli, a nutritional must. In my youth, sex was never spoken of. Indeed, homosexuality was considered a weak indulgence, confined to members of our class. Every family of good standing had a Funny Cousin. It was the lower orders who engaged in unbridled heterosexual activity, producing all those unwarranted children.

"We did not. Think of all the unmarried people we know. Maggie Carlson, though one suspects there was a man there sometime or another. Willy Mercer, who likes to drop heavy hints of passion requited in England but that may be pure romance . . ."

"And then there's Dr. John Fenton," Camellia added. "Promiscuous, they say, with a Woman Who Will Remain Nameless, but never married and one can only wonder . . ."

"After Kate died in the stable fire, John began taking Lettie around," Ruth said, cutting her sister off, addressing Wyn. "But Lettie escaped to New York, dyed her hair, went into the theater. John was too much a stick to put up with that and anyway, any idiot could see he was still mourning Kate."

"Dolly Carlson never married either," Camellia said.

"No, Cousin Dolly never married either," Ruth said, looking at Camellia, willing her to be quiet. Wyn symbolically rolled her eyes at the sisters, attempting to protect Dolly's good name when her illegitimate daughter by Jackson Hall and her Saturday-night romps with John Fenton were common knowledge. "I can't think of one substantial reason for killing Phineas," Ruth went on, changing the subject.

Wyn was going to say that the officials no longer believed Phineas was the intended victim, but Camellia forestalled her. "On the other hand," she said, "there are a good many people who want Jackson Hall dead."

"No doubt. But Jackson Hall doesn't seem much like a victim to me, either," Ruth said. "He believed he was badly used as a boy when he lived with us, and perhaps he was. We were singularly ill-equipped to be parents, foster or otherwise, and we felt, given his dubious bloodline, strictness was the antidote."

"Ruth was very upset when he left like that, without a word," Camellia said.

"You weren't?" Wyn asked.

"I was relieved. I never liked him, even when he was a little boy, so self-possessed, patronizing me from the time he could talk. I never wanted him in our house."

"He was the most interesting person who ever touched my life," Ruth said, with genuine feeling. "We did wrong, following Cousin Bull's lead. We should have offered him affection, not deprivation. I realize that now."

"He's a selfish, egotistical bastard," Camellia said, surprising Wyn with her anger. "Everything always has to go his way, no matter whom he hurts. And he hurt you, Ruth. I'll never forgive him for that."

"I suppose Camellia is right," the older woman said, looking tired and distracted. "Phineas was not the kind of man to get himself killed, but Jackson Hall is a likely victim."

"He hasn't been murdered *yet*," Camellia said brightly, passing the butter nut loaf around once again.

Fitz was waiting for Wyn in her office, which smelled, thanks to him, like one of the old Long Island Railroad smoking cars. He asked how she felt.

"Fine."

"You don't look fine. You look like Little Miss Muffet after the spider sat down beside her."

That's exactly how she felt but she wasn't going to admit it to Fitz. She wanted to tell him about her intruder but he wasn't looking so great himself, having enough to worry about; besides, there wasn't anything he could do. It wasn't as if this called for a police stakeout. Some kids in the neighborhood were having fun; she could remember similar tricks she and her pals had played, tying dead fish to the math teacher's Ford, painting the principal's poodle's tail black.

So she said she felt fine, considering the amount of napoleon they had knocked off the night before.

"I got some answers to those questions," he said.

"So quick?"

"Have you seen this morning's *Times'* Op Ed page? 'The Murder of a Small American Town' is the lead editorial. The town is Waggs Neck and the implication is that the governor's soft on crime, even when a murder happens in his hometown. Albany is anxious to help as fast as it can.

"Anyway, here's what we got. Turns out the bomb Jessica Stevens dropped when I had lunch over there was a live one. Jackson Hall is a married man. He wed a woman in a civil ceremony in New York over twenty years ago. All we know about her comes from the wedding license application: her name was Lee Le Verne, she was nineteen, and her profession was listed as 'entertainer.' There's no record of a divorce. So if she's still alive and kicking, Lee Le Verne gets a healthy chunk of Jackson's money when he dies.

"I don't suppose he's thought of that. We got ahold of a copy of his will, made only a few months ago in New York. Half of his money goes to fund a museum/ art school . . ."

". . . to be established at the old convent, which Jackson recently bought through a foundation he established," Wyn put in. "Maggie and Tony Deel are on the board."

"The things you real estate brokers know," Fitz said. "And keep to yourself."

"There didn't seem to be any reason to tell you."

"All the paintings in Jackson Hall's possession go to his new museum. There are several bequests, including a quarter of a million dollars to Maggie, if she survives him, and to her heirs, if she doesn't; and a like amount to Jessica Stevens."

"Where did all the money come from? His paintings sell for hundreds of thousands but . . ."

"A rich artist named Schlein—Jackson's French mentor—left him a block of blue chip property in Paris. He sold it at the right time and made a fortune. There's nearly ten million as we speak and a good chunk of it is left for his son, who we're attempting to trace, though I have a pretty good idea where and who he is."

"Ditto," Wyn said. "Want to elaborate?"

"Not until I'm certain."

"Any mention of Dicie?"

"None. That bastard has denied her since she was born," he said as he rose. "I'm going to the barn to see if the new, frightened Jackson Hall doesn't want to give me some relevant information. Like who his wife is and where his son is. And I wish the hell Billy Bell would turn up. I wonder what he remembered that he saw in the keeping room that set him off."

Maggie had a solemn lunch upstairs, thinking she probably would never eat in the keeping room again. A monosyllabic Dolly shared the meal, acting, Maggie thought, as if she were the one wrestling with a death sentence. Maggie was tempted to lay it on Dolly but decided the resultant sympathy and tears wouldn't be worth it. Belching lightly—the salad featured Annie's beloved tasteless, overseeded supermarket cucumbers—Maggie finally said, "Why don't you marry John Fenton and get it over with? You're the kind of woman who needs a man."

"You're not?"

"No," Maggie said, leaving the table, wrapping herself in a fake zebra fur-lined purple leather cape, studying her reflection in the long cheval glass mirror, thinking she looked like a Miracle-Gro eggplant. "Never was. Kate was the same and had she lived, I doubt if she'd have married. Neither Kate nor I minded carnal relations, but we refused to be subjugated by them."

"You've been talking about Kate a lot lately."

"I know. I suppose that as I get closer to the end of my life, I wonder what she would have made of hers."

"A good deal more than I made of mine."

Deciding that when Dolly was in her Pity Me mood there was nothing to be done except wring her graceful neck, Maggie left her. She strode down a breeze-swept Main Street, greeting a variety of acquaintances, and turned into the relative calm of brick-paved Washington Street. The Waggs Neck Harbor *Chronicle* building was situated on the east side of the street and consisted of four small rooms, two over two, in an undistinguished early nineteenth-century brick house.

A sharp but nugatory surge of pain charged through Maggie's body, and she stopped for a moment to catch her breath. It was gone so quickly she was tempted to comfort herself with the lie that it was imaginary; but she knew it was a precursor of the sort of devastating attack that would increasingly lay sieqe to her system and, perhaps sooner than later, incapacitate her. She was prepared for those last moments, but she wasn't going to check out just yet, having one or two things to accomplish. I can't stand here all day, she thought, looking with disgust at a pair of cocker spaniel fire irons in the Hearth Shop window. But she was unnerved, ill-prepared to deal with the *Chronicle*'s patronizing managing editor, and so she walked up to the Bay Street end of the street and sat on the unsteady bench thoughtfully provided by the Veterans of Foreign Wars, trying to bring herself back to the present.

But her rebellious mind didn't want to be there and she found herself sliding backward into the early days when her father had bought the *Chronicle*. He had been too expansive a man to be solely concerned with his inherited and doomed watch factory, and the newspaper, bought in an act of supposed good Samaritanism—it was on the cusp of bankruptcy—had given him a satisfying mid-life podium from which to air his views.

Maggie had eventually been forced to sell it, and the new owners had transformed the *Chronicle* into a literary curiosity, a folksy hometown paper laced with bite and intellect. Though she disdained the new *Chronicle*, Maggie didn't regret its success. She knew that she never would have been able to make anything of the *Chronicle* other than what it had been: a couple of sheets of local, parochial news. She was the last holdover from the old *Chronicle*, continuing to write her deliberately homey "Letters to Maggie" column, the new publishers wise enough to retain this bit of local color.

Feeling stronger, she left the VFW bench and entered the newspaper building, making her way up the memory-laden staircase to the small room where the letters sent to Maggie were kept. Leaving the office with the letters in a manila envelope, Maggie found herself, as she so often did of late, looking forward to home, to lying down on the old green sofa, having a cup of very sweet tea. Hot chocolate, she was disappointed to find, no longer agreed with her, and buttery cakes had lost their appeal. She regretted that she hadn't given in to all her temptations when she was younger.

Resisting the sofa, she sat down at her desk and opened the only envelope that looked promising, plain white, her name and address written in pencil in what might have been a child's hand. The sheet of ruled paper contained more of that neat, awkward, familiar Waggs Neck Harbor public school writing. It took her a second to remember where she had seen it: on the hand-written "Keep Out" signs Tony had ordered Billy Bell to make when the barn was being redone and attracting a lot of attention. The note read:

Dear Maggie,
If a person has proof that another person is a killer, how long do they have before they have to report it to the law? Answer in next week's *Chronicle*.

                                        Waiting.

It was obvious to Maggie that Billy didn't require an answer, that the letter was designed as a piece of public blackmail, a naive warning to the blackmailee to be quick. She read it twice, trying to decide how best to use it. And then, decision made, she got into the purple leather cape and went in search of Fitz Robinson, wondering if Billy Bell understood the danger he was in.

Wyn, shifting papers on the desk in her office, was feeling better after a relatively sane conversation over lunch at Baby's with Lucy Littlefield. Liz buzzed to see if she could see Lettie Browne, and Lettie, not waiting, entered her office, resplendent in black fox and controlled hysteria.

"You should get Liz a re-do, darling. She doesn't improve your image. Be that as it may, I've come to apologize. I was awful the other day and I am, sincerely, sorry." She removed the fur and sat in the visitor's chair, swinging one silk-trousered leg over its arm. "You do forgive me, don't you?"

"I wasn't so nice myself."

"Let's not get into a who-was-ruder contest. We'll put it all behind us, shall we? P.S.: your local CPA is a delight. Reminds me of a British character actor, doesn't he you? Of course all the British are character actors, but you know what I mean."

"We're going to have to wait for the government before I can dispense the major amount of the money, Lettie," Wyn began, trying to put an end to the chitchat, assuming money was the reason that Lettie had come.

"I don't care about that. I now have credit up the yin yang and everybody's being adorable about my little debts since Phineas bought his. I only dropped in to apologize and because I'm bored. And when I'm bored, I begin to get brittle and then I begin to age. How old do I look, Wynsome? The Truth."

"A good thirty-two."

"That's a lie and you know it. I look a well-preserved forty. Terrible age for a woman. I'm going to call that little frog of a surgeon who did my eyes and make an appointment to do the rest of me. I'll have him tell the police that it's imperative for my health that I jet down to São Paulo."

"Have you been asked not to leave town?"

"Everyone concerned has. I was lunching at the hotel with Ruth and Cammie yesterday when Captain Midnight came by our table and suggested that we all stay put. Cammie turned such a dark brick red, one could only suspect she had a ticket for Tierra del Fuego in her purse. The captain hinted that the case was coming to an end. That Phineas's murderer would soon be apprehended."

"I thought they thought the killer wasn't after Phineas," Wyn said. "That Phineas had accidentally drunk the poison meant for Jackson."

Lettie, in the process of lighting a cigarette, snapped open her ribbed gold Dupont and froze, the color beneath her expertly applied makeup fading. "Good God, Jackson?"

"You were at Mary Immaculate when he was there, weren't you?"

"I was insane over him. When Kate announced he was her date for the prom, I wanted to kill her. Poor Kate. That wasn't exactly a banner year, was it? The only good thing that came out of it was that I left Waggs Neck.

Thanks to Maggie's little loan, not to mention her end-
lessly appropriate advice."

"Jackson was in New York then, as well. Did you see
much of one another?"

"We lived in the same hideous building. It was owned
by Maggie's college roommate's family. The Monte Excel-
sior. Fifty ten-by-ten 'efficiencies' on West Fifty-eighth
Street with chorus girl kitchenellas and an elevator that
was a sometime thing. It was cheap and relatively clean
and beautiful Jackson Hall was my neighbor."

Lettie stared at Wyn with her cat's eyes for a long
moment and then shrugged. "I suppose the police will
find out sooner or later. Maybe they already have. Now
it's time, after all these centuries, that I went public. Pass
this information on to Fitz, will you, Wyn? Somehow I
don't want to."

She stood up and went to the big window that looked
out on Main Street and across at the New Federal. "I
won. Kate was dead. Jackson and I were in New York,
living cheek by jowl. I was taking classes at the Academy
and later at the Studio. He was studying with Bonet. We
were both alone. In the end—now hold on to your drawers, this is good—we married."

"Married?"

"Is there any way you could stop sounding like a parrot
in a vaudeville joke? I married him under my then-stage
name, Lee Le Verne. After a year of raw sex, I woke up
one morning to find I was not only pregnant but nearly
three months gone and too late for an abortion. Anyway,
I didn't want an abortion. I was wet enough to think that
maybe we would have this child and Jackson would settle
down to his painting and I would be one of those adorable
mothers strolling up and down Madison Avenue with Baby
in his Rolls-Royce carriage.

"Jackson disillusioned me quickly, but I was just old-
fashioned enough not to want to be an unwed mom.
He married me because I threatened inconvenience and
trouble—lawsuits and such—and then the bastard left for

Paris. I've never forgiven him, as you might imagine. It wasn't easy but I had the baby and gave it up for adoption and that was that."

"You told no one?"

"I tried to tell Phineas. He wouldn't listen; mostly because he didn't want to hear. And who else was there to tell? I assumed Maggie knew but maybe not. We've never discussed it. At the time I imagined I would eventually divorce Jackson but, as it turned out, I never felt the least inclination to remarry. I suspect Jackson never did either." She took a long puff on her cigarette as if it were an oxygen feeding tube and Wyn thought that for once Lettie did look her age.

"The last and only time I heard from him was five years or so after he dumped me. A New York attorney working with some Parisian law firm contacted my New York attorney wanting to know if I'd sign a waiver which would keep me from participating in Jackson's estate if he should predecease me. If I agreed, he'd do the same for me. I didn't get it but I said sure. I didn't want Jackson cashing in on my success. I was just beginning to make big money, but Jackson, as far as I knew, was still a pauper. His advisers, even then, must have known what he would someday be worth and, clever stinkers, got me out of the way early. Over the years, as he became richer and richer, my blood would boil at the thought of how he and his pals cut me out.

"So if Fitz is searching for suspects, I've just been graduated to *numero uno* again. Typecasting, *n'est-ce pas?* Fortyish and manless, a touch manic, she sees the husband who abandoned her and her unborn child years before and then made certain she'd never see a penny of his money. She takes the first opportunity to dispatch him, only she makes a wee miscalculation and kills her worm of a brother instead. Whose death, incidentally, makes her a rich woman. What do you think, Wynie-Poo? Will it play in Waggs Neck?"

CHAPTER

Eighteen

"I'M WORRIED ABOUT THAT KID," MAGGIE SAID, AFTER FITZ read Billy's note and told her the captain had been searching for him and couldn't find him. Fitz passed the note to Homer Price, who was having trouble equating the froufrou décor with Fitz's hardscrabble persona. It was his first visit to Fitz's house.

Maggie was squeezed into one of Jane's lady chairs, drinking Fitz's expensive Scotch, which, she was sorry to note, tasted acrid and medicinal. Her new body chemistry was having an effect on her taste buds but she was damned if she was going to give up Scotch.

"He's not an especially appetizing specimen, but we don't want him killed," Fitz said, pouring Maggie another shot.

"Is there time to get an answer in the next *Chronicle?*" Homer asked Maggie, distancing himself from the two friends, standing in front of the fireplace under the portrait of Jane Robinson.

"We can get in whatever we want at a moment's notice, one of the joys of computerized publishing."

"Let's not publish the letter," Fitz proposed. "Print a

message asking him to come round for personal advice. 'Answer too important for column. Please contact in person.' That sort of thing.''

"Won't fly," Maggie said, swallowing her Scotch, deciding she liked the new, medicinal taste, thinking it would be nice to put away her troubles for an evening, to get a little tight. "He'll never show but he might phone, and then only to see if there's anything in it for him. So what's the point?"

"You might find out what he knows," Fitz said.

"Being a police spy has never appealed to me." Maggie, who had been unusually prickly, left soon after, having agreed to print a personal message for Billy Bell.

Fitz, pouring himself another shot, asked the captain if he wanted another beer. He said he did. He was sitting gingerly on the pink-and-white loveseat and for a moment looked like a boy at his first dance. "Why do you think Billy Bell sent his letter to Maggie?" Homer asked. "It would have been published quicker in any of the other East End newspapers."

"Billy's known Maggie all his life, and in his twisted Bell way he trusts her. We all do." Fitz looked at Homer for a moment, not much liking him. "You're implying that he sent it to Maggie because he has something on her and she showed it to us as a sort of preprotection policy?"

"Only exploration, Fitz."

"No, it's more than that, Homer. You like Maggie as a suspect, whether it's Phineas's or Jackson's murder you're investigating."

"I do," Homer admitted, finishing his beer. "Especially for chilling Jackson. A quarter of a million bucks while avenging her sister and her niece isn't a bad motive."

Wyn locked her office, crossed Main Street, and started to walk with the wind toward her house, when she found Camellia Cole standing in the shelter of Dicie's Sizzle shop entry. Cammie was staring with wistful admiration at a bald mannequin wearing a black-and-white sequined two-piece dress made of some elastic material. *"You could wear that, Wyn,"* Camellia said. "On me it would look like two tourniquets. Let's go to Baby's and have a cup of something hot. The chill goes right through one, doesn't it?"

Wyn said she'd like nothing more, hoping that Camellia Cole would be an antidote to her nervousness. In spite of the new alarm system and cellar door lock and talking to herself of rowdy kids, she remained frightened. Cammie, sitting herself down at Baby's best table in the center of what had once been a family living room, said that the proprietors had done a "marvelous renovation, even if they did name the place after their dog."

"They didn't do all that much," Wyn said, thinking that if they cleared out the tables, Baby's would look like it had when it was just an unpretentious village house.

"That's the charm of it. Nothing like Jackson's barn, done up out of all recognition, they say." Cammie spooned more thick hot chocolate and whipped cream into her pre-Raphaelite mouth. "Uncle Bull kept a working gentleman's dairy there until Maggie pointed out how much money it was costing them. Not that he thanked her for it. Uncle Bull never did treat Maggie fairly.

"Oh, and how he hated Jackson, humiliating him whenever he could. I wasn't fond of Jackson myself, but Bull overdid it, as he did most things. One Veterans Day there was a party in the keeping room and we mistakenly brought Jackson along. I can still see Bull slamming Jackson against the wall, shouting at Jackson that he didn't belong there. Life is peculiar. Now Jackson's living in Bull's old barn, having turned it into the Taj Mahal."

Wyn agreed life was peculiar and found herself telling Camellia about Jackson Hall's new painting and the effect it had on her.

"I wonder who the woman is?" Camellia said dreamily. "Ruth has a theory that he paints the same woman over and over again. Maybe he does. Kate did, of course, die in a fire." She drank more hot chocolate and smiled, rambling along in her free-association conversational style. "Phineas is dead, too. Poisoned. So hard to believe. And Percy was electrocuted. Two Fat Boys dead in one year. And just when you think life is dull and what's the point, Jackson returns to Waggs Neck. I'd love to see for myself what he's done to the old barn. You know, I have a good mind to walk over and knock on the door. After all, I helped bring him up."

Wyn, leaving Baby's, thought of Bull Carlson humiliating a young Jackson Hall in front of his guests in the keeping room. There was some elusive memory about that incident floating around in her unconscious, but she couldn't bring it into focus. She lost all sight of it as she put off going home, went into La Pizzeria, and ordered a sausage-and-meatball hero with cheese to go. "Junk food junkie," John Fenton said amiably, picking up his double cheese pepperoni pan pizza.

"Physician heal thyself," Wyn said as he left, mentally going over the checklist for the morning's closing, praying that Lucy wouldn't do one of her famous off-the-wall numbers. Roy Stein and the Brooks Brothers–suited Grasslands attorneys were at the end of their patience.

She walked home, unlocked her kitchen door, deposited the football-sized hero on a counter, remembered just in time to switch off the alarm, turned on lights, and refused to consider the possibility of intruders. She found Probity's pink rhinestone lead and Probity in the yard tracking an oblivious wren and took that amiable animal down School House Lane. Waggs Neck seemed particularly dark and dreary, black clouds overhead, most of the leaves having fallen, the trees stark and unappealing. Only the tail-wagging Probity appeared happy to be alive.

Wyn had just turned on the six o'clock news on the postage-stamp kitchen TV and was unwrapping her odoriferous supper when the clouds opened and it began to pour. Knowing she should be eating broccoli—wolfing down, instead, a post-hero slice of packaged pound cake—Wyn wondered how Fitz and Homer Price were getting on with the investigation, not to mention with one another. She thought about checking in with her uncle but didn't, content to sit at the old kitchen table, listening to the rain, watching "A Hollywood Minute." Tommy called but she told him she had already eaten and no, she didn't feel like company on a rainy night but maybe over the weekend.

"You don't treat me very nicely, Wyn," Tommy said in an aggrieved voice. Wyn said she was sorry, she would try to be nicer in the future, but the truth was that she probably wasn't all that nice. Tommy, pushing what he thought was an advantage, wanted her to make a commitment, if only for Saturday night. "We'll pick up roast pork lo mein at the Amagansett Chinese, and rent a movie."

"We'll never agree."

"You get to pick. Anything you want, except foreign. How's that?"

Thinking of Tommy's earnest sweetness and innate sensuality, not to mention the fact that a date with him would be a legitimate way to avoid the horrors of her ex-husband's Saturday night dinner party, Wyn said fine.

Later, upstairs, she realized she had forgotten to activate the damn alarm again and went downstairs to do so. The rain beat against the French door panes and Wyn, reminded of countless horror movies, thought it wouldn't hurt to turn on the garden lights. She did so and screamed.

Standing on the other side of the French doors was what at first appeared to be an indistinguishable yellow blob until it took form as a man in a yellow sou'wester. Jackson Hall. With his ugly hands, he pantomimed Wyn unlocking the door. She hesitated but, after a moment, did so, taking his rain gear, carrying it gingerly across the long living room, depositing it on the covered front porch. She asked him if he wanted a drink.

"Do you have calvados?"

Wyn, keeping it together, refusing to let irrational fear betray her, assumed her mother's social hostess role, saying she was afraid she hadn't and would instant coffee do? When she brought his coffee, he was sitting in her father's old cane chair facing the fireplace, studying his painting above the mantel.

"You didn't have to break in to see it. All you had to do was ask. What was on this evening's schedule? Dynamite?"

With an effort, he took his eyes off the painting and looked at Wyn. "I do not sleep much or well and sometimes I end up wandering aimlessly around the village in the dead of the night. Which is what I was doing two nights ago. You had reminded me of Hap, and I was thinking of him when I walked into your garden and looked through your windows and saw the painting above your mantel. Seeing it again was a revelation; I thought that if I could examine it closely, I might find the clue I needed to finish the painting I am working on. I found some tools in the garage and removed the pane. I think I am on the right track but I still do not have the answer. I had to come back last night and tonight again. It is bizarre. Twenty years later, I continue to work on the same subject."

To Wyn, the huge woman in the barn painting and the two insubstantial masculine figures in the painting above her fireplace were as little alike as could be. But she hesitated to say so. Jackson Hall was so weird tonight. "I've been looking at this painting since I was a little girl," she said, thinking it might calm him to talk about it, "and I've always wondered if the two male figures are meant to be twins or the same person?"

"Twins? What would give you that idea?" He stood up, angrily taking the painting off the wall, staring intently at it as if he were seeing it for the first time.

Wyn, losing patience, said, "The fact that they look exactly alike might mislead one."

He seemed, Wyn thought, as if the proverbial thunderbolt had struck him. "They are the same person," he said quietly, setting the painting down on the mantel as if he were discarding it. "Thank you." He finally looked at her as if she really existed, but Wyn was exhausted by his corrosive presence and stood up, letting him know she wanted him to leave, leading him to the front porch and his raincoat. He stood under the yellow light for a moment and then he took her hand in his feverish one. "When I am finished with this painting, Wynsome, I want to make love to you."

There was no wobbly feeling now. Jackson Hall was the last person Wyn wanted to get into bed with. She thought he might be on hallucinogens, he was so far out there. She watched as he walked into the rain, down Madison toward Main. And then she locked all the doors, switched on the alarm, and fell into a sleep disturbed by images of twin Jackson Halls, cavorting around her bed like demonic children.

CHAPTER
Nineteen

THE CLOSING AND THE TRANSFER OF LUCY LITTLEFIELD'S property to Grasslands got Friday off to a fine start, being a model for such proceedings. Lucy had washed and done her hair and was very gay at a postclosing luncheon at the New Federal hosted by Roy Stein. The Grasslands' attorneys were happily self-congratulatory. They all received their checks, including Wyn, who handed it and Lucy's over to Liz, who sped across the street to the bank to deposit them with something like euphoria. Liz loved a successful closing.

Fitz was waiting in Wyn's office when she came in from the luncheon. She had meant to tell him about Jackson Hall's visit but, in her concern—Fitz looked so unhappy—she forgot. "I'm to fly to Albany this afternoon. The governor's men want a confab. What they really want is action. The *Times* piece stirred them up; they need someone to fry and I'm their goat."

"It hasn't even been a week, though it seems like a year," Wyn said.

"And all I have are suspicions. Billy Bell is still on the missing list and we think he can tell us something. More news came in from Albany this morning about Jackson's son. The boy's mother is, of course, Lettie. Neither she nor Jackson wanted the child, and soon after he was born he was adopted by a New Jersey family named Deel who called the boy Anthony. The adoption was not happy and when he was sixteen, Tony Deel, in Europe with his foster parents, visited his father—there had never been any secret about who he was—and Jackson was taken with him. The boy was allowed to join Jackson's household and has remained since."

"It's funny," Wyn said, "that he made a place for his son while he's determined to keep Dicie out of his life."

Liz rang through, saying Homer Price was on the phone for Fitz. Wyn activated the speaker with her index finger and the captain's resonant voice filled the room as if he were sitting there with them. "I'm at the barn. You had better get over here, Fitz. Someone's tried to kill Jackson again."

Like everything in Jackson Hall's studio–bedroom, the bullet hole was beautifully shaped. It lay in the exact center of the north wall, the glass intact except for that perfect cylindrical intrusion. An eerie whistling noise made by the wind from the bay set the tone, mock-scary. At any moment, Fitz thought, we'll hear organ music and Bela Lugosi and the creatures of the night will fly in.

The bullet had missed Jackson and lodged in a thick pad of paper propped against the headboard where Jackson had been sitting a moment before. The spare glass-walled room was silent except for that shrill whistle; Homer Price plugged the hole with a wad of Kleenex and everyone in the room felt a surge of gratitude.

A tranquilized Jackson was resting in a downstairs room. Jessica Stevens, Tony Deel, and Fitz stood waiting for someone else to speak. Homer Price, who had been at the head of his class in a police college ballistics course, obliged as he bent his long, muscular body in half and examined the visible portion of the bullet. He said that it came from a British hunting rifle, popular because of its wallop and highly developed telescopic lens.

The rifle had almost certainly been fired by a person standing at the deserted edge of the convent beach that jutted out into the bay for several yards and afforded a clear view of the central window in Jackson's bedroom-studio. The waters were too rough and the bay too public for anyone to risk shooting from a boat; only someone looking out of Jackson's barn or the boarded-up convent buildings could have observed the would-be assassin.

Fitz asked the captain if he'd examine the little rocky promontory where the marksman probably stood—not that the pebbles and weeds would reveal much—and to have his men ask around to find out if anyone had seen a man or a woman crossing the convent property since lunchtime. After Homer left, Fitz wanted to know where Jessica and Tony had been just before the shooting.

Pushing her mass of reddish hair back from her face with both hands, looking, for once, less than perfect, Jessica said, "I was on the yacht and, incidentally, so was Tony. I caught a glimpse of him coming out of Jackson's suite."

"I was checking the alarm system," Tony said. "Making certain it was secure."

"Against what?" Jessica asked.

"Against anyone coming on board, Jessica, for an afternoon assignation."

" 'Assignation!' " Jessica said, trying a smile, turning to Fitz, who had observed the sparring with interest. "I had coffee with an old friend aboard the yacht and I gather Tony was doing his usual spy turn. We did not engage in the activities the word 'assignation' implies. In other words, we didn't fuck."

"Who was the friend?" Fitz asked.

"David Kabot," Jessica said, after a moment's hesitation, deciding Tony would tell him anyway. "We were lovers when I was in school in Europe. I left him for

Jackson. David, who was even younger and angrier then, behaved like the macho dope he can be." She didn't seem all that unhappy about David Kabot's behavior. "But I doubt if he took a rifle down to the beach and tried to shoot Jackson. He's quite content these days with his little designer friend, Jackson's putative daughter." She stopped for a moment and looked at the bullet hole. "Funny thing is I never heard a shot."

"Nor did I," Tony said, suddenly garrulous. "I think Jackson should have police protection. We don't seem to be able to safeguard him. Maybe next time the murderer will attempt something more effective. What do you think a policeman could protect him from, Jessica? Poison in his brandy?"

"Tony, don't you think you'd better have a lie-down? You seem just a little stressed out."

"You stupid bitch," Tony said, ready to explode, but stopping himself before he detonated. "I think I'll go see how Jackson is," he said to Fitz, leaving the room without looking at her.

"Lots of suppressed anger there," Jessica said, smiling.

"How long will it be before Jackson comes out of sedation?" Fitz, uninterested in pursuing the Jessica–Tony wars, wanted to know.

"Not so very long," Jackson said, coming into the room, a cigarette clamped between his teeth. "You run along, Jessica, and have your rest. I am fine."

"You don't look fine," Jessica said, leaving nonetheless.

He didn't. The blue pajamas gave his skin a greenish cast and there were dark half-circles under his eyes; he seemed vulnerable. He put the cigarette out, walked across the room, removed the captain's wad of Kleenex, and the whistling began again. He didn't seem to mind. He went to the oversized pallet bed, plumped the pillows, and looked around to make certain everything was orderly before lying down. "Sit down, please, Fitz. You look like some vengeful figure of doom, standing over me like that."

Fitz, mindful of the time, thought he might have to try

for the next connection to La Guardia and then to Albany as he sat in one of the Corbusier chairs that seemed to sprout like mushrooms around the house.

"This has to stop," Jackson said, and Fitz began to wonder if the pressure on Albany had sources other than the media. "I am scared, Fitz. I do not think I have ever been so scared."

"We could put a twenty-four-hour guard on the barn. The captain's longing to organize one."

"I am returning to the yacht." Jackson's voice was low now and controlled, as if by making that decision he had taken charge of his life again. "She has an elaborate security system. If you could have Captain Price put some men in the yacht club and at the approach to the pier, I will be secure."

"No problem," Fitz said, disappointed. He had expected more. The late fall sun turned the room into a series of cubist refractions while the whistling wind added a surreal audio touch to the atmosphere. "I wonder why they didn't fire a quick second shot. Just to make certain."

"I dropped to the floor in unheroic fashion. Whoever it was believed they had completed their mission."

"That must be it." Fitz left him on the gargantuan bed in his magician's room, feeling uncertain. The wrongness that pervaded the place and the man threw him. He called Albany from a downstairs extension, saying he didn't think this was the moment to leave Waggs Neck, but Albany said the meeting was on and Fitz was expected.

Fitz might have said he was, after all, retired; answerable to no one; that he had taken this assignment as a personal favor and not for glory or money. But he had been a government employee for too many years of his life and he felt a genuine loyalty to the governor. Not without misgivings, Fitz left the new incarnation of Bull Carlson's old barn and prepared to make the trek—on a Friday afternoon, yet—to Albany.

CHAPTER

Twenty

A DESPONDENT MAGGIE, SIPPING AT HER TEA AS IF IT WERE a rare medicine, told Homer Price that she hadn't seen anyone or anything suspicious either around her house or on the convent grounds.

"Do you suppose your sister or Dicie . . ."

"Neither have been here all day," Maggie said, her attention on Main Street and the Friday night shoppers moving in and out of the stores. "And in any case we have only a very limited view of the convent."

"We're asking everyone in the immediate neighborhood," the captain said defensively. He looked directly at her for the first time and saw that she was distracted and pale. "Are you okay, Ms. Carlson?" He knew he should have called her Maggie—nearly everyone did—but somehow couldn't. Despite all the changes, Maggie Carlson continued to be the symbolic head of the village, which was why he hadn't sent Ray Cardinal to talk to her. Rank still had its privileges.

"Captain, I am not in the least 'okay,' " she answered with her usual asperity. "My oldest and best enemy was killed in my home. The murderer, who may or may not have made a world-class blunder, is still strolling around, planning to do in my nearest neighbor. What's more, we have a village board meeting scheduled tonight. Somehow a board meeting without Phineas and his pain-in-the-butt, pie-in-the-sky ideas for increasing village business revenues isn't imaginable." She felt the tears on her cheeks and wondered who the hell she was weeping for.

After the embarrassed captain left, she stayed put on the green sofa, trying to gauge just how scared she was. I'm not afraid of death, she decided. I might even welcome the peace. She imagined death as a tranquil sea-green coma, an endless nap in her broken-down sofa. It was the pain that worried her. The helplessness. The dependency on others. She was afraid that the pain would fool her into forgetting herself, into doing what she had never done: own up.

"If you're going to the meeting," Annie asked, "why don't you get up and go? Why do you look like your favorite dog has heartworm? You hated Phineas."

"They want me to take his place."

"Ha," said Annie, maneuvering the Bissell with renewed vigor. "The Lady Mayor. That's a hot one. I hope you're not going to ban all the brassieres." Annie, decades behind in feminist progress, glanced down at her own considerable chest. "My bosoms would bounce off my knees."

After Annie had gone home to feed her family, Maggie started to leave for the meeting, but the telephone stopped her. "You wanted me to call, right?" Billy Bell's insinuating down-island voice asked.

"Yes, I did," Maggie said, nervously picking up the locket from the side table, flipping it open, staring at the three aging photographs it contained. "You were supposed to call this morning."

"Hey, forget what I put in that letter. I got no info of any kind. Mind your own freakin' business, Mother Maggie." There was a click and a dial tone. Maggie moved quickly to the French windows. There was only one public outdoor telephone at this end of Main Street and that was attached to the post office. Billy Bell was walking away from it, keeping to the shadows of the post office's overhang.

Opening the French doors, Maggie stepped out onto the porch, shouting, "Billy" into the darkness. The only answer was the thumping sound of his motorcycle boots echoing along the pavement and then, as he moved onto the narrow strip of sand leading to the Waggs Neck Harbor Yacht Club, nothing.

Breathing fast, wondering what that call might mean to her and her plans, Maggie made her own telephone call. Then she left Carlson House for the Municipal Building. Main Street, for the first time in her experience, had a sinister quality and she moved along it as quickly as she could.

"Wonder how the bloodhounds are getting on?" the colonel asked in his best Mayfair accent. Wyn, who found it useful to attend village board meetings, was attempting to find comfort in the Municipal Building's unforgiving yellow pine folding chairs. The colonel, sitting next to her, wore an impeccably tailored safari suit, which gave him the aura of a mid-level Anglo official during the early years of the British raj.

"Fitz has gone up to Albany," Wyn said.

"Heard Jackson had a near miss. Deuced odd business." The colonel smiled, revealing dubious teeth.

"You don't seem to be crying in your beer over it."

"No harm done. Gives life a touch of excitement, what? Probably turn out to be some careless chap out hunting. When I was sent to Africa in seventy-eight . . ." Wilfred Mercer launched into a long, pointless tale. Wyn, having heard it before, thought that Waggs Neck had given birth to a number of eccentric men in one year. Jackson Hall. Phineas Browne. Percy Curry. The colonel. Even John Fenton had something of never-never land about him. Perhaps the water had been contaminated that season.

Finally, Maggie took her place at the board table between Ruth Cole and Betty Kunze, the owner–pharmacist of the Waggs Neck Drugstore. She was also the former chair of the Presbyterian Mothers and, though handicapped by a repugnant smugness, a woman who had high political ambitions. John Fenton, who did not, took a seat at the far end of the table, and the Waggs Neck Harbor village board closed their eyes while the very reverend Father Buffet stood up and turned his eyes heavenward.

"It's the Catholics' month," Camellia whispered loudly to a confused and somewhat deaf neighbor. Father Buffet, after giving Camellia one of his gentle, reproving looks, read the invocation and generously asked the board to pray for Phineas Browne's non-Catholic soul. At the same time, local citizens filtered in and found seats for that reliable monthly entertainment, the village board meeting.

Maggie was implored to take Phineas's place, but she was adamant and the honor fell to a pink-cheeked, delighted Betty Kunze, whose bifocals fogged over in the excitement. Various orders of village business were then discussed, ending with the president of the Main Street Business Society (MSBS) requesting that the village foot the bill for an extensive Christmas advertising campaign designed to keep local shoppers in local stores and resistant to mail order shopping.

The motion was defeated after Ruth Cole asked why the members of the Business Society couldn't pay for the campaign themselves.

Eventually the proceedings came to an end, but few felt a desire to go home. It was a slow television night and coffee and glazed cinnamon twists were being served by the village clerk, a custom instituted by the late mayor. The assemblage split into homogeneous groups to gossip about the attempts on Jackson Hall's life, already stale news on the village hot line; the ill luck (or consummate gall, depending upon one's point of view) of the MSBS proposal; the worsening state of the world in general.

Cammie Cole found herself standing next to Homer Price, who always unnerved her. "I've heard," Camellia Cole said, because she didn't know what else to say, "that Jackson has vacated Maggie's barn and returned to his yacht until the murderer is caught."

"Where'd you pick that up?" the captain asked, annoyed. The maneuver was supposed to be secret.

"Ruth told me."

"I did not. You came home from the IGA with that choice piece of gossip and an inferior cut of top sirloin. I'm going to have to have a talk with that new butcher."

"Someone must have told me at the IGA," Camellia, unabashed, replied. "I spoke to so many people. Carol Morrell was arguing with the new manager over the price of broccoli. Dicie and David were at the dairy case, looking as if they were committing to memory the dates on the skim milk cartons. A bunch of young people at the checkout were making rude remarks about Lettie's new fur. She turned on them and said she hadn't killed the minks personally and weren't their Birkenstocks made of leather? The Muzak was playing an old favorite of Mother's." Camellia sang a few bars of "I Can't Begin To Tell You" in a sweet and infinitely wistful voice.

Afterward, Maggie asked the captain to walk with her and she told him about Billy Bell's telephone call. "I don't suppose he really knows anything but he's the kind of horseball who would try blackmail, even if he didn't have much to go on. Nothing to lose, he would reason."

"Dumb reasoning," Homer Price said.

"Do you think," Maggie asked, changing the subject, "that Jackson is safe aboard the yacht?"

"He's got an alarm system Fort Knox would envy, and I have two men in the yacht club, eyes trained on his boat. Jackson's safe."

"I wish Fitz were here," Maggie said, heedless of Homer Price's feelings. "I'm worried."

"About Jackson?"

"It's not Jackson I'm thinking of," Maggie said, hugging herself, looking at the telephone attached to the post office.

Ray Cardinal, redheaded and broad-shouldered, possessed a delicate white skin through which blue veins showed like secondary roads on a rental car map giveaway. He was having the time of his life, having been given his most exciting assignment to date: guarding Jackson Hall's life.

He glanced at the special—Jerry Rotz—who was sleeping on a badly used wicker sofa, the principal piece of furniture in the Waggs Neck Harbor Yacht Club social room. "Specials," ordinary Waggs Neck residents willing to perform police duty for five dollars an hour, were looked down upon by the regular constabulary and most everyone else.

Ray was disappointed by the clubhouse, thinking it should have been grander. The low-ceilinged board-and-batten room smelled of gin, beer, mildew, peanuts, salt air, tobacco, and Jerry Rotz.

"They think it's fun to play poor," Rotz had said several hours before as he attached the submarine yellow Walkman earphones to his head and taken possession of the sofa. "Wake me when it's over." Rotz had closed his bloodshot old-dog eyes.

Ray stayed alert throughout the long, comfortable night, keeping his eyes on Jackson Hall's yacht as if it were a South Seas volcano prone to eruption and he was responsible for alerting the sleeping villagers. Once each hour he left the shelter of the clubhouse and walked the decks of the glistening boat, hearing the sound track from *RoboCop 2* and later *The Terminator* emanating from the stereophonic VCR in Jackson's suite during the early hours. After midnight the only sound to be heard was the bay waves lapping against the yacht.

Ray waited for something, anything, to happen. Nothing did. He was disappointed when the pale morning sun began to come up and Mary Jane Eden, Thelma's daughter, arrived with coffee and a box of the Eden's cardboardlike doughnuts covered in sugar. "What's the deal with the murderer?" Mary Jane asked, chewing Doublemint in time to some inner rhythm. "Get him, yet?"

"Nope," Ray said, rubbing his colorless eyes, reaching inside his flannel shirt, scratching himself under his arm, and giving other indications of lusting after Mary Jane in his own quiet way.

Mary Jane, not unaware of Ray's interest, cracked her chewing gum through several cycles before she said, "We have a date on Saturday night, or what?"

"If I ever get off this stakeout," he said, moving next to her, unable to resist her furry pink sweater, pulling her to him, looking over her shoulder to make certain Rotz was still out. There ensued several moments of enjoyable kissing, hugging, and tugging until Rotz made a grunting noise. "Your partner's about to rise and shine," Mary Jane said, pulling away.

"I'm about to rise and shine." Ray reached for her but she was already on the way out, giving a twist to the flip of her Clairol blond hair.

"Saturday night," she said, exiting.

" 'That a gun, honey, or you just glad to see me?' " Rotz asked, sitting up, looking at Ray's expanded trousers, amused.

"Go fuck yourself, Rotz."

"Wish I could," Rotz said, headed for the men's room.

Ray took it upon himself to tour the yacht one last time before the captain turned up. The diluted yellow sun coming up over the horizon, reflecting across the foamy gray bay waters, struck Ray, who was not without a mute appreciation of beauty, as particularly poetic. The enormous yacht, all white and gold, seemed permanently fixed in place, a monument to the mysteries of the rich.

Moving quietly about the upper deck, anxious not to wake Jackson Hall, Ray peered into the corridor leading to the main suite. A bathroom door was ajar. Ray, lost in the reflection of fourteen-karat-gold faucet taps, nearly missed the fact that the double doors leading to the master suite were swinging open on their chromed piano hinges.

He stood still and listened. Ugly gulls were cackling from their perch on the mast of a neighboring sailing sloop but there was silence aboard. Too much silence.

"Maybe he's an early riser," Ray said. "Maybe he's on shore." But that didn't seem possible because he would have had to walk by the clubhouse—or on water—to get by Ray. Unless he took one of the yacht's smaller boats, Ray thought, knowing he hadn't. He still checked on the cigarette and the dinghies and the put-put, and all were where they were supposed to be.

Ray Cardinal ran his flat, bony hand through the stubble of maroon hair on his head and sighed, watching his breath turn to steam as it rose in the crisp morning air. He thought about getting Rotz but decided that Rotz wouldn't be much help. And so, carefully, he disarmed the alarm system as Homer Price had taught him, punching in the appropriate numbers. His hands at his sides so as not to leave fingerprints, he moved along the corridor and in through the open doors. The blinds were partially closed and the stateroom was in half light.

Turning on the lights by grazing his elbow across the panel of switches, he saw that no one had slept in the giant bed. Or if they had, they had made the bed afterward. The room felt unused. He took off his shoes and walked across the tiled floor to the circular iron stairs that led up to Jackson Hall's shipboard studio. At the top, he let out a little unmanly shriek of which he was unaware.

What Ray Cardinal would always remember—thanks

to that freeze-frame lodged in his mind—was the harrowing agony communicated by the tortured body on the painted wooden floor. The oversized hands were clutching at nothing. The poor bastard, Ray guessed, had tried to crawl his way to help. The long, muscular legs were twisted like pieces of wrought iron, a configuration of horror and pain. The convulsions, Ray thought, had to have been unbearable. The white-and-gold skipper cap Jackson had liked to wear aboard ship was crammed down around his head like a hat in a Three Stooges short. There was gray and red matter strewn across the room, splattered over the mirrored wall so that it appeared in duplicate. The sweet, nauseating odor that assailed Ray indicated that final humiliation, the loss of sphincter control.

There was no doubt, in Ray's mind, that Jackson Hall was dead, but he forced himself to go to the body, to kneel down, to take the lifeless wrist between his thumb and forefinger. There hadn't been a pulse in that wrist for hours and one infinitesimal ashamed piece of Ray was relieved. Had the hand been warm, had there been even the slightest chance of revival, he would have had to turn the body over and administer the kiss of life.

The thought made him aware of the Eden's doughnuts and he nearly brought them up. He used all his willpower to resist the need, getting out of the room, with its corrupt sweet perfume, and off the yacht as fast as he could. Gulping the bay air, he sped into the clubhouse and called Captain Price at home. "Jackson Hall bought it," Ray said succinctly.

A grim Homer Price took one look at the body, which was face down on the floor, about-faced, and returned to the yacht club, taking a swipe at Rotz's peaceful head resting on the wicker sofa arm. "Get Rotz out of here," the captain told Ray, calling Suffolk, and then, after a moment's thought ("Cover your ass, man," he warned himself), Fitz Robinson at the governor's mansion in Al-

bany. Fitz was en route to a breakfast meeting but a
nasal-voiced secretary assured him that he would receive
the message that the captain had called.

The photographic unit and the medical examiner were
already on the pier, clad in plastic booties, taking in what
little warmth the sun gave, talking to the lab men from
Hauppauge. Captain Price himself, along with Ray, put
up the yellow scene-of-a-crime demarcation barriers and
tape to keep everyone else off the yacht club pier and out
of the clubhouse. Then he and Ray led the ME aboard the
yacht. The sun had moved far enough across the sky to
illuminate the stairwell and the place where the body lay,
still seemingly clawing at air.

"Something's not right," Homer Price said as the three
men bent over the body and prepared to turn it over.

"What is not right?" a voice asked from the bottom of
the staircase. The new arrival climbed the stairs, reaching
the top just as the body was turned face up. Homer Price
removed the cap from its head and Billy Bell's yellow-
blond curls spilled onto the wooden floor.

A confused Ray Cardinal, looking up at the new arrival—Jackson Hall—was the first to react. "Hey, man,
you can't be here. You're dead."

CHAPTER

Twenty-One

IT WAS AN OVERCAST, DRIZZLY SATURDAY MORNING AND Colonel Wilfred Mercer took his time getting out of bed. Half-asleep, he inserted his partial bridge, brushed his thinning hair with matched silver-backed initialed brushes, and got himself into suitable breakfast togs (smoking jacket and trousers). Sipping at Earl Grey, he studied the photo of the titled English woman he had convinced himself he loved. Her death had caused Wilfred to take early retirement and return to his homeland. He wondered whether he had done The Right Thing. Waggs Neck Harbor didn't seem to appreciate him. I would have been better off, he thought, staying on.

He entered the narrow room he called the smoker, avoiding the sight of the glass-enclosed gun case. He knew definitively that he hadn't done The Right Thing in regard to the .223 caliber semiautomatic—and missing—rifle. He had told himself that he hadn't reported its theft because: (a) it would turn up eventually; and (b) he wasn't certain he had a legal right to own it, since it was equipped with a silencer that he knew couldn't be legal. The Great Walpole Street shop clerk had confided that all the really super hunters used silencers. "Don't want to frighten the game away, do we?"

And there was a (c): the colonel had smuggled the rifle into the States, saving at least fifty dollars. Certainly an excessive fine and possibly confinement were in the offing if this transgression was uncovered.

Adept at not facing the consequences of his acts, let alone examining them, the colonel skipped breakfast and mixed himself a Scotch and soda. "Bloody laws," he said to himself as the doorbell, a melodious device, commanded his attention. "Who the devil . . ." he asked himself, setting his drink on the Benares table, pleased—though determined not to let on—at the interruption.

"Why hullo," he said, opening the door wide, recognizing his caller. "Come in and have a cuppa. Nasty out, isn't it? What's that you got there? My rifle? Wherever did you get hold of that?"

The rifle was casually raised. "Just don't hit me," the colonel begged, believing for a split second that he was only going to be punished. The barrel was pressed against his chest. "It wasn't my fault," he said as the gloved trigger finger began to tighten. Then, realizing this was "it," the colonel looked up in search of heavenly intervention. His eyes found the framed miniature flag of Great Britain he had nailed up over the door. England and all things English had been his escape from the realities of who he was; or rather, who he wasn't. The bullet tore through his chest, ripping apart his admittedly dickey heart, exploding out through his back, lodging itself in the masonry surrounding the decorative fireplace.

Wyn lay in bed, a smelly Probity at her side, wondering if she had the energy to drive over to the Route 114 McDonald's for an Egg McMuffin, grateful that for the first time in weeks she had no weekend property showings scheduled. Even more relaxing was the belief that her house was again sacrosanct; she sensed that Jackson Hall wouldn't be making any more unexpected visits.

What's more, the specter of having to become Lucy Littlefield's keeper had evaporated when an eminently sane Lucy called to thank Wyn for her patience. Now that she was filthy rich, she was having her sister's oldest come and live with her. "She has strong opinions. She'll keep me on my toes." Wyn knew and liked Lucy's niece, who was moral and sensible and forever immune to the lure of the home shopping channel.

Her second call of the morning was from Fitz, in Albany, who told her about Billy Bell. "He was poisoned with cyanide, just like Phineas. Hauppauge just faxed me the lab report. Person or persons unknown dropped enough cyanide into a decanter of calvados sitting on the salon's bar to kill the proverbial horse."

"Don't you think Billy would've been smart enough to stay away . . ."

"No. Besides, he didn't know what it was. He saw a cut-glass decanter filled with some dark alcohol and poured himself a drink. He wouldn't know what it was supposed to taste like."

"You think it was again meant for Jackson?"

"It's widely known he's addicted to calvados, and Phineas's death hasn't turned him off it. Tony Deel claims the decanter has been on the yacht since late summer. Until recently, they've been careless about switching on the yacht's alarm system. Anyone could have gotten aboard and poisoned the stuff, pretty certain that eventually Jackson would drink it.

"His would-be assassin doesn't seem able to get anything right. Poor Billy. I can see him eyeing the decanter, wondering how much he could drink without it being noticed. He was the kind of kid who had to try everything. And, except for Tony Deel's visits, he was alone on the yacht, bored. I suppose he thought he was living the life, drinking brandy out of that fancy decanter." Fitz paused. "I wish to hell he had told us what he knew."

"Who was aware that Billy had taken Jackson's place aboard the yacht?"

"Jackson's household, Homer Price, myself." The "myself" was said somewhat sheepishly.

Not that Wyn was going to let Fitz get away with it. "Yourself? You mean you were pretending to be all worried about Billy while you knew where he was? Who was I supposed to tell, Fitz?"

"I didn't like it but you know Homer, a literal letter-of-the-law man; he swore me to absolute secrecy. I'm sorry."

"Humph."

Taking this for tentative forgiveness, Fitz went on. "We let it leak that Jackson had moved onto the yacht. It seemed safe for everyone: safe for Jackson who stayed in the barn; safe for Billy because the boat was intruder-proof."

"Whose idea was it?"

"I'm not sure. Price and I went to a meeting called by Jackson at the barn. The damn idea just seemed to be there. Tony Deel confessed that he let 'Beautiful Billy'—his words—'camp out' in the convent playhouse. Homer and I went and had a little talk with Billy, who changed his mind, insisting he remembered zip about Phineas's murder and knew nothing about a note. What were we going to do? Beat it out of him? Tony had come with us and it didn't take him long to convince Billy to move from the unheated convent to the yacht and play stand-in for Jackson."

"How long will you be in Albany?" Wyn asked, feeling her uncle's frustration, wishing she could help.

"Only a day or two. They're bringing in the big guns and I'm to brief them."

"You're a big gun, Fitz."

"I was."

Wyn chewed on an overmicrowaved bagel and then unenthusiastically bathed a for-once sullen-eyed Probity in the old basement sink, unable to get Billy out of her mind until the phone rang again. It was Nick. "Do I have to drive over to Waggs Neck in the Land Cruiser and drag you to this dinner party myself?"

"Please leave me alone."

"What could be so important that you want to miss this dinner? Cook's working her butt off over the food."

"That's an appetizing visual."

"Get this: clams aux blinis; vichyssoise à la Ritz; Pakistani pigeons and pilau; avocado pear grand duc; oeufs à la neige. I'm not even going to mention the wines because it'll be too much for you. Tell me you're not coming."

"I have a date, Nick."

"Who with?"

"Tommy, not that it's any of your business."

"That *schmendrick*? Get real. Besides, Allie's got someone she wants you to meet. Someone special."

"Cousin Martin. She introduces me to Martin at every one of your charming little get-togethers and don't think I don't appreciate the fact that he's worth umpty-dumpty million dollars, but even you have to admit there might just be something off-putting about a man who doesn't bathe."

"Martin's a financial wizard."

"Don't you think, Nick, it's time you consulted your psychiatrist about your obsession with fixing me up? Other divorced couples go their own separate ways and leave each other alone. That's why they got divorced in the first place. So they can live independent, detached lives. I leave you alone, Nick. Why won't you leave me alone?"

"Because I want the best for you. Because I love you."

"If you loved me, you wouldn't have divorced me. I was content to be your slave for life."

"I made the sacrifice. I knew it would be better for your personal enrichment if we split."

"You're a saint, Nick."

"Come tonight."

She got off the telephone by promising she might consider Thanksgiving dinner. Fat chance. I'd rather spend it in a snake pit, she thought, knowing both Nick's and Allie's parents would be at Thanksgiving, along with Martin. She knew Nick—and yes, even Allie and the rest of their combined, carnivorous family—genuinely cared about her and were not, deep down, bad people. But she wished he and they cared a lot less.

Needing to get out of the house, Wyn put on a sweater and jeans and took the temporarily clean Probity downtown. There was a small, thick knot lodged in the back of her brain that was, she sensed, important to unravel, but she couldn't find a thread to begin. Working at it, she knocked over ten-year-old Brendon Slaff, who was wearing roller blades and having a conniption fit in front of Zero's, where expensive sporting goods were sold. "He wants a two-hundred-dollar tennis racquet," his father, Harris, a monied Manhattan orthopedic surgeon and Waggs Neck Harbor weekender, whined.

"You can afford it, Harris," Wyn told him, helping Brendon, momentarily silenced by the collision, stand up. The resemblance between Brendon and his father was always startling, but especially so this morning as they were dressed in matching Gap sweaters, Gap corduroy trousers, Gap tartan caps.

"We don't want to spoil him."

As she looked at Brendon and Harris, so directly one after the other in the hereditary lineup that it was scary, the knot in Wyn's mind began to unravel. "There's worse things, Harris. Buy him the racquet." She managed to pry Probity's attention away from a piece of discarded fried chicken in the gutter with a friendly kick in the heinie and raced her home.

She went directly to the bookcase in the study where her father's collection of journals and Waggs Neck Harbor memorabilia was stored and immediately put her hands on the old red leatherette binder, its hand-pressed gold letters declaring it to be "A History of the Fat Boys, 1925–1947," by Hap Lewis. Painstaking boy that he was,

Hap had complemented his handwritten narrative detailing the Fat Boys' past with appropriate photographs and newspaper clippings.

The photo she was looking for was just where she remembered it, on the second page of the scrapbook. It had been taken in 1925 and the subject was in a Mary Immaculate blue blazer, looking privileged—or "fat" as they said in those days—and radiating attitude. Hap had written under it, "Photograph Courtesy of Miss Margaret Carlson."

Wyn found the other photo she wanted printed in the first pages of the book she had borrowed from Maggie. It had been taken forty-two years later, the subject was in a Mary Immaculate blue blazer, and though he didn't look especially privileged, he certainly had his share of attitude.

Wyn already knew, but her training and her heritage made her thorough and she took the two photos downstairs, comparing them to the figures in the painting. It can't be, she told Probity. But it was.

She returned to her father's old office and sat on the wide-planked floor searching through his meticulous journals, blessing Hap for his sure sense of organization. It took only a moment to find the entry she was looking for, written the day after the last Mary Immaculate Academy Senior Class Promenade in his neat, circular handwriting.

Early this morning Jackson Hall came in through the kitchen door and found me drinking Nescafé. He wanted me to accompany him to Bull Carlson's house so he could get his money, thinking my presence would help.

We found Bull in the keeping room eating a huge breakfast—sausages and eggs and biscuits—furious over his burned stable. Maggie was there, smoking a cigarette, drinking hot chocolate, looking pale. Jackson demanded his money and Bull, cramming fried potatoes into his mouth, asked what money and Maggie, coming out of her blue funk, said you know very well what money. The money put aside for him by his mother.

Bull and Maggie looked at one another as if they were going to lock horns across the breakfast table. Despite the differences in their ages, at that moment father and daughter seemed evenly matched. To break the tension, I harrumphed and Bull asked what the hell I was doing there and I said Jackson had asked me along to see to his interests. There was another long moment until Bull told Maggie to go get his ledger, which she did, and he scrawled his name at the bottom of one of the checks.

"Good riddance," he said. Jackson asked me to do him one more favor, to drive him to Bridgehampton for the early morning train to the city. He had hinted, earlier in the week, that he and Kate were going to elope, one sure way to get revenge on Bull. But I gathered that Kate had backed out and she was either going to meet him later or that he was going on his own. I tried to help him count his blessings: he had gotten his money from Bull and his diploma from Mary Immaculate, he was eighteen and leaving town. But he seemed frightened and I suppose the idea of cutting off all his old ties, no matter how painful some of them were, was scary.

We had time and so we stopped at the Clover Diner but he couldn't eat. He was furious over some fool trick Phineas and the Fat Boys played on him at the dance. I never did get the details but Ruth and Cammie were chaperones and they're sure to tell.

Eventually I got him to the station and waited with him until the red-eye came in. He left a painting in the back of the station wagon and I caught up with him just as the train was moving out. He told me to keep it, that it was a present for being such a great guy. I didn't feel like such a great guy, standing there in the early morning fog, letting that kid go off to New York all by himself. But what was I to do? It was right that he leave.

After you look at it for a while, the painting makes you feel like you've swallowed a ticking bomb. Linda took one glance and said it was "corrupt," whatever that means. But Wynsome, my eleven-year-old sweetheart, thinks it's "interesting" and together we managed to convince Linda to let it be hung over the mantel.

Later: Ruth called with the terrible news that Kate died in the stable fire. The theory is that she set it herself, smoking a marijuana cigarette in the hayloft. Bull has fallen apart and the village is in mourning.

Wyn closed the journal and decided she had better go see Camellia and Ruth.

Ruth and Camellia were delighted, leading her into the sitting room alcove that faced the side door to the Curry mansion where Percy Curry had lived and died. Cammie was pouring, Ruth talking. "Who could forget? It was the night of the senior promenade, Mary Immaculate's last dance. While the monsignor and the Girls—as the irreverent called the nuns—were planning an elaborate graduation ceremony for the following day, Phineas was plotting to get even with Jackson Hall.

"Even for what, no one was sure. Except that Jackson was everything Phineas was not. Beautiful and gifted to the point of genius. Mary Immaculate's lay headmaster had recognized that genius, as did several others, Maggie Carlson included. Kate may or may not have. She was a spectacularly good-looking girl, as self-centered as Phineas, with the same mean sense of humor.

"Phineas begrudged the time she spent with Jackson while Kate resented the hours Jackson devoted to his work. Jackson was studying with an artist named Holtz in West Sea and working every afternoon and most evenings in Holtz's studio, none of which sat well with Kate. She used to call here, demanding to know where Jackson was.

"I'm half-convinced the joke was Kate's idea. On the night of the dance Jackson was to meet her in the convent playhouse where the promenade was being held. He couldn't have picked her up at home; Bull was certifiable on the subject of Jackson Hall.

"I overheard snatches of a telephone conversation they had that afternoon and I knew Jackson hadn't wanted to go to the dance in the first place. It was his eighteenth birthday, and the following day he would receive the money Bull was holding for him. He finally agreed to go to the promenade as a concession to Kate."

"We were chaperones," Camellia piped in. "I wore a long pink dress I had for centuries. Maggie, even then going in for color rather than taste, was in a bright red dress that made her seem angry. All the young girls wore those birthday-cake gowns popular that year in Waggs Neck . . ."

"But nowhere else . . ."

". . . tiers of chiffon. Kate was the exception, appearing in a short black cocktail dress that made her seem decades more experienced than the others. We thought the monsignor was going to send her home, but he was a peace-loving man. It would have been better if he had."

"Jackson had rented a tuxedo," Ruth said, recovering the narrative, "and he was late, having trouble with the tie and cummerbund. While she waited, Kate danced with John Fenton. They made a lovely couple, John tall and dark and Arrow-shirt handsome; Kate and that red hair of hers and that sophisticated dress and that aura of sheer devil-may-care glamour.

"Willy Mercer was out on the porch, waiting for Jackson, and when he saw him coming across the convent grounds wearing that shiny tuxedo and his old brown loafers, he gave the signal. Kate, taking John by the hand, led him through the dancers, down to the first-floor cloakrooms. When Jackson asked where she was, Phineas directed him down the stairs, where he found John in what he thought was an amorous embrace with

Kate. Jackson pulled them apart and in his jealous fury, kissed Kate with full passion. Then he pushed her away.

"It wasn't Kate at all, but Percy Curry. He had on a red wig and a black dress just like Kate's. He was all made up: a hideous transvestite version of Kate. Jackson knocked poor Percy down and left.

"Kate went after him, no doubt realizing that the prank had gone further than anyone thought it would. They hadn't really known Jackson. He was supposed to have been embarrassed. Or he was supposed to have laughed. After all, they were little more than children. But Jackson has never been a child in his life.

"Kate, it was guessed, couldn't find Jackson, probably assuming he had come home to our house. Even Kate wouldn't have dared appear here in that dress and at that hour, so she went to the old Carlson stable and up to her secret place in the hayloft. She was evidently smoking marijuana—just the sort of rebellion Kate would engage in—when she fell asleep. If Kate screamed, no one heard her. By the time the Waggs Neck Volunteer Firemen arrived, nobody could have saved the stable— or Kate, had they known she was in there.

"She wasn't missed until the next day. Mary Immaculate seniors traditionally spent the wee hours after the promenade skinny-dipping in the bay and then, at dawn, going on to the Greek's place for breakfast. Kate's friends thought she was with Jackson. Everyone else thought she was with her classmates.

"Early in the morning Jackson left here with a suitcase, a portfolio filled with paintings, and one canvas under his arm. He went to your father and convinced him to accompany him to Carlson House, where he got his money out of Bull. Bull Carlson couldn't have refused, not in front of your father.

"When Kate hadn't come home by noon, and no one knew where she was, Maggie called the police, who found what was left of Kate in the stable. It was the

Carlsons' dentist who offered definitive proof that Kate had died in the fire, and then Bull had his stroke."

"Jackson was long gone," Camellia said in that wispy voice of hers. And then, looking out the bay window at the old Curry mansion, she said, "Do you think Percy was murdered, too?"

CHAPTER
Twenty-Two

RAY CARDINAL'S SISTER, DAWN, TELEPHONED HER BEST friend, Heidi Lum, early on Saturday afternoon to inform her, with appropriate menace, that the colonel had been murdered. Heidi told her mother and Liz, genuinely dismayed, called Wyn, who had just that moment come home from tea with the Coles. "This has got to stop," Liz said.

Wyn agreed it had to stop. She tried calling Homer Price, but Ray Cardinal told her that the captain was on a conference call with Albany and would get back to her, maybe. John Fenton's service operator said that he was out of town for the weekend and that Dr. Marshall, over in West Sea, was taking his emergencies. Wyn said, "Thank God," and the operator said, "I beg your pardon," but Wyn had already replaced the receiver.

She thought of calling Tommy, but decided she'd had enough of the telephone and went to the cedar closet in the attic, found the old mouton fur coat her mother had left behind, and put it on, for warmth. And comfort. Sometimes, Wyn thought, a girl does need her mommy. As unsatisfactory as that mommy might be.

She walked up Main Street toward Carlson House, seeing a familiar figure in the second-floor living room, her back to the village and the French windows. The front door was, as always, open and Wyn, without announcing herself, climbed the narrow stairs to find Lettie Browne pouring herself a drink.

"You always let yourself into other people's houses?" Lettie asked, but her heart wasn't in it. Despite the smart dress and the careful makeup, she look tired, her eyes dull and defeated.

"We're past etiquette," Wyn said. "Is Maggie here?"

"She and Jackson have gone over to the convent playhouse. He's finished his painting and they've had it temporarily displayed on the stage. Maggie's planning a gala opening for the Jackson Hall Megalomania Museum of Art. You want a drink?"

"You've known all along, haven't you?"

"I've suspected all along. There's a difference." Lettie sat on Maggie's old green sofa and picked up the locket Bull had given his daughter for her twenty-first birthday. "Such a perfect Bull Carlson present, don't you think? Ten-karat gold. Same quality as his heart."

"He was, I suppose, your father-in-law."

Lettie Browne laughed. "I've never thought of that but you're right. My son Tony's grandpa, as well. What a bastard the old man was." She used one of her long, enameled nails to pry open the locket, glanced at the three photographs, and then handed it over to Wyn. "A family portrait," Lettie said.

Wyn looked at the three people pictured in the locket. The first photo was the original of the blown-up version Wyn had found in Hap's album; the second was a snapshot, taken when the subject was in his twenties. Except for the difference in ages, the two men might have been twins. The young woman in the old school photo had to be a close member of the family, her plain features displaying that chin-up attitude that bound them all together.

"What are you going to do about Tony?" Wyn asked, anxious to move on, but still curious.

Lettie took a long pull at her drink. "Not much." Wyn left her contemplating the faded photographs of Bull and Jackson as boys, Maggie in her youth.

The late afternoon sky was low and darkening, the salty air bitter. Wyn walked quickly along the narrow strip of sand as the pale sun, half obscured by clouds, began to disappear. She kept her hands clenched in the pockets of her mother's coat, thinking that the inner chill she was feeling sure didn't come from the weather.

The three blood-brown onion-domed convent buildings looked like monuments to a long-dead civilization. The wind plastered the heavy coat to her body as she made her way to the playhouse that had fascinated her when she was a girl. There was light inside, a dim orange-yellow glow seeping through and around the playhouse's boarded windows, promising warmth and shelter. She stopped for a moment, asking herself what the hell she was doing. She should wait, she knew, for Fitz to return, for Homer Price to get off the damn phone. But she didn't. The massive double doors opened too easily.

They were sitting on the stage, their heads together, smiling at some shared memory. An oversized kerosene lamp placed on the stage floor illuminated them, reminding Wyn of the shadow monsters Hap once made for her on her bedroom wall. Behind them, hung as if it were a movie screen, was Jackson Hall's finished masterpiece, its technical virtuosity and emotional force staggering.

And now that the last brush strokes had been put in, there was no doubt that this was Jackson Hall's family's portrait. Jackson and Bull Carlson, nearly identical, fading into the fire while the dominant figure, angst steaming off the canvas, ignited the earth in an unquenchable conflagration.

"*C'est moi*," Maggie said as Wyn approached the stage.

"Big Mama." They were sipping calvados, a newly opened bottle sitting on a fragile piecrust-top table beside an amber-colored pharmaceutical vial. Jackson was serenely stoned, silent, his serpent eyes half closed as he chain-smoked his "occasional" cigarettes, flicking the ashes into the air. "Sit up here with us," Maggie invited, as if she were Granny Goose, "while I tell you the story of our lives."

Wyn chose a seat in the front row, knowing this was to be a performance in which she was merely the audience. And then of course, fear, slipping in its knife, alerted her to the fact that she had a better chance of survival if she remained where she was, out of reach.

"I gather you know the broad outline. If you like, I'll fill in the details."

"Please."

"It began with Bull," Maggie said, taking Jackson's ugly hand in hers, resting her head against the back of her chair, smiling as if they were all old friends, reminiscing. "Inside all that beef, Bull Carlson was a sad, tormented pigmy who desperately wanted to make his mark in the world, to overshadow his own big-balled entrepreneurial dad. Unfortunately, no God-given opportunity— or talent—presented itself. Bull stayed on in Waggs Neck, overseeing the failing watch factory he inherited, fooling with the failing newspaper he bought.

"He let me go to college—big whoop—but after two years Bull ordered me home. His third wife had died and there was the newborn Kate to be taken care of along with three-year-old Dolly.

"Through with marriage, he found other uses for me besides nursemaid. The first time he had to rape me, but after that, when I realized he liked the struggle, I lay passive; though not, I admit, totally unresponsive. He had, after all, elevated me from daughter to wife and, in a matter of six weeks, mother-to-be, Bull once again living up to his name.

"When he noticed that I had become somewhat rounder

about the edges, he lost it and beat the hell out of me. The scandal of his daughter having his child struck terror in his teeth, but it didn't stop him from coming to my room for his morning release—though he began using precautions. Always late in the day when it came to precautions was Bull Carlson.

"When I was nearly too far gone, he hired a housekeeper for Kate and Dolly and sent me off to a doctor friend of his who ran a clinic for asthmatics—abortions on the side—in a place called Jackson Hall, Mississippi. Jackson Hall, get it? Halfway between nowhere and Biloxi. I knew all about thin blood and incestuous idiots, but I didn't believe half of it and I had no intention of having my child aborted. It was my chance to be a mother and I desperately wanted a child. That the child was the spitting image of Bull was just one more example of life's nickel jokes.

"I stayed away four years and then gave in. I was out of money and prospects. I called Bull. He broke down on the phone; said he and the girls needed me. Even so, negotiations took time. I wanted concessions. When I had them, I returned to Waggs Neck with my son, concocted the orphan fable, and made Bull arrange for Ruth and Cammie to take Jackson."

"Didn't anyone recognize the resemblance?" Wyn asked.

"There was no resemblance then, Bull by that time being a hefty two hundred and fifty pounds of balding, wasted, jiggling flesh. I forced Bull to set aside money for Jackson's eighteenth birthday and publicized the fact so Bull couldn't renege. Jackson was everything he wasn't, and Bull would have done him real harm if I hadn't had such a powerful weapon in public opinion. Bull knew that if he hurt Jackson, I'd go public with our sex life. Mother-love made me strong.

"It was when I was teaching English at Mary Immaculate that I had my epiphany: I happened to see, in a school art show, Jackson's first paintings. I hadn't planned to tell him I was his mother, but when I saw those paintings, so imaginative, so vivid, so alive with fury and creation . . . I was so proud. Everyone deserves one prize in life, Wyn. Jackson is mine.

"I told him who his parents were. His reaction was rage. He understood, finally, Bull's need to humiliate him. He wanted to take a knife to Bull, but eventually he calmed down and realized there would be other ways to settle his hash.

"I manipulated that horseball, Mary Immaculate's headmaster, into believing he discovered Jackson's 'gift,' as he called it. Together, we got the German painters to take a look and Jackson was on his way.

"I don't mind admitting now that I was afraid someone would take him from me. Even when he was in his early teens there were women of every age who would have eaten him alive, given the chance. Without me his genius would have dissipated. He had his father's sexual appetite and he had to be taught that sex was merely a biological urge, that art was his life. I had to show him the way."

"So you gave him Kate," Wyn said.

"So I gave him Kate," Maggie agreed. "She had no idea of our real connection and she was genuinely in love with Jackson. But despite a superficial bravado, Kate was a child of her extremely tight environment and she needed, you'll excuse the expression, that little extra push. I provided it with the setting—our stable—a talk about the rewards of sexual experimentation with the man one loved, and appropriate safety precautions; at eighteen she didn't want to get stuck in Waggs Neck with a kid. Jackson did the rest."

"The stable reeked of aged dung but it did not matter," Jackson said, coming awake, bending over the kerosene lamp, lighting a new cigarette by its flame. "Kate was so beautiful." Dreamily, he clamped the cigarette between his teeth and talked around it. "And snake mean. She was irresistible."

He opened his eyes and focused on Wyn. "You have imagination, Wyn. You must know how I felt that afternoon in the keeping room with Phineas showering me with his foul saliva, confessing that it was he who had thought up the trick that led to my killing Kate. I had always believed it was her doing. 'I knew you would be a good sport about it,' Phineas said after he told me. So I offered him my glass for the toast."

"You always carry cyanide in your jacket pocket?"

"I had planned to kill him from the moment I decided to return to Waggs Neck. I needed to kill him. To resolve what Jessica calls early conflict. Not long before I left France I joined the local version of the Hemlock Society, which offered quick release via double doses of cyanide. I brought the pills with me, waiting for the right opportunity. And what better one was there than the Whalers Festival reception? When the lights went out, I put a pill in the calvados and when Phineas needed a drink for his toast, I handed him mine. I do not think I have ever felt more fulfilled than when I heard Phineas writhing on the floor."

He sat back, exhaling smoke though his nose like a lean dragon, watching Wyn with ancient eyes. "I killed Phineas for revenge; I killed Kate out of passion. Killing Kate was wrong. It meant I had to leave Maggie."

"He had to leave anyway," Maggie said. "He'd hardly have made a world-class reputation in Waggs Neck. Only this was sooner than we thought. Kate had followed him when he left the dance and found him in the stable. He wouldn't speak to her, much less make love to her. She taunted him, telling him that her father—well, *their* father, but she didn't know that—was right, that Percy Curry was more his type after all. He strangled her and came to me.

"I forced him to go home to Ruth's and Cammie's while I went to the stable and made certain that Kate was dead. Holding her body in my arms, I had a great many feelings I don't think I'll share with you, but uppermost, I will tell you this, was that atavistic instinct to save my son. The wind was right, blowing away from both the house and the dairy barn. The stable was all ancient dry wood, filled with old straw; it was easy enough to set a fire that would destroy it and Kate's body.

"That was a busy night. I found Jackson shivering on Ruth's and Cammie's front porch, all packed and ready to go. I talked him into asking your dad to help him get his money from Bull, knowing Bull couldn't renege in front of Hap. My fear was that Bull, when he learned Kate was dead, would intuit that Jackson killed her and then he would go after him with all his hate and energy. Kate meant to Bull what Jackson means to me."

"Maggie would have made a great conspirator," Jackson said, turning, looking up at the painting, pouring himself more calvados. "She had a room waiting for me at the West Side Y and somehow got through to Bonet, who was willing to see my work."

"Luckily," Maggie said, belting down her own brandy, "Bull had a stroke when they told him and then the police had to deal with me. They wanted to launch an investigation; they wanted to know if Kate had been alone in the stable. They had heard of the scene at the dance, of Percy Curry's masquerade, and they were suspicious. I stopped them. I told them that Bull couldn't stand an inquiry; that I didn't want my father to suffer any more than he had, for an unnecessary investigation. The coroner, a malleable Fat Boy alumnus, brought in the report I wanted—accidental death—and my son was free.

"But needy. He's the kind of man who must have sex every day or his work suffers, and I didn't trust the women he would meet on his own. So I sent him Lettie. She had always loved him and she wanted to be in New York, to be independent of her own miserly father, so I gave her money and other support. I never dreamt Lettie would be stupid enough to get pregnant. She made him marry her then, thinking maybe they were all meant for the family life. Papa Jackson. Mother Lettie. Baby Tony. Can you imagine? The Addams family would have had heavy competition.

"After Jackson decamped for Paris, with a little assistance from yours truly, Lettie came to her senses. It was too late for abortion so she had the child and gave him to a family recommended by her doctor. Ergo Tony Deel."

"And after Jackson had gone to Paris, I suppose you sent him Dolly?"

"Bull was finally dying," Jackson answered. "Maggie wouldn't leave him or Waggs Neck and I was lonely. Dolly worked out nicely in the beginning, a docile version of Kate, though without her incandescence. But one dreadful day she found her own voice and, unfortunately, it was one of chalkboard-grating complaint. I asked her to leave and she moved in with a man I had introduced her to, thinking that by going to bed with him, she would get me back. Instead she got Dicie.

"There was a touching scene when she came to me, baby in her arms. But I had to tell Dolly that I had myself fixed soon after my first and only child was born. Dolly still maintains that Dicie is my child, but that obviously does not work." Smiling, tuning out, Jackson closed his eyes and put his head back, inhaling smoke, listening to the voices in his mind.

"Jane Robinson," Wyn said, prompting Maggie. "Fitz's wife."

"Jackson was depressed and couldn't work. Jane had been flitting in and out of beds for years and I didn't see what harm it would do if I brought the two of them together. You may not believe this, but I have a great affection for Fitz. He was so much better than Jane; I thought it a good idea to liberate him."

"Omniscient Maggie," Wyn said. "Jessica Stevens?"

"Her aunt and I went to college together. Eileen brought her around and when I found she was going abroad to study . . . she was perfect. I hadn't taken the boyfriend into consideration. David Kabot tried to punch poor Jackson's lights out over her."

"I suppose you were the one making all of Jackson's career decisions."

Maggie laughed. "Hell, no. The French public relations man I hired was brilliant. Though he had what to work with, you have to admit. Once in a while I offered a suggestion, timing being my forte. Yet it seems to have deserted me now. I'm leaving just when the going's getting good." She leaned over and touched her son's pale forehead. "But there it is."

The accumulated odor of a hundred years of incense, sweat, and makeup was being made piquant by the heat of the kerosene lamp on the stage. "You've been acting," Wyn said, "as Jackson's procurer for the last twenty years or so. I suppose it was one way to keep in touch with your son."

"You have a narrow mind, Wyn, like your mother. From your limited point of view, I've been working as a white slaver to satisfy one man's not, after all, overwhelming lust. You envision me as accessory to my sister's murder.

"From my side of the mountain the vista is more acceptable. I see myself as having helped sustain for the world the ongoing work of this century's greatest artistic genius. I'll go down in the history books not only as Jackson Hall's mother, but as the woman who made his art possible."

"You'll go down in history, if at all, as a murderess, Maggie."

"I was the one who killed Percy, Phineas, and the colonel," Jackson said, eyes still closed. "I had to. The Fat Boys deserved to die." He sat up and drank the calvados noisily, as a child might drink his milk. His consciousness, like an unpredictable sun, seemed to slip away again as he lay back in his chair.

"But you killed Billy Bell, didn't you, Maggie?"

"How could I have let him live? And why? It took Billy

a while but he finally realized the import of what he saw in the small circle of light from his flash: Jackson handing the glass to Phineas. He made the mistake of confiding in Tony, whom he regarded as a friend. Tony, not believing him for a moment, told Jackson, who told me. We got Tony, who thinks his father is a god, to hide Billy here in the convent until it was time to take him to the yacht, where Billy expected the payoff. Tony—my grandson, and don't I just deserve it?—was led to believe we were humoring Billy, keeping him from bothering Jackson until the painting was finished and it could all be sorted out. It can never really be sorted out. Can it, Jackson?"

Jackson smiled at her from half-closed eyes, his head leaning back on the chair, one hand holding a cigarette, the other holding hers. "That tired, Maggie darling."

"God must be an over-the-hill barren American woman, don't you think, Wyn?" Maggie asked, kissing the back of Jackson's ugly hand, holding it to her cheek. "Just another desiccated bitch taking her frustration out on anyone happier than she. Jackson is finally returned to me and I'm told I have incurable cancer." She laughed her bark of a laugh. "Well, I won't engage in self-pity. Not my style. I've had years of a fulfillment most women can only guess at."

She took a pill and swallowed it. "Don't worry, it's not the cyanide. Only a mega-tranquilizer, deadly if enough are taken, guaranteed to ease one out slowly." She looked at Wyn and smiled. "I am the greater criminal, of course. I killed Billy with premeditation and would have done the same to anyone who threatened my boy. Jackson, his father's son after all, killed out of revenge, emotional turmoil, mental upset, if you will. He's been obsessing over the Fat Boys for three decades. Right, Jackson?"

He could no longer speak, barely able to keep his head up. But he smiled at his mother as his body went slack in the oversized chair. She put her arms around him and held him to her, placing her lips against his black hair. "We had decided he had nothing to gain by remaining in Paris. His reputation has been secure for a long time and besides, he was lonesome and wanted to come home. While Tony oversaw the transformation of the barn, Jackson spent the summer on the yacht, creating his masterpiece. It was halfway finished when Percy, still incurably in love, sent Jackson a note, inviting him for tea and seduction.

"The twenty-year-old virulent boil popped. Jackson, reliving all those early humiliations at the hands of the Fat Boys, found Percy, who had grown progressively nuts over the years, waiting for him in a bubble bath, coming on all seductive, his mother's old radio plugged into the electric shaver outlet, tuned to easy listening."

"He invited me to join him," Jackson said, sounding far away, as if calling in via a remote satellite. "Instead, I threw the radio into the tub. It made a satisfying crackling sound but the smell was terrible."

"Afterward, Jackson found it increasingly difficult to finish the painting. Phineas's demise nearly made him abandon it altogether. He needed time, he said. I had Tony steal the rifle from Willy Mercer and shoot at Jackson's window, telling him we needed to ensure that Jackson got real police protection. Tony, who is extremely naive under all that surface sophistication, also believed that if everyone thought Jackson was living aboard the yacht, protected by Homer Price's minions, he would be that much safer. He began to look a little worried when Billy Bell was found but still bought the story—because he wanted to—that Jackson was the intended victim.

"Now we can put all that hogwash aside. The painting was finished—just this morning—and Jackson returned the purloined rifle. He was least lucky with Wilfred's murder; had I been consulted, we could have made it look like something else. But what was the point? We knew that sooner rather than later someone would figure out what was happening."

"It is a pity John Fenton's luck held out," Jackson interjected.

"*You* don't really believe that, do you, Maggie?"

"I had to watch those stupid boys torture my son every day of his school life. Do you know what they called him? Queenie. Those Philistines thought art and manhood couldn't go together. They drew little coronets and tiaras on his desk. They burlesqued his walk and the way he spoke. They didn't give him a moment's peace.

"Typical of the Fat Boys to attack my son with an arrogance that had neither intelligence nor creativity to back it up. Jackson makes arrogance moral. Oh, I know what you think, you're so like Hap: arrogance is never justified; no living human being has the power of life or death over another. Give me a break, Wynsome. I would kill thousands of Billy Bells to protect my child. Millions."

She sighed. "At any rate, it's done now. The ultimate masterpiece is finished, Jackson and I have taken our medicine and said our good-byes privately." She reached over and kissed his cheek, which had turned the color of parchment. If he isn't dead, Wyn thought, he will be soon.

Wyn stood up and glanced back at the doors. "You'll never manage to get help in time," Maggie said, reading her mind. "And think about it: Do you really want to be responsible for resuscitating an old woman dying of a painful cancer to face a doubtful prosecution?"

"I can't let you die, Maggie."

"Forget about me. Imagine Jackson brought back to life to face accusations and recriminations and a defamation of his art. I haven't worked and schemed for that indignity, thank you very much, Wyn. My son—my glorious son—is going to die here, on this spot, below his masterpiece, in the building that is going to be his museum, a shrine to a late-twentieth-century genius." She staggered over to the dainty piecrust table, suppressing a spasm of pain, shaking another pill from the amber vial.

"Suppose you're wrong?" Wyn asked.

"About what?"

"Jackson. Think of all the painters declared geniuses in their day and look at their nonexistent reputations now. In five years your museum may be a Holiday Inn."

"This painting secures his reputation forever." Maggie looked up at the canvas and then back at Wyn, unwillingly recognizing the truth in her words. "You're a regular comfort to a nearly dead woman."

"I don't intend to be a comfort, Maggie." Wyn turned and, shedding the heavy coat so she could move faster, ran up the endless playhouse aisle and out the doors, heading for a telephone and help. As she left, she took one last look at the stage and saw a shaky Maggie moving around the kerosene lamp, reaching for her somnolent son.

Wyn had just reached the deserted Carlson House living room and was standing with the telephone at the doors to the summer porch, willing someone, anyone, at the police department to pick up, when the evening dark exploded into light. Homer Price answered but it was far too late. Wyn watched helplessly as the flames enveloped the playhouse along with Maggie, Jackson, and his final, lost masterpiece.

PART THREE

Spring Again

CHAPTER

Twenty-Three

AGAINST HER JUDGMENT, WYN HAD PURCHASED FOR THE
Memorial Day celebration a short piqué dress almost the
color of her hair. "You look like a zillion bucks," Tommy
Handwerk said unoriginally but admiringly.

Tommy, nude, was lying on the bed, watching her, a
paperback copy of *Pride and Prejudice* splayed across his
spare, white, muscled stomach. He was taking the Infi-
nite Art of Jane Austen course at West Sea College,
mostly because Wyn had maintained, during one of their
minor arguments, that they had nothing in common.
"Do you think Mr. D'Arcy ever took off all his clothes?"
Tommy wanted to know.

"I doubt it," Wyn said, applying a silvery lipstick Dicie
had talked her into, looking at herself critically in the
mirror, wondering if she looked more like a dollar ninety-
eight than a zillion bucks. "Mr. D'Arcy never struck me
as a fellow who gloried in nudity." Tommy was enjoying
the course, reading the novels as sociology rather than
fiction. Now Wyn had to admit, Tommy argued, that
they did have something in common. They were into the
third trial month of Tommy spending weekends in Wyn's

house and she wasn't, she allowed, exactly unhappy about the arrangement.

"He's sweet, he's even-tempered, he's gorgeous, he's not stupid, and he's willing to do anything in the world for you," Liz Lum had lectured her. "There isn't a woman in this town who wouldn't trade places in bed with you, myself included. But you're too much of a snob, Wynsome Lewis, to marry Tommy. If he came from money and had gone to an Ivy League college and used you for a couple of years and then left you high and dry for some rich yuppie witch, only then might you consider him marriage material."

"I'm the one who's not marriage material, Lizzy," Wyn said, thinking of Nick, who had sent her a Memorial Day bouquet of calla lilies which Wyn, remarkably guilt free, threw in the garbage along with the engraved invitation to a Meyer family barbecue.

She left Tommy getting into his volunteer fireman gear and walked down Madison to Main in low, but still too high, heels. The sun was shining, the sky was blue, the lilacs and the weekenders were blooming.

"Phineas couldn't have asked for anything more," Camellia Cole was saying as Wyn reached the New Federal Inn porch.

"He could ask to be alive," Ruth said, offering her hand to Wyn, who gladly took it. There had been a lot of touching hands, of kissing cheeks, of heretofore unheard-of demonstrations of affection in postdebacle Waggs Neck. It was as if the entire town was in mourning over the death of close relatives and needed the comfort of touching one another to help dispel the sadness.

But with spring, Waggs Neck seemed to be coming out of its collective unhappiness. The official verdict was that the murders of Phineas Browne, Billy Bell, and Wilfred Mercer (Percy's death was left alone) were by person or persons unknown, though everyone knew Jackson Hall had been the killer. Wyn's deposition, never made public, was not considered definitive proof—so much of it was hearsay—and though the case was still officially open, it was reluctantly agreed that there would never be a tidy ending.

If local citizens still talked about the grislier aspects of last autumn's mayhem, no one else did. The media had forgotten Waggs Neck Harbor and Wyn thanked the village's lucky stars for that.

Wyn did not thank the village's lucky stars for the grade, junior, and senior high school bands, which might have, for once, expanded their repertoire. They were playing—what else?—"When The Saints Come Marching In" with their trademark yet regrettable gusto as they marched past Main Street's red, white, and blue-festooned shops. Camellia put her gloved fingers in her ears until they went by, a gesture disapproved of by her older sister.

Nor was Ruth Cole amused by Heidi Lum and her Waggs Neck Harbor baton-twirling compatriots in their very abbreviated and heavily pom-pommed costumes, tossing their instruments, their heads, and their hips with abandon. No surprise to anyone, the poor Gold Star Mothers, crammed into the huge-finned pink Cadillac convertible, were again being spritzed with brown steam from the chronically defective whale float.

Tommy Handwerk gave Wyn his dimpled, ingenuous smile and a "thumbs up" from his seat high atop the Waggs Neck Harbor Volunteer Firemen's antique fire engine, and several impressionable young and not-so-young Handwerk fans in the crowd put hands to beating hearts and sighed. The VFW followed the firemen in a World War I ambulance, which seemed particularly appropriate, given their ages and physical conditions.

Mayoress (she was insistent on the title, no feminist or pro-abortionist she) and pharmacist Betty Kunze had refused to listen to the naysayers who wanted to call off the celebration in light of the last parade. "Nonsense," she had said, often and loudly. "The Whalers Day Parade was a great success. That Phineas got himself poisoned and we had a mad artist loose in the village is no reflection on the positive aspects of our parades. The Memorial Day celebration will go on as scheduled." She did concede, however, that there would be no grandstand, and only she herself, Chief of Police Homer Price, and a few of the village board members stood in front of the Municipal Building on a narrow platform, reviewing the parade.

David Kabot and Dicie Carlson were sitting on the curb in front of the Marjorie Main Laundromat, holding hands. Jessica Stevens had returned to Europe and Dicie almost forgot that she ever existed. "Did you say something about getting married?" Dicie asked over the roar of "When The Saints . . ." and David Kabot said, "No. Did you?"

"Yes."

"All right," David Kabot conceded, bringing her hand to his lips.

"You look much too fashionable in that dress," Camellia Cole was saying to Wyn as the Girl Scouts tripped by. "Careful, or Lettie will have you removed from the premises."

Lettitia Browne, recently returned from South American surgery, and looking it in a new orange-and-yellow Galanos with matching hat, had invited a small group of friends to watch the parade from the New Federal porch.

Her son, Tony Deel, who had chosen to wear body-sculpting black bicycle shorts and a matching shirt festooned with zippers, was thinking of going ahead with his late father's and grandmother's plans for a Jackson Hall Museum of Modern American Art on the old convent site, only now there were only two onion domes to worry about, rather than three. As the BPOE float (a stuffed, motheaten elk, circa 1922, in a pickup truck) cruised by, Tony and his mother shared a momentary look of chilly understanding across the New Federal's porch.

Dolly Carlson was standing next to Tony, amused by

his comments on the parade. Despite all expectations, Dolly had survived the winter's tragedy with equanimity and even, of late, seemed to blossom. She had recently sought Wyn's assistance with the legal ramifications of turning Carlson House into a pricey bed-and-breakfast establishment.

"Maggie will be doing cartwheels in her grave," Wyn had said.

"Let's hope she has a good spin." Dolly was becoming more like Maggie every day.

Wyn, who still felt the urge to call up Phineas and tell him the latest news, had survived the winter through hard labor, taking on as much as she could, as if she were punishing herself for the deaths of the previous fall. Fitz confided to Ruth Cole that he thought Wyn was overdoing it, working overtime with Roy Stein on the Carlson Watch Factory condominium project.

"Not to mention earning fat commissions from the sales of several choice waterfront properties," Ruth observed. "And sleeping with Tommy Handwerk every weekend. Oh, I know, she looks as if butter wouldn't melt." Ruth Cole laughed, genuinely amused. "Wynsome indeed."

Ruth was irritated that Wyn—and Fitz—knew a lot more about last autumn's goings-on than anyone else, and even she hadn't been able to worm it out of them. "Though I haven't given up trying," she warned Fitz.

"Very trying," Fitz said, under his breath.

As the school bands made their return pass down Main Street, John Fenton took his place beside Dolly. He was as handsome as ever, but somehow less substantial, like a fading ghost in a romantic movie. Wyn had only realized how sentimental he was when she found he still took Monday lunch at the New Federal, now at a table for one.

The bands had reached lower Main Street and there was a blessed moment of silence into which Camellia, noticing John Fenton's late arrival, observed, rather too loudly, "The last of the Fat Boys."

"Praise the Lord," Ruth said, standing, taking her sister's hand, leading the way into the dining room, where Lettitia had provided a lavish and elegant midday meal.

Fitz, an unlighted White Owl jammed into his mouth, sat on for a moment, staring down Main Street at Carlson House. He had been so ill during the winter with some difficult-to-diagnose—much less treat—pulmonary disease that Wyn had closed shop for the suicidal month of February and taken him to Key West, where the subtropical Florida colors and weather and denizens helped restore first his sense of humor and then his health.

She sat next to him and put her slim hand on his old paw, bringing a smile to his craggy face. "You miss her, don't you?"

"The village, not to mention life, isn't the same."

"She was a monster, Fitz."

"But she was a magnificent monster."

Wyn agreed that Maggie Carlson had been a magnificent monster and then, with a last glance at Carlson House, she linked her arm in her uncle's and walked with him into Phineas's New Federal Inn, where Lettie and her exclusive luncheon buffet were waiting. How Phineas would have loved it.

POCKET BOOKS
PROUDLY ANNOUNCES

THE
WINTER WOMEN
MURDERS

DAVID A. KAUFELT

**Available in Hardcover
from Pocket Books**

The following is a preview of
The Winter Women Murders. . . .

THE
WINTER WOMEN
MURDERS

A Wyn Lewis Mystery
by David A. Kaufelt

For over fifty years the Annual Literary Arts Symposium has provided entertainment, enlightenment, and a raison d'être for Waggs Neck Harbor's "winter women"—upper-middle-class, upper-middle-aged fugitives from marriages and careers gone aground. Founded by the late grande dame Sophie Comfort Noble, the Symposium is now in the hands of her daughter, Rhodesia. This year's topic is feminist in theme and features Sondra Confrit, the sixtyish "mother of the sexual revolution," novelist Keny Blue, who has stolen Sondra's thunder and then some, and Annie Vasquez, who seems on the verge of stealing Wyn Lewis's live-in boyfriend, Tommy Handwerk.

Stopping for a moment at the "V" where Madison met Main Street, Wyn took a loving, exasperated sweep of her village thoroughfare. The weathered statue of the Union soldier presiding over an elderly cannon stood beside her, looking in an easterly direction. The redbrick shops and the hotel and the monstrous Municipal Building were near-perfect illustrations of nineteenth-century-after-the-fire building style. The shingled ex-Carlson mansion and the futuristic barn attached to it (both now compromising Dolly's elegant B&B) sat squarely at the far end of Main Street, blocking the view of the bay, but not the winter winds.

Normally, on an early Thursday evening in February, there would be half a dozen cars on Main Street, mothers and retirees getting in their weekend shopping, maybe taking a cup of coffee at the Eden before closing time (six P.M.). But today only a couple of brown town dogs were strolling past the shops while every parking space was filled with costly foreign runabouts. The runabouts belonged to the mostly female participants, come to combine a love (well, at least a like) of literature with the titillation of hearing the outspoken Keny Blue speak on such celebrated new feminist topics as self-induced orgasm and multiple sex partners and the brave new world of sexual freedom as depicted in her novels.

Wyn walked east on Main Street, following several pairs of attractive, middle-aged women dressed in tweeds and suede into the expertly Victorianized New Federal lobby. Flocked wallpaper, Turkish carpets, chesterfield sofas, and a fire in the fireplace created a Sherlock-Holmesian atmosphere that even the most diehard modernist found hard to resist.

The only person Wyn knew who disliked the New Federal was her ex-husband, Nick, who disdained charm, preferring the efficiency and anonymity of an AAA-approved chain motel. On their honeymoon in Hong Kong (grudgingly paid for by his mother), Wyn had longed for the venerable Peninsula; Nick had booked them into a suite in the Sheraton.

Wyn, who normally viewed any sort of sentimental arrangement—furniture or otherwise—with suspicion, admitted to herself that she was a sucker for the sort of Victorian charm the late mayor and hotel owner, Phineas Browne, had managed to create.

Today the lobby was organized chaos. Her fellow FALAS executive committee members plus half a dozen winter women were doing their duty: greeting the paying participants, leading them to the appropriate sign-in desk (Unpaid or Prepaid or Media); helping them with the hand-lettered, color-coded badges; providing them with Xeroxed maps indicating their lodgings (either the New Federal, the Carlson B&B, or the budget choices out on the highway); escorting them to the large dining area where Liz Lum, Patty Batista, and other FALAS members presided over an extraordinary array of finger food.

Soon after she inherited the New Federal from her brother, Lettitia Browne had had a cutting-edge electronics system installed and the ground floor's nonbearing walls replaced by artfully designed (Dickie ffrench) folding wall panels. Thus, the entire first floor could be turned into one large public space, ideal for meetings and such. But it rarely was, the convention planners Lettie courted drawn to larger, more accessible hotels.

The conversion, however, worked for ALAS; most Symposium social gatherings, aside from panel discussions, took place in the New Federal.

Wyn was immediately pressed into service by chief hostess Ruth Cole who passed on David Kabot as if he were her partner in a square dance. Kabot had a deliberate two-day growth, a sweater with a hole in its sleeve, and a gold stud in his ear. The rumor was that he was having trouble giving birth to his fourth novel. Kabot, who had once lusted after Wyn, only to be rebuffed, refused the proffered badge (red ink for authors) somewhat abruptly.

"So refreshingly modest, David," Wyn said, handing the badge to his wife, the raven-haired beauty and Main Street dress shop owner (Sizzle), Dicie Carlson. Dicie, more than a touch pregnant, her black curls cut short, and her film vamp's lips painted Real Ritz Red, rolled her eyes behind her husband's muscular back. "Thank you, Wyn," she said in her child's whiskey voice. "The boy's worried that the baby will take his place in my affections."

"Yeah, right," David Kabot said, turning around. "Sorry, Wyn. I hate these things."

Wyn didn't ask why he attended because she had already seen, set up in the small dining room, the long table with local authors' works piled on it, David Kabot's prominently featured. "Would you sign my copy of *Six Months*,

Mr. Kabot?" a woman with a diva's bosom asked. "Pretty please. It's my favorite novel of all time. That peanut butter scene. Do make it something personal. My name is Iris."

A *Chronicle* photographer took a photograph of David Kabot signing his book, a heavy-breathing Iris looking on. "Kabot Smiles" should be the cut line for that photo, Wyn thought, wondering not for the first time how Dicie stood him.

Iris broke out in uncontrollable giggles. "Look what he wrote," she said, holding the book under Wyn's eyes. " 'For Iris, In memory of that night in Chicago.' Bad boy," Iris said, clearly delighted. Wyn's mood darkened.

The lobby was turning stuffy, what with the fire and two hundred or so women swarming around. Three local authors who had gone to the trouble and expense of having their books privately printed were haranguing poor Frank Taylor (of Frank E. Taylor's Antiquarian Book Store), demanding to know why he hadn't stocked their efforts for the Symposium sale.

Frank, very tall and very adept at slipping out of tight situations, suggested they have a natter with Rhodesia Noble about the ALAS policy of not purveying privately printed books. While angry and righteous, none of the three felt quite up to facing Rhodie, as Frank well knew. He dodged Sondra Confrit, winked at Wyn, and faded toward the bar.

Wyn, taking care not to touch his shedding sports jacket, escorted Sondra's husband, Rupert Hale, to his place behind the sales table. "I never do this," Ginger said, as they all did, searching his pockets for a pen. Wyn supplied him with one that had the Lewis Real Estate Company logo on it. She left him to his fate between a cookbook writer who specialized in local dishes (e.g., baked tuna fool) and a deranged-looking woman who had written a cautionary paperback on the dangers of radar ranges, electric toothbrushes, and other household apparatus.

Making her way across the room, which smelled increasingly of Estée Lauder's venerable Youth Dew, Wyn caught sight of Tommy. He was leading Annie Vasquez to the more exclusive sales table, a half round reserved for the three principal speakers.

Sondra Confrit had found her own place there and was lecturing four women with spiked haircuts who said they had come by truck from Elizabeth, New Jersey, and were great admirers. "So buy a book," Sondra said, holding up a copy of her *One Woman's Sexual Manifesto* (Cannabis Press, 1967). Cowed, they bought books while Tommy introduced Annie to Sondra.

"Very nice to meet you," Sondra said, concentrating on autographing the recently purchased books. "Love your stuff."

"I love your stuff, too," Annie said and for a moment Sondra really looked at her.

"You do?"

"You're a brave woman and we all owe you a great deal."

Oh, no, Wyn thought, coming up to be introduced. She's sincere, too. As well as long and lean and glamorous in a dark, retiring, confident way. She was wearing jeans and a jacket to match and a white lacy blouse underneath and red high heels and a big, fat turquoise and silver bracelet on her elegant wrist. Though they were about the same age, Wyn felt years older. She also felt a burning desire to race home and put on red high heels, if she only owned a pair.

What's more, Annie Vasquez radiated integrity and niceness and Tommy was looking at her in a way that Wyn acknowledged she didn't like. Worse, Annie was deferring to Tommy in a way Wyn absolutely despised. Wyn said a few words of welcome and asked after Annie's child. Caitlin was upstairs, Annie said, watching what was probably a triple-X-rated film on the VCR. "She's twelve. The hormones are raging."

Wyn commiserated and then moved off as Annie Vasquez's admirers, realizing she was present, started buying her books as if they were original Gutenberg Bibles. Irene Handwerk, Tommy's mother, was swamped at the cash box. Sondra, whose only sales had been the four she had brokered—*One Woman's Sexual Manifesto* had, after all, been in print for a number of years—said she'd had enough and was going to help Rupert, who "couldn't give away free gold."

Her only comfort, she went on to say, was that Keny Blue was not present. "That woman can suck the life out of any room she walks into, just like that." Sondra snapped her long fingers, making a castanet sound. That was when the lights were dimmed for a moment and, in the silence that followed, Jane Littlefield's clipped, amplified voice asked everyone to pay attention: the Symposium's chair had been persuaded to say a few words of welcome.

Rhodie was standing at the podium between Jane Littlefield and Lettitia Browne. Behind them were Peter Robalinski and the executive committee members: Dolly, Dickie, the Cole sisters. Ruth Cole gestured impatiently for Wyn to join them. Wyn did so while Rhodie was giving what she described as an informal welcome to Waggs Neck Harbor's fifty-first Annual Literary Arts Symposium.

She had arrived at the part that her dead mother had really loved—asking those who had been attending the Symposium for more than ten years to raise their hands—when the outer doors to the lobby noisily opened. A short woman, buxom in the great Dolly Parton tradition, strode in.

She wore an ill-advised floor-length blue fox kimono coat that emphasized her lack of stature, despite (this gave Wyn a second of happiness) her red high heels. Her mass of expertly disarranged Wonder Women blue-black hair featured a vintage blue aquamarine barrette over one ear. With all the artifice—huge, blue-shadowed eyes, expertly bobbed nose, inflated lips—Wyn wondered if anyone knew what she really looked like. It didn't matter, she supposed: the impression was extravaganza, all brass, no strings. She was as out of sync in the New Federal, Wyn thought, as Rhodesia would be in Caesars Palace.

The newcomer stared into the awed silence facing her and, taking her time, counting the house, finally allowed her gaze to settle on Rhodie, Peter, Jane, and the FALAS executive committee. They were fast-frozen at the far end of the large space, looking as if they had been caught engaging in some naughty activity.

"Well, look who's here," she said in a voice that was one part Tallulah, the rest Brooklyn, waving a short, be-ringed hand with very long, painted fingernails. With the gesture, her coat fell open, revealing a skintight blue snakeskin-print jumpsuit and an oversized bleached bone necklace with a crucifix resting in her considerable cleavage. ("It couldn't be human bone," one thrilled attendee whispered. "Could it?")

Lettie Browne, possibly not realizing that the microphone was still "live," said, "What—in God's name—is *that?*"

"How quickly they forget," the newcomer said, proving she didn't need amplification. "This is a Keny Blue, dolls. So hello, girlfriends. That includes you, too, Dickie love."

* * *

Long after Keny Blue had been shown to her suite and her half-dozen matching pieces of Louis Vuitton (blue) brought up and her rented Saab Turbo convertible (blue) stashed in the hotel parking lot, the tongues wagged.

"She could be worse," Jane Littlefield said hopefully in the back booth of the Nonesuch Bar, sipping at one-star brandy, taking her pink eyeglasses and placing them on the stained oaklike table. "She apologized again for not turning up this afternoon. Said she decided at the last moment to drive herself out here and save everyone time, trouble, and money. Of course, she's billing us for the rental car."

"She's a model of economy and consideration." Wyn's voice was steady but her insides felt like jelly on a plate. Though she had no rational right to, she felt betrayed. As she and Jane had escaped from the New Federal and made their way up Main Street to the Nonesuch, she had glanced into the window of the new Japanese restaurant and hated what she saw.

Tommy, his mother, Annie Vasquez, and presumably her

issue—a devastating twelve-year-old strawberry blonde named Caitlin—were seated at the round table, laughing and eating what Tommy had always heretofore considered inedible.

It had looked like a happy family gathering, Tommy's good-natured and somewhat dizzy mother, Irene, chatting away to Annie Vasquez while Caitlin—clearly and forever enthralled—talked up to Tommy. Wyn could imagine Annie's and Tommy's private smiles to each other as they patronized one another's closest relative.

*　　*　　*

On Day Two of the Symposium, Keny Blue, the sexpot author, fires Dickie ffrench, her longtime ghostwriter, tangles in public with rival Sondra Confrit, and manages to turn the high-minded library lecture into a verbal sexual free-for-all. At tea with Wyn afterwards, she confides the story of her life—or some of it. From what little she hears, Wyn knows major fireworks are in store for Waggs Neck Harbor. . . .

Once again Tommy did not arrive home until early morning and then slept in the guest bedroom. The guest bedroom mattress had not been aired in some time; the sheets hadn't been changed since Wyn's ex-sister-in-law, Natalie Meyer, had visited over the Christmas holidays. Natalie favored the pulsating scents of Jungle Gardenia—a perfume that made Tommy gag—and Wyn hoped the sheets still reeked of it. She heard him toss and turn as she lay corpse-still in her big, lonesome bed.

Tommy performed none of his usual Saturday morning capers. He rose early, showered, and quietly went downstairs, feeding Probity her disdained but healthful and wildly expensive vegetarian breakfast purchased from the health-oriented pet shop in West Sea. Wyn could hear him opening and closing the old Kelvinator door, preparing his own roughage-laden cereal breakfast.

She sat up in bed, uncertain how to proceed. A screaming fit had its attractions but, in Wyn's experience, usually didn't do much but delay the inevitable.

Besides, it wasn't her style. Maybe it was time for a new style. She stared up at the wooden ceiling, remembering a peppy Judy Garland song about a trolley that her father had liked. But Judy had been high on new love while Wyn was experiencing the painful zing of the strings of her heart breaking, one by one.

She forced herself to get out of bed, determined to present a business-as-usual face, telling herself that women of the nineties didn't cry. Brushing her teeth vigorously with a *Consumer Reports*–recommended toothpaste, she felt moisture around her eyes and decided that, all right, she did love Tommy after all. She had been loath to show it, to make too much of her involvement, in case of just such an eventuality as faced her now.

"Bastard," she said, finding a small release in controlled anger. Damn mother and, yes, damn Hap for all those sane, polite conversations about control around the dinner table. Wyn knew what Keny Blue would do in the situation: she'd stomp all over Mr. Thomas Wainwright Handwerk with her stiletto heels and then go have Annie Vasquez and issue for breakfast.

Getting into her leopard-print leotards and her Nike Airs, Wyn marched noisily down the stairs lest Tommy remain unaware she was up and ready. Stopping at the door to the dining room, she felt her anger ooze away as self-pity and a terrible longing seeped in.

Tommy sat at the round pine table in the French-doored octagonal room, drinking tea stewed the way he liked it, chomping on his Granola. Wyn couldn't stand looking at the sympathetic back of his head and the way his ears stood out and so she went into the kitchen and got her caffeine from an open diet Coke can before returning to the dining room doorway. Wishing Tommy an early baldness—no man deserved that corn-blond hair—she resisted the urge to put her arms around those knobby shoulders and nuzzle one of those protuberant ears.

"Morning, Wyn," he said in his deepest, dolorous voice, not turning around.

"I have three requests for you, Tommy," Wyn said as casually as she could manage.

"Wyn . . ." he began, but Wyn wasn't to be stopped.

"Well, two are hopes. I hope that Caitlin has her own bedroom at the New Federal."

"Jesus," Tommy said, turning but looking just above her at the molding atop the doorway. "Do you think that I . . ."

"And two, I hope you're using what we modest ones call precautions. That was our pre-living-together arrangement, was it not? That we were absolutely free to have sexual relations with anyone we wanted as long as we used the above-mentioned precautions." She knew she was sounding like a hybrid between her academic mother and a Bush Supreme Court nominee but she couldn't stop herself. "Not that I ever intend to sleep with you again, Handwerk."

"Wyn . . ."

"My last request is that you remove your belongings from my household as soon as possible and no later than noon, today."

"Wyn, I love you . . ."

"You have a remarkable way of showing it."

"I thought we had this agreement . . ."

"It's null and void."

"Wyn . . ." Tommy said, looking at her with helpless, pleading eyes, so handsome and appealingly manly in his own boyish way that she almost gave in. But the last two eon-length sleepless nights and all the long-ago sleepless nights she had endured waiting for Nick the Rat kept her from going to him. "Listen, Tommy," she said, "I want you to have a great life, and Annie Vasquez may just be the one to give it to you."

"Wyn . . ."

"As always, I'm overwhelmed by your way with words, Tommy."

He stood up and she knew if he touched her, she was going to lose her resolve and they would only be going through this again in a week's time, and so she turned and fled out the kitchen door. He and Probity, salivating on Tommy's bare feet, watching as their mistress jogged down School House Lane toward the Old Railroad Spa for whatever solace or distraction the red-eye aerobic-step class might provide.

"You okay?" Dice asked as Wyn joined the dozen other aerobic animals—mostly of the younger winter women ilk—prepared to give their bodies and souls to Patty Batista for the next sixty minutes.

"Is this a coffee klatch or you here to work?" Patty shouted, obviating the need for Wyn to answer Dicie, whose New Wave obstetrician encouraged exercise. As the rock sound of "Have Mercy" reverberated through the not insignificant stereo system Patty had had installed, Wyn, catching a glimpse of concern in Dicie's memorable green eyes, wondered what had happened to her own famous poker face.

After class, rather than face Dicie's interested empathy, Wyn went home. She found it not unexpectedly empty, save for a bewildered Probity. She showered, changed into an all-purpose dress, and got the Jaguar out of the garage, noting that Tommy's motorcycle and truck were gone. I won't think about it now, Wyn told herself. Tomorrow is another day. Et cetera.

Tommy's mother, Irene, had recently realized a lifelong dream and had become the Swap 'n' Shop announcer on WWAG. She was a great success, airing music she liked between sale announcements of flatbed trucks and nearly new washer-dryers. This morning she was playing a lugubrious Peggy Lee rendition of "Am I Blue."

"Lordy," Wyn said, shutting off WWAG, deciding this was not going to be her day (month, year, or decade). She drove around into the New Federal parking lot, the Symposium attendees and area book lovers having taken up all Main Street spaces. Frank E. Taylor—tall, handsome, and a well-intentioned cook (his specialty: veal tonnato)—was hosting yet another event, an early morning coffee at his Antiquarian Book Store.

She sat in the car for a moment, not wanting to go into the New Federal's lobby. Knowing my luck, she thought, Tommy and Annie will be coming down the main stairs in wedding whites, Caitlin throwing brown rice in their wake.

Packing up her troubles in her old kit bag, as Camellia Cole would advise, wondering what the hell a kit bag was anyway, Wyn used the New Federal's never-locked rear entry, which led to a long and narrow wainscoted corridor, which in turn led to the lobby. The entry also contained richly carpeted back stairs that at one time had been the private ingress to the late mayor's spacious, high-tech apartment. It had taken up most of the mansard-roofed New Federal attic and had been a source of wonderment to that fellow's friends.

Lettie, soon after inheriting the inn, had Dickie design and oversee the creation of several suites carved out of her brother's former "aerie." Dickie had "done" the new suites in what he called Billy Baldwin Victoriana ("tons of leopard-skin throw pillows").

Keny Blue had demanded and been given the most lavish of the suites. Wyn ascended the steep stairway in what she assumed was the vain hope that overnight Keny had seen reason, that her Vuitton was packed and that she was ready to take the helicopter back to Manhattan, where she belonged.

She might have called first, but keeping on the go was the prescription for the day. The image of Tommy and Annie and Caitlin, strolling hand in hand through an urban wonderland, was permanently acid-etched in her mind.

Wyn knocked on the door where a pink-beige rose-encumbered ceramic plaque read Suite Sue. Phineas, she thought, must be having conniption fits in decorator heaven. There was no response. Perhaps Keny was in the shower, an elaborate hydra-headed "minispa." Wyn thought about trudging downstairs to the main lobby and trying the house phone, but then she heard Tommy's voice coming from the neighboring suite's (Suite Pea) half-open door and, finding Keny's door unlatched, she escaped into Suite Sue.

Keny Blue was not in the minispa. She was in an elaborately canopied bed, nude, a thin black wire twisted around her neck, red seeping out from around its edges, staining the pillows. Her trademark aquamarine barrette had been repositioned once again. It now adorned her pudenda.

Look for
THE
WINTER WOMEN
MURDERS
Wherever Hardcover Books
Are Sold